P9-DUU-269

WRONG SIDE OF
THE COURT

WRONG SIDE OF THE COURT

H.N. KHAN

WITHDRAWN

Penguin Teen
an imprint of Penguin Random House Canada Young Readers,
a division of Penguin Random House of Canada Limited

Published in hardcover by Penguin Teen, 2022

1 2 3 4 5 6 7 8 9 10

Text copyright © 2022 by H.N. Khan
Jacket design by Jennifer Griffiths
Jacket art by Anju Shrestha

All rights reserved. Without limiting the rights under copyright reserved above,
no part of this publication may be reproduced, stored in or introduced into
a retrieval system, or transmitted in any form or by any means (electronic,
mechanical, photocopying, recording or otherwise), without the prior written
permission of both the copyright owner and the above publisher of this book.

*Publisher's note: This book is a work of fiction. Names, characters, places
and incidents either are the product of the author's imagination or are
used fictitiously, and any resemblance to actual persons living
or dead, events, or locales is entirely coincidental.*

Manufactured in Canada

Library and Archives Canada Cataloguing in Publication
Title: Wrong side of the court / H.N. Khan.
Names: Khan. H.N., author.
Identifiers: Canadiana (print) 20210090650 | Canadiana (ebook) 20210092718 |
ISBN 9780735270879 (hardcover) | ISBN 9780735270886 (EPUB)
Classification: LCC PS8621.H36 W74 2022 | DDC jC813/.6—dc23

Library of Congress Control Number: 2020951760

www.penguinrandomhouse.ca

This book is for Regent Park, no longer a housing project, no longer a slum, but forever a gathering place for those yearning for new beginnings and dreaming of something more.

PROLOGUE

I can't believe I didn't shoot. Agh. I could've won us the game, but no, I was too busy worrying about what Omar would've done to me if I didn't pass it to him. And what did he do? Miss.

Can't do anything about it now. I'm exhausted. I just want to close my eyes and sleep like a baby. I can't remember the last time I did that. Like, it's literally the one thing we should all be proficient in. It's all we did when we were fresh out of the womb and not crying or shitting ourselves.

Blame it on technology: all the glare from this stupid phone, the highlights of Curry draining threes on YouTube, getting sprung off Cardi B videos . . . wait, scratch that last part. Or at least don't tell my mom.

It doesn't help that my room and Gerrard Street don't have much between them. Sure, there's a wall and a large window, but I can hear *everything*. Cars whizzing by, people talking, dogs barking, and streetcars flying by like they have somewhere to be. Who needs to go to Main Street subway station at this hour at lightning speed? I feel like someone jolts me awake with one of those resuscitators every time one passes. Maybe I need to put a sign outside my window, like those stickers on the backs of cars

1

announcing there's a baby on board, but something more to the effect of "growing teen who's an insomniac and would really benefit from sleep lives here." Not that anyone would pay attention. It is Regent Park, after all.

Wait, it's starting to rain, I've got the pedestal fan on high, and the ambient noise is starting to make me a little drowsy.

I'm not tossing and turning as much. I start to feel my body give in. Thank you, Lord. I will repay you by not replaying those Cardi B videos in my sleep.

Bang!

I jolt up. What the f—

Where's my phone? My hands scramble to find it. My heart's pounding a mile a minute and don't get me started on the sweat. I hear nothing for another moment. Is it over?

Bang! Bang!

A car roars down Gerrard Street. I'm feeling around on my body. Am I hit? Am I bleeding? It's outside—whatever went down is right outside my window.

Mom barges into my room. The doorknob smashes into the wall. She's heaving and disheveled.

"Fawad, beta, are you okay?" she screams.

1

"You gotta hold the ball with your finger pads, see?" says Abshir, showing me the ball in his hand. "And leave space between the ball and your palm."

It's Friday afternoon. We're both sweating from our one-on-one game, which was after playing a few pickup games with some randos. Came right after Friday prayers at the mosque.

I nod, wiping beads of sweat off my forehead and brushing my hair back. I can feel the side of my skull where I just got a high fade from Mary-Jo, the local Chinese barber me and the boys have been going to since forever. My cut-off tank top is drenched, and my only pair of Nike sports shorts aren't doing much better. Mom's going to hate me for stinking up the laundry, *again*.

Abshir has his Afro back in a bun and he's rocking a long black T-shirt, black sweats that he's pulled up toward his knees, and oh, those sweet monochrome black Air Jordan 11s.

"How do you line up your shot, though?" I ask, taking the ball from him, pressing my finger pads to it, and spinning it in the air, trying to practice the motion Abshir's just shown me.

"All right, I'm going to tell you and only you, so you'd better keep this between us," says Abshir, taking the ball from me and getting a few steps closer to the rim. "Keep your elbow and wrist in line with the basket, but the real key is right up there. See them rim hooks?"

I look up at the rim. I've seen them about a million times and never paid them much attention. "What about them?"

"That's how you take aim," says Abshir, dribbling way past the three-point line, shooting, and hitting nothing but net. That swoosh sound . . . if it were up to me, I swear, I'd just listen to that on a loop all day long.

"Okay, let me try," I say, grabbing the rebound and going not as far as him but far enough. I line myself up with the basket and eye those hooks before I let it fly. *Swish*. Holy shit, it works.

I let another one fly and hit again.

"One last thing, always, and I mean *always* . . . extend your arm all the way every time you shoot," he says. "And that's all the free advice you get out of me today, unless your mom's making some of the seekh kababs or whatever you call 'em."

"I can bring some. This shit's priceless."

"I'm joking. Keep practicing, I'ma go hang with Irv," he says, walking toward the exit. There's a lounge just a few steps away.

We're in the North Regent recreation center, or my second home, but don't tell my mom that. It's not a crazy nice gym, but coming down the flight of stairs whenever I enter, I swear I feel like a king strolling about his kingdom. I didn't always love ball this much. I wasn't even good up till recently.

But this year was different. Not only did puberty work in my favor and have me shoot up five inches so I can officially say I'm six feet (okay, five foot eleven), but also I've been training all summer. Hell, I might finally try out for the school team when school starts back in a couple of weeks. Tenth grade is going to be different. I don't want to sit on the bleachers wishing I was on the court. I want to be in the game. Sure, I gotta get my mom's permission first, but who's keeping score?

I'll figure out a way to get her to say yes. First things first: there's an inner-city summer league championship this Sunday. The league pits neighborhood recreation centers from all around the city against one another. My best friend, Yousuf, and I have been training with the Regent Park team and playing all summer. Yeah, my mom knows. At first I thought there was no way I could keep up, and now I'm up for sixth-man award with the stats I've been averaging. No big deal.

Arif and Yousuf stroll in. They'd better not have been smoking up . . . I hate it when dudes show up high to the court. Straight-up disrespectful.

"Took you both long enough," I say, practicing dribbling the ball low around my ankles. Really, I'm just trying to show off.

"Yo, there's more to life than basketball," says Arif, removing the duffel bag from across his shoulders and placing it to the side. He's been working out all summer and posting photos on his Insta. Even started doing workout tutorials on TikTok. Why? Not to spread his love of fitness to the masses, but for the DMs from girls across the GTA and beyond who can't stop gushing over his six-pack. Agh.

"Y'all missing out. Abshir was dropping some serious knowledge and now you'll never know," I say, taking a shot and hitting nothing but net.

"Man, he don't even do that shit for me," says Yousuf, removing his baseball cap and taking out his ball sneakers from his bag.

"I swear if I asked him to come train with me, he'd just laugh at my ass."

Yousuf is a little on the heavier side, likes his head shaved, and wears glasses, which he takes off and puts on a ledge. He's got a bit of a baby face, with big eyes and thick lips. There's an inkling of a beard along his jaw, but it's super patchy.

The two of them start warming up. Yousuf wasn't lying exactly when it came to Abshir. Ever since my dad passed, Abshir has taken me under his wing. I know Yousuf's a little jelly, but his older bro looks out for all of us.

We're shooting around when someone kicks open the backdoor. It's Omar, Johnny, and the rest of Omar's crew coming in. They usually hang in South Regent, but the gym must be closed for some kids' camp or something.

At six foot four, Omar's got a solid four inches on me. That's just height. If we're talking muscle, that's a whole other story. His Afro is poking out from under his hood. I stare at his unlaced Timberland boots and baggy jeans and imagine how much damage he could do if I ended up on the floor and he stomped on me.

Johnny's Vietnamese and has a stocky build with broad shoulders. He rocks a ponytail, and despite his size, dude can shoot. We all went to the same middle schools together.

"Hey, it's Fuckwad and his little bitches," says Omar, dribbling and taking a shot at the other side of the court. That gets Johnny and them laughing. It irks me, but I know better than to bite. It's nothing new at this point. I keep shooting, but I can tell Arif and Yousuf are pissed off. Besides, there's six or seven of them and only three of us.

We ignore them as they get their ball gear on and keep shooting. The funny thing is, when Omar first came to Canada, we were in the same class in seventh grade, even friends, and he was as clueless about Regent as I'd been when I first moved here two years prior. Hell, we even used to get bullied together.

What changed? He was really athletic and tore it up no matter what sport we played, and as for me, let's just say I was better with numbers and an easy target. His crew changed quick and I mostly just hid behind Yousuf and Arif. I'm not a straight-up nerd now; hey, we all gotta adapt. I can hold my own on the court, which helps.

Arif jumps to grab a rebound to my shot, and I had no idea he could jump that high.

"How'd you that?" I say, jumping up to try and touch the backboard and missing. One day, I wanna tap the backboard after a layup. It's not a dunk, but it's close.

"Check this," he says. He hops and grabs the net to pull himself up, goddamn Spider-Man that he is, and hangs off the rim, his muscles flexed. "Give me the ball."

He's hanging with one arm and holding out his other hand.

"Damn monkey," says Yousuf, chuckling and putting a ball in his hand.

Arif grabs the ball and then "dunks" it. I'm still shaking my head. He then slowly lets himself down.

"If I had your hops, I swear, I'd be unstoppable," I say, jumping again, unable to even touch the tip of the net.

I turn and see Omar and his crew walk up to the center of the court.

"You pussies wanna play a game?" he says.

"Hey, who the fuck you calling a pussy?" says Arif, cracking his neck side to side, then walking up to him.

"Why you gotta talk shit all the time?" says Yousuf, shaking his head in Omar's direction.

"Whatever, let's just play threes," I say. There's only one way to shut him up.

"Which ball?" he says.

"This one," I say, feeling my NBA Official Wilson leather ball for good measure before I dribble to the top of the key. I'm guarding Omar, Yousuf's on Johnny, and Arif grabs Steven, the lone white guy who runs in their crew. "Shoot for ball."

I drain a long three-pointer. Our ball.

Omar checks it to me and doesn't even bother getting up close. If I didn't have to pass the ball, I'd love to chalk it up just then. I swing it to Yousuf, who's in the paint, his back to the rim, bodying Johnny. He fakes right, then spins and lays it up.

"Fluke," says Omar, checking it back up.

This time I dribble in and find Arif cutting, so I give him a sweet dribble pass that he catches en route to the rim, and he lays it up.

"All right, enough of this shit," says Omar, tightening up the laces on his sneakers. Now he's got a hand up. I lob it to Yousuf, but Omar quickly double-teams him and strips the ball from his hand. I've got my knees bent and arms up. He pulls up and nails a jumper.

"Come on, Fawad, get up close to him," says Yousuf.

He's right, my defense is weak. Omar throws the ball to Steven, who shoots and misses. I grab the rebound and dribble out to clear the ball, and stare down Omar, who's just standing there. I jack up a shot and drain it.

"3–1," I say. "Up to 7."

His crew and some of the other players are gathered around watching close. He checks me the ball. I throw it to Arif, who passes it back to me.

I line up and drain another shot.

A dude from Omar's crew says, "Ooooooh, Omar, you gon' let him do that to you?"

Omar gives him a dirty look and a middle finger, then turns to stare me down. "Fuck this shit."

He checks me the ball, but this time puts a hand up and sort of bends his knees. There's a part of him that refuses to think I'm any better than I was back in grade seven. Oh well, I guess he's gotta face the music. I'm quick off the dribble and fly by him, drawing Johnny toward me. I dish it out to Yousuf, who hits the jumper.

"5–1," I say, this time with a smirk on my face. I can tell he's cooked, ready to blow. I so badly want to drain the final jumper on his ass. He thinks he's all that. Well, this ought to show him.

Except he intercepts the pass, and this time he's not letting Johnny or Steven put up a shot. He gets them to pass to him every time as he shoots off the dribble or drives and lays it in, emphatically tapping the backboard. A few more rounds of this and he says, "5–4."

Arif grabs a rebound from his missed shot, dribbles it out, then spots an open Yousuf by the rim, who lays it in easily.

"What the fuck are you dumbasses doing?" Omar yells at Steven and Johnny, while slamming the ball between his hands and shaking his head. "Man up. If they score, swear on my mom's life . . ."

"6–4, game point," I say. I tell Yousuf to come up top because I want the final shot. I wanna shut Omar up.

Yousuf checks the ball to Johnny and when he gets it back, he hands it off to me. Now it's just me and Omar. And he's playing defense all right. He's on me, trying to steal the ball. I push off, giving him a stiff elbow, and he's livid. Next thing I know, I cross him up and his whole crew's losing it, erupting in *ooohs* and *damnnns*. I get myself an open look. But before I can get the shot up, he quickly gathers himself and shoves me so hard I get the wind knocked out of me, and I hit the floor hard.

"The fuck you push me for?" says Omar, jumping on top of me, grabbing my tank and yanking me up. His boys rush over and circle around us.

"I didn't push you—you were fouling me," I yell, bracing my face while trying to squirm out from under him.

"Get off him, you piece of shit," says Arif, pushing through.

"Watch your lip, son," says Johnny, cocking his head sideways.

"Or what?" says Yousuf, giving him a shove.

The rest of their crew's ready to pounce.

Abshir rushes in from the lounge, clears the way, grabs Omar off me, and throws him to the floor.

"Wallahi, I'ma fuck you up the next time you touch him," says Abshir to Omar, before saying something else in Somali. Omar responds and they exchange a few more words before he nods and starts walking off.

"Fucking lucky punk," says Omar under his breath, taking one more look at me still on the floor, his lower lip trembling even as he bares his teeth, his face tight.

Omar and his crew exit from the back and it's just me, Arif, Yousuf, and Abshir left. I'm breathing heavily, still lying down. That was a close call.

"Why you three always getting into trouble?" says Abshir, helping me up. "Like, I literally let you out of my sight for five minutes."

"It wasn't our fault. Omar's a dick," says Yousuf. "Though you should've seen Fawad break his ankles. Man, I wish I got that on video."

Arif inspects me. "I swear if he hit you, I would've lost it."

"Yo, y'all need to stop getting involved with them dipshits," says Abshir, sitting down on a bench. "Let them play gangster and see where that takes 'em. Only two places you end up playing that game: dead or in jail. You three got bigger and brighter things to look forward to."

He lectures us for another few minutes before he sends us packing. Outside, the August sun hits hard, but I'm just glad I don't have to go home and explain no bruises to my mother. She'd have a heart attack, and I don't think I'm ready to be an orphan just yet. We catch Arif's cousin Nazmul hanging with his boys in the parking lot behind my building, standing by the trunk of his BMW. Long hair slicked back, baseball cap so low you can barely see his eyes, wearing a dark denim shirt over a black T-shirt and jeans. He runs the Bangladeshi crew, and just like the Tamils, Somalis, and everyone else in Regent, they don't fuck around.

"I'm gonna say what up to Naz," says Arif, throwing up his hand so we can do our man-hugs. "Y'all still good for catching a movie tonight?"

"I'm down," says Yousuf.

"I still gotta ask my mom . . ." I say, not making eye contact.

Yousuf and Arif snicker, before Arif breaks off and heads over to them other guys.

I try to invite Yousuf over for dinner, but he tell's me he's good. Also, I bet a hundred dollars my mom won't let me out of the house that late for the movie.

...

I hit Gerrard Street and head left, keeping a slow pace. I want to make the most of one of the, like, twenty summer days we get living in Toronto. It's the best feeling in the world. At least it helps me not think about Omar knocking out my front teeth. Though I did cross him up pretty good. He's going to remember that one, and so are his boys. A couple of chipped teeth would've been worth it. Thank God for Abshir—it wasn't the first time he's saved my ass from being beat down. Fingers crossed, it won't be the last.

I look across to Cabbagetown. One road separating the ghetto from million-dollar homes. And yeah, it feels shitty to be on the wrong side.

My family didn't always live in Regent, or Canada for that matter. We immigrated eight years ago and lived in the west end of the city, in a neighborhood called the Junction, in a crammed two-bedroom apartment on top of a country music bar for three years. For those years, I went to an elementary school where the worst thing that ever happened to me was someone making fun of my lunch. Got invited to proper birthday parties in backyards and everything.

I didn't even know what a "community housing project" was up until my dad came home to that apartment one day looking like we'd won the lottery.

Our name was apparently on the list for a minute before they'd assigned a first-floor three-bedroom apartment to us at

407 Gerrard. Subsidized rent when you're living on social assistance and driving a cab makes a big difference, I guess. Like two trips for groceries to No Frills a month instead of just one.

I was going to miss my friends, but at the same time I was excited to finally have my own room like any ten-year-old—but that was before my bike got stolen, I got picked on for my clothes, and every day felt like something was going to go wrong.

Like some asshole coming up behind you on a basketball court and putting you in a chokehold just because he felt like it. Then laughing like some psychopath as you struggled to keep taking in just enough air to stop yourself from passing out. Or watching fights break out and not being sure when a punch, a knife, or worse, a bullet could come flying your way.

It wasn't all rosy like my dad imagined. Or at least not from what I remember. He still drove a cab. He was a senior naval engineer with a master's degree back home in Pakistan. Here, he was no one. Suddenly, an uncle or family friend presented an opportunity to co-invest in a Tim Hortons franchise, and Dad wanted in—but he needed capital.

We had land back home that he said he was going to go back to sell. A month later, we got a phone call. He was riding a motorcycle and got struck by a transport truck. He died on the spot. No Timmies franchise. No moving out to the burbs. From then on, I knew it was on me to get us out of this shithole.

That was two years back. He never made it to my middle-school graduation, where I got the math award. My mom told me the plan had been to save money for a down payment on a house. I laughed when she said it . . . like that's ever going to happen now. Twenty percent of a million dollars is $200,000. That's five zeros. Who's got that kind of money?

I kick a plastic Coke bottle onto someone's lawn and start walking over to my brick apartment building just a few steps down.

To be honest, whenever I walk through Cabbagetown, all I can think of is what it'd be like to have a front lawn, a backyard, and a bathroom I didn't have to share with my sister. Fantasies of the highest order.

Instead, outside my crusty-ass building, which literally looks like some builder shat out bricks and didn't have enough money for the concrete to put between them, I see my white next-door neighbors sprawled out having a little BBQ. Looks like they invited a whole lot of their extended family from across Regent.

They're sitting on lawn chairs, smoking, sipping on beers tucked in brown paper bags. Older dudes wearing Hawaiian shirts they leave unbuttoned, letting their guts hang loosely like they live on an island or something, with their wives or girlfriends sitting on their laps. Everyone looks like they took a hit of something and are stuck in a perpetual after-party.

I don't know if the showers work in their units or not, but I gotta hold my breath every time I pass by. There's rock music blaring from a Bluetooth speaker. I have no idea how people live in Regent and still manage to have enough money to spend on shit like that.

There are some kids my age, one I even went to elementary school with, hanging on the steps, blocking the entrance. I don't want to have to talk to them, but I say, "Excuse me, coming through," before one of them gets up and shuffles to the side.

As I pass by, I notice the girl who's usually making out with this skinny dude that went to school with me. I can never remember his name. Kyle? John? Ronny? One of those, for sure. She's got a large bump showing.

The way he's keeping his hands on her tummy makes me realize that she's pregnant. I shrug and keep moving.

The buzzer system has got so much grime that if you used it, you'd probably get infected with some nasty-ass shit in no time. I wouldn't touch it with latex gloves on the real. I pull out my fob. When I put it close to the little scanner, I realize I don't need it.

Someone broke the front door lock. Again. *Broke* meaning ripped off or pulled on the handle so hard that the magnetic strips or whatever keeps it closed—and all the drug dealers out—doesn't work. The superintendent may fix it next week, but it doesn't matter . . . someone will just bust it again a few days later.

There's a sign inside emblazoned with the words "THIS AREA IS MONITORED BY CLOSED-CIRCUIT TV." My ass it is.

My apartment is on the left, down a mini-hallway. I get hit with a whiff of shit. Someone must've taken a dump in the stairwell leading up to the second floor again. Happens at least once a month.

I hold my breath and rush to my door. I've got this habit of just twisting the knob like I expect it to be open, even though you'd have to be batshit crazy to leave your door unlocked in this hood. Just saying.

2

I could hear Bollywood tunes from outside the door. Lo and behold, Shah Rukh Khan is dancing on the Swiss Alps with Kajol, the two of them playing in the snow like they're on the beach. Never made any sense to me. Not now. Not ever.

My sister and mom are lounging on the couch, each with her own blanket, streaming music videos from YouTube to the TV. On the coffee table, there's cups with remnants of chai and next to them, a plate with rusk cake and cumin cookies.

Jamila keeps her hair short, recently got purple streaks, and also has a nose ring. All of which really annoys Mom. I think that's mostly why she does it. She pays for it herself working retail part-time at Old Navy at the Eaton Centre, so not much Mom can do either.

My mom's long salt-and-pepper hair is tied back into a bun, and she's looking at me through her bifocal lenses. She's got moles on both sides of her nostrils and a long, narrow nose.

"Again?" I say, dropping my duffel bag and kicking off my sneakers. "These songs are so old and crusty. Just like Shah Rukh."

"Don't pretend like you don't love him," says Jamila, looking over and rolling her eyes.

I don't. Okay, maybe just a little. I mean, I did grow up watching his movies over and over again. It's impossible not to like something you've been exposed to that much. Even if I never had a choice in the matter.

"We could watch something else once in a while," I say, relaxing on the couch adjacent to theirs.

Jamila shrugs.

"What took so long?" says Mom, pushing herself up to stare at me. "You said you'd be home by one."

I glance at the clock on the wall. It's now six thirty. Big whoop.

"Lost track of time. You could just text me, you know."

"Don't talk to me like that," says Mom, cocking back her hand. "One slap and you'll be straightened up right now."

I just smile back.

"You'd better stay put at home for the rest of today," Mom says. "Your room's a mess, and I'm tired of picking up after you like you're some two-year-old. When are you going to take a break from that stupid sport and do something useful? Like tidy up?"

Ouch. Somebody call a medic. Someone is in a sour mood. Mayday.

I just nod because it's pointless arguing with mothers. This is not only from my own experience. I've seen it with all my other friends too.

Her phone starts vibrating. She picks it up. It's a video call from Pakistan. It's *her*. Mom's definitely going to try and get me to talk to *her*. Agh.

"Assalamu alaikum, Aunty," says a loud, high-pitched voice from the other end.

"Wa-alaikum assalam, Nusrat. How are you, beta? You look beautiful today," Mom says. It's over-the-top and enough to make me want to throw up.

Jamila sees me squirming as I get up and head into the kitchen. I'm starved after that pickup game. I hit the goldmine. Aloo keema parathas.

They're cold, but that has no impact on how savory they are. Not when there's some mint raita and mango achar. Lots of mango achar.

"Fawad, come speak to Nusrat," my mom yells from the living room.

I feel like I'm being yanked into the depths of hell. Here she goes again.

I can hear Jamila giggling and losing her shit. She's getting in on the fun, bragging about how I've become such a superstar basketball player, waiting to see the look on my face. The cruelty that only an older sister can inflict.

"I'm busy eating, Ammi," I yell back. This is not a lie. I am eating. I am busy. It's not that Nusrat and I aren't cool. We actually hit it off when I was in Pakistan, but as cousins, not as in I-want-to-marry-you or whatever my mom's hell-bent on arranging.

"FAWAD!"

Okay, that does not sound good.

I drag my feet out into the living room, still chewing on a morsel of that aloo keema paratha dipped in raita.

My mother hands me the phone.

Nusrat has a scarf over her head. She's petite and, like, a little pretty, only slightly, but *eww*, she's my cousin. What's wrong with my family?

"Salaam, bhai," she says. I am a few months older than her. That's the messed-up part, right? She just referred to me as "brother" out of respect.

I garble up, "Salaam, Nusrat. How are things?"

This is just as awkward for her as it is for me. Her eyes are shifty and she finally responds with, "Here, let me show you around."

She does a panorama of my uncle's home in our ancestral village, with its front yard so wide and open it could actually be a school playground.

In one corner, they have these massive cattle grazing on freshly cut wheat from the field. There's even a goat tied up to a tree, nibbling on something. My favorite bit of the tour is catching the little chicks roaming around pecking feed off the ground, looking all cute and shit.

Off to the side, I catch a glimpse of my mom's mom, my grandma, lying on a manji in the shade.

"Everyone is missing you," she says. "Come visit."

"We'll book his ticket today," says Jamila, smirking.

I nod my head like I'm entertaining the thought. Then I give Jamila a kick in the shin for being such a witch. She lashes right back and takes a swipe, but I dodge her, the phone still in my hand.

"Okay, I have to go. Talk to you later," I say, waving.

I give Mom her phone and dash back to the kitchen. I feel like I've lost my appetite, but nope. I'm an addict. It's impossible to eat too many parathas. Then I lock myself in my room, which is pretty bare-bones: a double bed; a full-length mirror next to a built-in closet that has a curtain drawn across it; a study table next to the bed, which has a laptop on it that belongs in a museum. There's also a bookshelf with random binders and a participation trophy from a basketball tournament.

After a few more minutes, I hear my mom hang up and breathe a sigh of relief.

When I come back out into the living room, it's finally one of Shah Rukh's more recent songs that they're streaming.

In the video, I catch a glimpse of the one girl I'd do anything to be with. Like, literally anything. You can have it in writing. I know she's older than me, but I can't help it. I have the biggest crush on her.

"You can sit, you know," Jamila says, eyeing me like I'm some weirdo.

"Oh yeah," I mutter.

The queen of hearts, specifically my heart, is none other than—wait for it—Deepika Padukone. I fawn, I faint, I melt watching her in this ridiculous dress swirl, smile, and flash those goddamn dimples. Kill me. Tell me I'd never eat another meal cooked by my mother in exchange for one kiss from her and I'd gladly say yes. Crazy. Right?

Jamila whips a cushion at me. "Stop it, you creep."

"What?" I say, throwing one right back.

I go back to watching Deepika twirl.

After the song, I head into my room to unwind. There's a WhatsApp message.

NUSRAT: Khala's gotten a little crazy, no?

I laugh. If only Mom really knew how Nusrat felt about her antics.

ME: Just a little. I swear something's gotten into her the last few months.

NUSRAT: Yeah, she's been talking to Abbu a lot too. Have you talked to her about this?

ME: I wish. I think she'd bite my head off.

NUSRAT: Lol. I don't know how to talk to Abbu either. Ahmed's baap and him don't get along unfortunately. :(

ME: Who's Ahmed again?

NUSRAT: You ask me every time. He's my aunt's cousin's son. We have a property dispute with them. But we both really like each other.

ME: Sounds complicated. Okay, I'll do it. I gotta set her head straight. This is getting out of hand.

NUSRAT: Promise? When? I don't want her and Abbu to do something silly.

ME: Uh, soon. Promise.

NUSRAT: :) okay, have to go. Salaam.

I put away my phone and play out my mom's reaction. If I told her directly to back off, she would 100 percent throw a fit and become even more adamant. I gotta think strategically, look for the right moment to strike.

Besides, if Jamila can date whoever the hell she wants, I ought to be able to. There's no way Jamila would even hear my mom out if she ever brought up her marrying some guy from our village back home. The only difference is Jamila can stand up to her. And me? Well, it's complicated.

Ever since Dad died, it's a sure thing that I'll be the one to take care of her as she gets old. Unless she moved back to Pakistan or something. And every damn Pakistani soap opera that's ever on television is all about mothers-in-law quibbling with daughters-in-law. It's a thing.

So yeah, she's trying to make her life easy. She likes Nusrat. She knows Nusrat. And if she brings her all the way over here, she's basically guaranteed to have someone to do the chores, make her chai, and all that.

On top of that, all her life she's talked about how badly her brother's wife treated their mom. I don't know the ins and outs of that, but it's left its mark.

Ugh. So really, I'm screwed. *Dad, thanks for bailing.* I look up at the ceiling. *I'm being sarcastic, in case humor isn't a thing up there.* I imagine his face crinkling, his enormous mustache hiding his upper lip.

. . .

I go back out into the living room after a short while and look out the window. I can see right out onto Gerrard Street. Yousuf's townhouse is the first of three by the intersection. Coming from that direction are three men dressed in thobes, which are kinda like long robes, sporting well-groomed beards and stern faces, as most religious men do, walking toward our building.

"Jamila, your best friends are coming," I say.

"Not them again," says Jamila, getting up and looking annoyed. "I'll be in my room."

"Don't forget to cover your head in case you come back out," says Mom, busy adjusting and fixing a thin fabric scarf, or dupatta, over her own hair. She too gets up and heads for the kitchen. "Just tell me if they want chai."

I nod. One of the things about being the man of the household is having to field these visits from men I'd prefer to only see at the mosque, if and when I go. I have no idea how they know where I live, and why they feel entitled to knock, sometimes enter, but mostly lecture me and make me feel like shit for not coming around the mosque more often. Sigh.

There's a knock. I look through the peephole for good measure. Standing there is Imam Aziz, my Quran teacher and Omar's father, along with Abdullah, an older student of his who's Afghan. The third man is short and Bangladeshi. I've seen him around but don't remember his name.

"Ah, Fawad," Imam Aziz says as I open the door. "You know, you really must show your face at the mosque more. It's not enough just coming to Saturday's class. You are coming tomorrow, aren't you?"

"Yes, Imam Saab," I say, scratching the back of my head. "I've just been busy."

What I really want to tell him is his son's a dirtbag. That he should really keep an eye on him because he's always gunning for me.

"Can never be too busy to visit the mosque, my child," he says, patting the top of my head. "It's all that counts when this temporary life is over. Death comes to us all."

Morose, possibly true, but I'm skeptical. Not about the death stuff. Mostly about the religion stuff.

"Do you guys want to come in?" I say.

"Oh no, we don't want to trouble you or your family," says Imam Aziz. "I believe you've met Abdullah already, budding scholar that he is. This here is Mohammed. He just moved to the community and is eager to help out."

I shake hands with them.

"So, Abdullah, will you do the honors?" says Imam Aziz.

Abdullah holds out a pink sheet of paper; on it is a picture of a guy with a turban and beard.

"Brother, we're very honored and privileged to be hosting Maulana Umar Qadri next week. We're inviting all the brothers in the community to come and bask in his knowledge," says Abdullah. He's so giddy while talking—it's like Arif when he's bragging about going to third base with some chick. "He's doing a Canadian tour for our benefit. Traveling all the way from Saudi, no less. We want our mosque to be full for such an honor."

I nod politely. "Sure, I guess."

"Oh, and if you don't mind," says Mohammed, taking out a stack of flyers from a bag and holding them out, "we need to spread the word, so if you'd like to go around and put these in coffee shops, give them to your friends, or help us promote this event on social media, it would mean a lot. Thank you, brother."

I take the stack. I mean, it's not like I have a choice.

Imam Aziz pats me on the head again and tousles my hair. "Good boy, see you soon, then."

They start heading off. I slowly close the door, staring at the face of this maulana on the poster. He doesn't look all that different from countless other religious scholars. He'll probably regurgitate the same things I've heard before. Pray, fast, don't do anything that's haram, which is a lot, and when all's said and done, you'll live happily ever after in the afterlife.

Jamila strides in and takes a flyer from me. "He's a looker."

Mom appears from the kitchen and takes the stack from my hand. "We have a place in the thrift store for community events. I'll put them there."

"Thanks, Ammi."

She's been working part-time at Double Take, the local thrift store, ever since Dad passed. Her English has come a long way too. Before the ESL classes, she barely got by, but now she doesn't need me or Jamila with her at the grocery store or the bank. She can do it all on her own. No thanks to Dad, but that's in the past now.

I watch her put the stack of papers on top of the fridge.

"Oh, also, Arif wanted to go see a movie tonight," I say, picking up and washing a glass in the sink to earn some extra brownie points.

"That stupid boy has too much time and money on his hands," says Mom. She's tidying up the kitchen—God forbid there be a stray dish lying here or there.

"So can I go?" I say, drying the newly washed glass in the dish rack.

"No. Invite him home and watch something here," she says. "It's not good to be out so late."

"But Ammi . . ."

"But nothing. But Ammi ka bacha."

I slouch and walk back to the couch, defeated. I text Arif I can't make it. He already knew my mom wouldn't let me; then again, so did I.

She was a worrier even when Dad was around, but now it's at a whole other level. She'd monitor my breathing while I slept if she could. Suffocating as hell.

Jamila continues to pick songs with Deepika. This time, I watch along a little more nonchalantly, because I think Jamila is right. I do get a bit creepy watching her videos. Need something to shake off how nervous I'm feeling about the big game on Sunday.

3

The gym is sweltering hot. Hotter than the kitchen when my mom decides she wants to bake naan, which is ten times better than store- or restaurant-bought naan. Wallahi, ask any of my friends.

Fuck, now I'm hungry. I need to focus on the game. The rest of the guys are waiting for us on the bleachers. They get up when they see us walking into the gym with Jerome, our coach. Jerome was my fifth-grade teacher, and I still trip and call him "Mr. Williams" every so often. Other dudes sometimes call him Dr. J, since he can pull out the hook shot like Julius Irving, but he doesn't like it. It's Jerome or bust.

Yousef and I hitched a ride in Jerome's 2012 Honda Civic from the South Regent community center, along with two other dudes. Abshir said he wasn't up for driving us. He was out late or something. He said he'd be at the game, though. Yousuf doubted it. I bet him a chicken shawarma sandwich that he'd make it. How could he not want to come see me use his tips and tricks to light up the other team?

I put my NBA Official ball back in my duffel bag. I've got a weird habit of having it in my hands all the time. I'm not a fiend, but then again, there are worse things to be addicted to.

Jerome drops the two black garbage bags he's had in his hands onto the court. He lets us loose to dig through and pick out our jersey numbers. As usual, I take 30, because no one shoots better than me from behind the arc. I also do the best Steph Curry impersonation when I sink one. To be honest, all I'm missing is a mouth guard to chew on—and to throw when I'm pissed.

"Let's move, fellas. Big day ahead of us," says Jerome. He's got his typical thick, black glasses on and a T-shirt with Nelson Mandela's face on it. He must own at least five of those. Other favorites include Malcolm X, Gandhi, and Maya Angelou. Still my favorite teacher of all-time.

The energy in the gym is electric. We're repping Regent Park hard against Moss Park. The game's happening at John Innes Community Centre, though, so we're on their turf. I'm not too worried. I think we got this in the bag.

The grin on my face is wiped clean when I feel a shove from behind and get knocked off balance as Omar cuts through to pick out his jersey.

"Get out of my way, Fuckwad," says Omar as he rummages through and takes out the jersey with the number 23 printed on the back. He turns to face me and waits for a reaction.

But I don't say anything. My lips are sewn shut. My sweat glands are working overtime, and my heart is racing. The adrenaline pumping through my veins is for running away, not for gearing up for a fight. Besides, there's no Abshir here today.

"Eh man, leave him alone," says Yousuf, stepping in between us. I wouldn't put my money on Yousuf if they got into a fight, but maybe the two of us could take him.

"You wanna make me?" says Omar, towering over him as he shoves him back.

"Do we have a problem here, gentlemen?" says Jerome. He walks over with a pissed-off look on his face.

"Nah, Coach, I was just messing . . ." says Omar, shriveling up. It's the only time I get to see him squirm, so I savor it.

"Well, it's game time, so let's start warming up," says Jerome in a firm, deep voice, giving Omar one of his stare-downs.

Omar shakes his head and walks off.

Yousuf and I smirk at each other. We start the trek across the gym to the locker room behind the rest of the team. I'm taking copious mental notes, watching the guys from Moss Park warming up. My eyes follow each shot.

In the locker room, I'm realizing I gotta start hitting the gym more. Some of the dudes on the team have full-fledged six-packs. I think the furthest I ever got was a four-pack. I'm sitting at three abs right now. I hate odd numbers.

Coach is on the phone in the corner. He ends the call and walks over, looking distressed. We huddle around him.

"Boys, we've got a situation," he says, crossing his arms. "Kevin's mom called and said he's got a funeral to attend. We're down a starter."

My eyes widen. Kev plays point guard and so do I. I'm fantasizing about walking onto the court for the tip-off. I've been waiting to start all summer.

Licking my lips like I'm about to bite into my mother's aloo keema parathas, I'm anticipating Coach saying my name. My real name. Not Fahd, Fa-ad, Faaaad, Fuckwad, Foooowad, but *Fawad*.

"Fawad, do you want to start?"

I want to scream "Hell yeah!" from the top of my lungs, but I look over at Yousuf, who I know has been wanting to start all summer too, and shake my head.

"Put Yousuf in, Coach."

"All right, then, we got our five."

Everyone nods. The guys are lacing up their sneakers. Some of those kicks look way too expensive for kids from Regent. But I know money doesn't just grow on social assistance trees. There's plenty of other kinds of trees.

I've been playing in my beat-up Under Armour Curry 1s for the last three years. I can feel my big toes stub against the tips.

Yousuf backhands me across the chest as the locker room clears out.

"What the hell, man?" he says. "You've been literally practicing ten hours a day all summer waiting for this. Now you pull this shit?"

I play it off as no big deal. But it's true: I've been eating, sleeping, drinking, and breathing ball for the last two months.

"How you gon' back down like that?" he continues.

I shrug. "Just figured you'd want a shot."

"I should slap you silly sometimes, man," he says, throwing up his hands. "Who does that?"

"You dummies done jerking each other off?" says Omar as he's about to exit.

"Fuck off," I say.

He turns, looking angry. "You grew a backbone today?"

My body tenses, and I elongate my spine and stick my chest out a little. "Yeah," I stutter. "I did."

"Well, don't make me twist it and spit it out, shitface."

He gives me a shove and heads out onto the court. I hold Yousuf back from retaliating. It's not worth it. It's the last game of the summer.

On the court, during the warm-up, I'm sinking jump shot after jump shot. There's a group of older dudes from Regent in the stands. No Abshir, though. Those guys have all been training and playing for Jerome for years. Some of them are poised for big things, like college basketball in the States.

One of them, Kingsley, better known as King, reigns supreme. Highest-rated prospect in Canada headed into his final year of high school. Rumors are flying around that he's headed to North Carolina. Like, the same school Jordan played college ball at.

How. Fucking. Amazing.

Yousuf says I'm a fanboy. I like to think of myself as an early adopter. He could be the next LeBron.

There's also parents and friends of my teammates in the stands to cheer us on. I can't imagine my mother or Jamila sitting there—they'd be bored out of their minds. I feel like my dad would've wanted to see me play, but he's gone, so there's no point in thinking about that now.

We're doing layups to warm up. I drive in for my turn. Boom, out of nowhere, Omar swats the ball away.

"Ha!" he shouts. "Weak."

I pick up another basketball off the floor. I'm ready to whip it at him.

"Omar, that's not part of the drill. Get back to the top of the key," Jerome yells from the sidelines.

The referee blows his whistle. We huddle around Coach by the bench.

"All right, listen here, everyone," Jerome says, looking proud. "You've worked your butts off all summer to get to here, but I want you to know, no matter what happens, you should all be proud of what we've accomplished. I see a lot of potential, and this is where the rubber meets the road. Before the game, I wanna share words from my hero. Everyone recognizes the man on this shirt, right? By now, everyone's head should be nodding."

I love it when Coach shares a quote. He used to start each morning the same way when I was in his class. Had most of his top quotes memorized by now.

"Mr. Mandela once said, 'Do not judge me by my successes, judge me by how many times I fell down and got back up again.' So I want all of you to focus on that. You get knocked down, jump back up, and keep count. That's how we win. Okay, 'Regent' on three."

"Regent," we shout.

I'm watching the tip-off from the bench with all the intensity of the pressure cooker my mom makes lentils in. I'm rattling and shaking like one too. The guy next to me cups my knee with his hand and looks at me like I'm crazy. I was making the whole bench vibrate.

What can I say? I'm a nervous guy who's overexcited, over the moon, and overjoyed to be watching some ball. I stop shaking and imagine a basketball instead of a heart beating inside me. *Thump. Thump. Thump.* Plus, wait, is that . . . ? Yup, Abshir, sitting with some of those older dudes from Regent. Free chicken shawarma, here I come.

Moss Park is kicking our ass but Omar's keeping us in the game. Yousuf's long arms aren't doing him any good today. He's been poking around looking for steals and picked up two fouls. At this point, we're only five minutes in.

He does score four points. Each time he gets a bucket, I'm on my feet cheering. We got a pact. One game I scored nineteen off the bench. He was acting like I hit a game-winner every time the ball went into the net.

"Fawad, you're in," Coach yells, motioning to Yousuf to come to the bench.

Those have to be my three favorite words in the whole wide world. We're down by ten. I've got the ball in my hands, staring down this guy who's guarding me real tight.

I swerve, I criss-cross, I shake, and I bake. I find Omar down in the post. He bodies the dude guarding him, who's a whole foot shorter, to get an easy lay-in.

The assist is a stat only. Omar feels entitled to the ball. He never registers where it comes from.

On defense, I'm trying to stay steady, watching a guy named Darius do things I thought only NBA players could do. He's hitting fadeaway jump shots like they were free throws. Someone call the fire department. We're being torched.

Morale is low, so I pick up the pace and before the other team can react, I'm already at half-court, speeding down like thunder when I pull up not one, not two, but three feet outside the three-point line. I jack up a shot that hits nothing but net. The crowd *oohs* and *aahs*. The bench jumps in joy.

"Booyah! That's what I'm talking about, boy," I hear Abshir yell. I point at him and smile. Hard work does pay off.

I hit three more threes just for good measure before the second quarter ends. Half-time came way too soon—I was just getting into a rhythm. Damn. Rather than head back to the bench, I go over to dab Abshir. He's wearing a long red hoodie with no sleeves over a black T-shirt with the words "RP 4 Life" printed on it, along with gray sweatpants and white Air Force 1s. Looks like he didn't sleep much. There are serious bags under his eyes.

"I see you, boy. That flick of the wrist we talked about? You got it down pat," he says, ruffling my hair.

I rub the back of my neck. "Thanks for the tip. You doing okay? You're looking a li'l rough."

"Just haven't been sleeping much. Here, let me intro you to this dude."

Sitting a few feet away is *him*. He nods his head to acknowledge me. I'm stupefied.

"Eh yo, King, this here's Fawad," says Abshir, putting an arm around my shoulder and pulling my head close to his chest.

"That's some legit sharpshooting," says King.

Never in my entire existence did I think myself worthy. I fist-bump him and his crew like I've known 'em for a minute. There are a few fine girls with them.

"You from Regent? How come I never seen you around?" says King, sitting up and leaning forward. Dressed in a green Adidas track jacket, he's got cornrows, big fake diamond earrings, and a chain around his neck. In other words, he's the definition of smooth.

"First summer playing with Jerome," I say. But really it's because my mom barely lets me out of her sights.

"Oh word, he'll do you good, stick with him," he says. "You got Steph Curry vibes, homes. That jump shot ain't no regular jump shot." He then looks up at Abshir. "You been showing him the ropes, dawg?"

Cloud nine. Did he just say I have Steph Curry vibes? Pinch me. Earth to Fawad.

"Here and there, but he's a hustler. He'll wake up crack of dawn and start messaging me."

"Fawad," yells Coach from the other side of the court, snapping me out of my daze.

"Looks like you gotta go, little man," King says.

"I can't stay till the end of the game," says Abshir, hand on my shoulder. "But just merk 'em for me. You and Yousuf can probably hitch a ride back with Jerome or just walk home."

"We'll probably walk."

"Cool, and if that punk Omar says anything, just let me know. Now go get 'em," he says, giving me a strong pat on the back.

I nod. I'm still a little bit in shock. "Word," I say, running back to my team.

"What was that about?" says Yousuf as we're sipping on some Gatorade.

"Oh, nothing," I say, playing it cool. "Your bro just told King about me and he said I got Curry's jump shot."

"Word?"

I nod.

"My homie," says Yousuf. We're both like kids in a candy store. Getting praise from a legend is no small feat.

"Fellas, curry boy thinks he's the next Curry," says Omar, cracking up. "Smelling and shooting are two different things, guy."

His cronies are wilin' out like he's a stand-up comedian.

"What did you say, Omar?" says Coach.

"Nothin'," says Omar, looking away.

The third quarter is in full swing. Yousuf is on the court, but I'm itching to go back in. Yousuf catches his third and fourth fouls halfway through the quarter.

I'm shaking my head, but that also means I'm back in.

We're down by five.

I'm driving in, splitting defenders hard. I spot an open teammate in the corner, who hits a bank shot. We do our little celebration gesture, thumping our chests.

Darius, on the other end, does the most serene and cleanest spin move I've ever seen. Completely catches Omar off guard, and he's wide open as he lays it in. Poetry in motion.

Fourth quarter. Yousuf fouls out. He leaves the court cursing the referee. Coach is pissed at the ref too. I get my butt slapped as I head in. "Go get 'em, son."

It's all or nothing now. We're still down by five. Eight minutes remaining. Tit for tat. We score. They score. Two minutes. We're down by four. It's boogie time.

I fly up the court. Omar's screaming for the ball. I got other plans. My defender thinks I won't shoot from where I'm dribbling. That I'm too far out. That I'd be crazy to jack up a shot from there with this much on the line. He gives me a confused look when I put the shot up. I see him watch the ball fly out of my hands and hit nothing but net. Down by one. Everyone's on their feet.

"Pass the fucking ball next time," says Omar, running past me. "Or else."

I gulp. We're back on defense. The clock's winding down. We need to get a stop. Darius is cutting through us like a whirlwind. I sneak behind him and poke the ball out from his unsuspecting hands. A teammate picks it up and passes it to me. I'm in the clear. Omar's a few feet down. Defenders are rushing back. Do I take it all the way? Or do I not?

I'm hesitating. I'm scared. I pass. Omar jacks up a shot. It rolls around the rim but just as the clock winds down, it spins right back out.

We're not champions. The other team is jumping for joy. Meanwhile, I still have no idea why I didn't shoot. Fucking Omar.

On top of it all, he's glaring at me like *I* missed the shot and not him. "You fucking took too long," he yells, confronting me in the team huddle. Everyone's giving him the same crazy look.

"That's enough of that," says Coach. The other kids laugh. Omar is pissed. "You did good, Fawad."

Everyone's patting me on the back.

"We'll get 'em next year. 'Regent' on three."

"Regent," we shout half-heartedly. We shake hands with the winning team and watch as they're presented with a big trophy, then wait until we get our second-place ones. Darius wins MVP. We head back to the locker room. I really should've taken it all the way. We could've been the ones out there celebrating right now. I take a photo of my trophy and text it to Abshir: Almost . . . and throw in a grimace emoji.

. . .

Yousuf and I decide to walk home after the game. The entire summer feels like a waste. I'm feeling like I let everyone down . . . especially Jérome, after everything he's done for me. I'd be half—no, a quarter of the player I am now if I hadn't trained with him the last few months.

I finish the can of Coke in my hand and crush it.

"Whoa, easy there, homes," says Yousuf. "You know you killed it, right?"

I don't know about that.

"We still lost," I say, eyeing a garbage can and lining up a shot. I send it flying in the air and Yousuf swats it down to the sidewalk.

What an asshole! Just when I thought he was sympathizing with me. He picks it up and does a throw behind the back to have it land in the can. The smile on his face is unbelievable.

"C'mon, man, you didn't think I'd let you have that," he says. "Also, it wasn't your fault. So quit sulking."

"Agh, I fucking hate Omar so much," I say, stomping my foot and clenching my fists. "Then he tried to pin it on me. What an ass."

"Nothing new," says Yousuf, flipping through a song playlist on his phone. He's got one side of his Beats Solo^3 wireless headphones on his ear. They're bright red and shiny. Abshir copped them for him. They're the type of thing that makes you nervous walking through Regent, wondering if someone will just walk up to you and snatch them. Unless you're Abshir's younger brother. Then you're cool.

"You remember the time he tried cheating on that math test in eighth grade?" he says, getting close and pretending to look over my shoulder. "He was so blatant about it that when Mr. K caught him, he said you were the one showing him your sheet."

I laugh. "Yeah, you're right. It's nothing new."

School was pure hell with Omar. I remember telling my dad how badly I wanted to change schools. Every time, he'd listen and then just tell me to stick with it. That running never solved anything.

I counted my blessings every day when I found out we were going to different high schools. There's still no getting away, though, when you live in the same neighborhood.

"Forget him, man. Anyways, looks like Abshir did show for a bit," he says, eyes wide like whenever he's cooking up a scheme. "That means I'm treating yo' ass to a shawarma from Kabul Express."

The shawarma from the Afghan spot next to the mosque is the best, bar none. My stomach starts grumbling at the thought of all the garlic sauce they throw on there.

"Double meat," I say.

"Done."

Oh man, nothing like food to shake me out of a funk. I may not look it, but I can eat. Yousuf would know. One time a crew of us went to the Mandarin all-you-can-eat buffet and every single dude there couldn't believe their eyes when I was the last man standing, helping myself to my eleventh plate.

"I knew that'd cheer you up," he says, taking off his headphones and handing them over. "Here, listen to this."

I put them on. Damn, now that sounds like a serious update to what I have to work with. He's bumping a J. Cole track. I'm straight-up vibing with it now, bopping my head.

I take my ball out of the duffel bag and feel like I'm on a different planet. Yousuf's looking at me, laughing. I don't care, though. I'm going to just let this song ride out.

4

We're unwinding at Yousuf's home after the game, both of us still reeking with the stench of disappointment. Our second-place trophies are next to one another on his bed, at the foot of which is the Yamaha guitar that Yousuf "plays," though he's played it, like, once in front of me. We're taking out our frustration playing *NBA 2K19* on Yousuf's PS4 Pro that Abshir copped for him a couple months ago.

I'm Steph Curry. Yousuf is Kawhi Leonard. I'm dominating. Obviously.

Arif barges in.

"Damn. Look at you two," Arif says, picking up one of the trophies. "You guys won something? Holy shit."

"Second-place trophies," I say, turning to face him for a quick second before going back to the game.

"Put this on Insta yet?" he asks, still inspecting them like they're some archaeological marvel.

We both shake our heads.

"Y'all tripping, girls go cray for shit like this. Keep telling Yousuf to post videos of him playing guitar, but does he listen? Nope."

We shrug.

Arif knows a lot about the opposite sex. Yousuf had a girlfriend back in fifth grade, so he knows a little more than I do, even though they broke up two weeks later.

I just get nervous as fuck around girls. Can't get my shit together long enough to say something that will make them smile. That is the goal, right? Because if they smile, that means they like you. If they like you, that means they want to kiss you.

At least that's what I think. But what do I know? Like I said, my track record with females is zilch. The only girl I can act normal around is Nermin, but she's a friend so that doesn't count.

"Oh, I know who'll get a kick out of this," says Arif.

I stare at him like he's crazy—which he is, for the record.

"Nusrat."

I jump up and tackle his behind to the floor. He's still laughing. We're both pretty evenly matched, so he retaliates quickly.

Yousuf's way bigger than both of us, so he quickly jumps in and rips me off Arif.

"My mom catches us like this, and that's the last time I'll ever see you losers."

I'm still pissed he said *her* name. He doesn't get secrets. I should've known better than to tell him.

"Don't say her name, like, ever," I warn him.

"Bro, you're talking about your future wifey. You do know that, right?"

"Arif, c'mon, man," says Yousuf, leading him a few steps back.

"Whoa, chill, I'm playing," says Arif. "On the real, though, if you don't start dating, your mom just might eventually pull the trigger. Happened to my cousin just a couple months ago."

"Over my dead body. Arranged marriages are fucked," I say.

"Word. Like, to your first cousin too, man," says Arif. "So nasty."

"Eh, Arif, why don't you hook this dude up with some cute white girl at Northern?" says Yousuf. He puts his arm around me. "Like, who wouldn't want to be with this guy?"

Like that's ever going to happen.

"I've tried, bro," says Arif. "He just freezes up like you wouldn't believe."

"Whatever. Can we go back to finishing the game?" I say, pointing to the TV.

"I'm worried about your wrist," says Arif, shaking his hand up and down near his waist. "Trust me, it's way better with a girl."

Another dagger. Arif's ruthless today. I give him a hard shove. "Punk."

"Why you still going to Central, man?" I say to Yousuf. "Switch to Northern already."

"Abshir, remember?" he says. "Mom wants us to go to the same school."

I'd do anything for the three of us to be at the same high school. Don't get me wrong, I love Arif, but school without Yousuf sucks balls.

Plus, I've known Yousuf from the time I first moved to Regent Park. His mom met my mom at the doctor's office across the street and they hit it off. They didn't speak much English or know each other's native tongues, but the mothers seemed to have some weird bond. Turned out his mom had a bad knee and trouble walking him to school. My mom offered to drop both me and him to school every morning. So yeah, it was a little forced at first, but then we just hit it off.

Oh, and he introduced me to the love of my life: basketball.

I didn't have an athletic bone in my body when he first waved me over to play with him and his friends during recess one day in fifth grade. I had no idea it would take over my life.

I met Arif a few weeks after moving into Regent too, at mosque after my mom enrolled me in Quran class. But once the three of us hung out, it was game over.

We sit back down and pick up the controllers. Arif joins Yousuf because he can't wait for someone to knock Golden State off their championship ways. Like that's ever going to happen. It's 2018 and they've made the finals for three years straight.

There's a loud bang on the door just before it's flung open. Startled, we turn around and see Abshir, fuming.

Uh-oh. He doesn't get mad very often but when he does, boy, better watch out.

"I told you not to go through my shit," he yells, stomping in. He's pointing his finger at Yousuf, who looks like he's about to shit his pants. "Where the hell's the duffel bag?"

"What are you talking about? I ain't going through your room," says Yousuf. "Fatima must've put it somewhere. She was cleaning up earlier."

"We've been playing *NBA 2K*—" I say.

"You stay out of this," he screams at me.

I zip up fast. Angry Abshir is not one to mess with.

He starts rummaging through Yousuf's room. Knocking the trophies off the bed with a swipe, throwing his comforter off, checking underneath the bed before moving on to plow through a pile of clothes in Yousuf's closet.

"Fuck," he says, ready to lose it.

Just as I think he's about to leave, he grabs Yousuf by his shirt.

Arif and I jump up. What if he hits him? We get a mean mug, and we sit back down.

"I swear if I find out you took it or put it somewhere," he says, cocking back his fist.

He lets go of Yousuf's shirt and flings him back to the floor before marching out. We hear him running down the stairs and yelling, "Fatima, where the hell's my duffel bag?"

We hear Fatima respond. He runs back up, sorts through something in his room, and runs back down. He slams the front door and we hear a car screech off.

What. The. Fuck.

He was cheering us on at the game a couple hours ago. I'm losing it, staring at Yousuf. He wants to cry, I can see it, but he won't. Not while we're around. I'm so confused.

"You all right, man?" I say, patting his shoulder. "You wanna take it easy? We can head home."

"I'm good," says Yousuf, staring at the floor. "What the hell's his problem?"

"What did he think you stole?" says Arif, picking up the comforter and putting it back on the bed. "It's not like we're smoking up his stash or any of that bullshit."

"I don't know, man," says Yousuf, throwing some of his clothes back into the closet. "He's just been trippin' hardcore lately. Like almost got into blows with my dad. Nearly got kicked out of the house type of shit."

"That's wack," I say. "Abshir's graduating and going to college next year. He can't be getting involved in hood shit."

"Forget it, let's just finish the game," says Yousuf, sitting back down in front of the TV as if the last two minutes never happened.

43

I try to relax, but I'm still shaken up. I'm also hella worried about Yousuf should Abshir ever decide to rampage into his room again. I don't say anything, though. I can tell he's trying to forget it.

We play for another half hour or so. Long enough for me to glance over at the clock and realize what time it is. Oh boy, Mom's going to murder me. I do our shake with the two of them, leave them to keep playing, and make my exit.

. . .

Later on, in bed, I glance at my phone to check what time it is: 2:00 a.m. Why is it so hard to fall asleep? I still can't believe I didn't shoot. Agh. I could've won us the game, but no, I was too busy worrying about what Omar would've done to me if I didn't pass it to him. And what did he do? Miss.

Can't do anything about it now. I'm exhausted. I just want to close my eyes and sleep like a baby. I can't remember the last time I did that. Like, it's literally the one thing we should all be proficient in. It's all we did when we were fresh out of the womb and not crying or shitting ourselves.

Blame it on technology: all the glare from this stupid phone, the highlights of Curry draining threes on YouTube, getting sprung off Cardi B videos . . . wait, scratch that last part. Or at least don't tell my mom.

It doesn't help that my room and Gerrard Street don't have much between them. Sure, there's a wall and a large window, but I can hear *everything*. Cars whizzing by, people talking, dogs barking, and streetcars flying by like they have somewhere to be. Who needs to go to Main Street subway station at this hour at lightning speed? I feel like someone jolts me awake with one of those resuscitators every time one passes. Maybe I need to put a sign outside my window, like those stickers on the backs of cars announcing there's a baby on board, but something more to the effect of "growing teen who's an insomniac and would really benefit from sleep lives here." Not that anyone would pay attention. It is Regent Park, after all.

Wait, it's starting to rain, I've got the pedestal fan on high, and the ambient noise is starting to make me a little drowsy. I'm not tossing and turning as much. I start to feel my body give in. Thank you, Lord. I will repay you by not replaying those Cardi B videos in my sleep.

Bang!

I jolt up. What the f—

Where's my phone? My hands scramble to find it. My heart's pounding a mile a minute and don't get me started on the sweat. I hear nothing for another moment. Is it over?

Bang! Bang!

A car roars down Gerrard Street. I'm feeling around on my body. Am I hit? Am I bleeding? It's outside—whatever went down is right outside my window.

Mom barges into my room. The doorknob smashes into the wall. She's heaving and disheveled.

"Fawad, beta, are you okay?" she screams.

The sound of her voice throws me into a panic. I start hyperventilating. My breathing is some next-level shit.

"I . . . I . . . think so."

She hugs me really tightly. I'm already having trouble breathing, so I need to tap out.

"Ammi . . . Ammi . . . I can't breathe."

She relaxes her grip, holding my face in between her palms, inspecting every nook and cranny.

I motion that we should look out the window. I crack mine open. There's a body in the middle of the street. Not just any body. It's in front of Yousuf's home. That's Yousuf's mom. She's kneeling on the ground, holding the body, caressing its head, screaming. The rest of the family runs out. Everyone except him. Then it hits me.

"Ammi, I think that's Ab-sh-sh-ir," I stutter. My muscles start feeling weak, and it's as if the ground starts moving underneath me.

Ambulance sirens, cop car sirens, fire truck sirens—every damn department is on the scene in no time.

Caution tape is put up. We creep slowly into the living room and stare out the bigger window. I see Yousuf's family speaking with police officers holding notepads. Paramedics are attempting to resuscitate Abshir.

They've finally got Abshir on a stretcher and they load him into the ambulance. Yousuf's on his knees, bawling his eyes out. I can see it all happening and still I feel way too far away. I need to go out there. My chest is so tight I swear it's a struggle to get a single breath down.

Jamila stumbles in. "Did you guys see all that?" She grabs me and holds my shoulders. "Kiddo, you all right?"

I shake my head with the only obvious answer. Then I can't hold it back any longer. Snot, tears, unintelligible slurs toward whoever did this. "Abshir . . . Abshir . . . they shot Abshir . . ."

I want to go see Yousuf. I bolt toward the door. I need to go to the hospital. He's gotta make it. No way he's fucking leaving me too. I can't even right now.

My mom's hand latches onto my arm before I can slip on my sneakers and unlock the door.

"Fawad, you can't go out right now," Mom screams.

"Ammi, Yousuf's out on the street crying. Abshir's in the hospital. What don't you understand?" I'm struggling to get her to loosen her grip. "Let me go."

"It's too dangerous."

"No, it's not," I scream back, falling to my knees. "Let me go." I'm losing feeling in my body. There's a numbness shooting down my arm. I'm trying my best to simultaneously tamper with the lock and fight Mom off. My hands are too unsteady, though. I've never experienced a tremor so strong.

Am I losing my mind? Mom finally lets go. I struggle to get back up.

I've got the door open but my body is feeling too heavy, frozen. It's as if I'm staring at myself from up above.

Jamila wraps her arms around me. She shuts the door, locks it. I'm shaking and I can't stop crying. He was just at the game this morning. There were still things he had to show me. He can't be gone. Not now.

"Hey, come here. Just relax. His family just left in a taxi behind the ambulance," she says, stroking my back. "There's nothing you can do for them right now except pray. He still might make it."

"Fuck," I yell. "I hate this fucking neighborhood."

I run to the couch and throw a cushion to the ground as hard as I can. I punch a wall, leaving it with a dent and me with bruised knuckles. "It's the same shit over and over again."

My brain's flooded with memories of Abshir.

He didn't deserve this. No one deserved this. Bastards, whoever did this. All of them. Straight-up cowards. Hiding behind guns. All for what?

I try to imagine what Yousuf must be going through. I grab my phone and text him.

ME: Fuck. Fuck. Fuck whoever did this. We're gonna get 'em

I don't get a response, so I chuck the phone away. Mom and Jamila watch me closely. My body is too weak to yell, resist, fight, move, breathe, any of it. It's done.

Jamila helps me up. She takes me to my bed and tucks me in. Mom's sitting in a chair next to the bed. After a few moments, Jamila goes to her room.

I try to fall asleep but I just stare at the ceiling. Did he make it? Dear God, please just let him make it. All I see is Abshir's dead body. He'd just sat next to me on that big-ass roller coaster earlier in the summer, when he took us to Wonderland, after both Yousuf and Arif backed out. He'd bought us funnel cakes, shit-ass expensive pizza, and won us those huge Pokémon stuffed toys from throwing baseballs into tin bottles.

We'd gone up, down, then round and round until I felt like I was legitimately going to die. The only reason I knew I'd be okay was because I was sitting next to Abshir. I knew he wouldn't let me fall. He always had our backs.

My mom strokes my hair, sitting beside me while reciting a surah to protect me. Finally, my eyelids are so heavy that I can't keep them open any longer. They close at last.

Except all I see is caution tape around my best friend's home.

5

Arif is over early the next morning. It's Monday, and he's sitting at the foot of my bed as I start coming to. I feel like I've been run over by a truck.

"This is fucked," he says, scrolling through his phone. "I saw something on Twitter and couldn't believe it."

I don't have words to respond.

"Did you message Yousuf? Have you heard from him?" he says, leaning forward.

Still don't have it in me to say something. I want to open my mouth, but I can't. It's sewn shut. Abshir's gone.

Arif's getting frustrated having a one-way conversation.

He gets up and starts giving my body a shake. "Fawad, snap out of it, man. We gotta talk to Yousuf and find out if he made it."

The thought of Yousuf hits me. "You're right," I blurt out at last. Then I start bawling again. "Abshir's gone, Arif. They took him. I saw. I saw . . . outside my window . . ."

"Fuck, dude," he says, grabbing me a box of tissues and putting a hand on my shoulder. "I don't even feel nothing no more. Feels so messed to be desensitized to this shit. Part of my brain's like, *Abshir's gone.* Another part of my brain's thinking, *No duh, stupid—you live in Regent. What else is new?*"

He sits back down, buries his head in his hands, and starts sobbing, his body collapsing underneath him. I've seen him cry before, like when his dad has an episode and loses it on him. But never like this. I grab him some water. I'm grinding my teeth thinking about last night. Heat flushes through my body. I want to scream so hard that every organ inside me bursts.

Arif gathers himself. "Yousuf. We gotta see how he's doing."

He's right. I grab my phone. We give him a ring on speaker . . . no answer. He still hasn't responded to my last text, so I shoot him another one. We stare at the screen but then I put my phone away.

Things like this have a history of spiraling out of control in Regent.

"We gotta fuck up whoever did this," I say.

"It's not going to be easy. We're still kids, and those dudes who did it are convicts, bro," says Arif, flipping his fitted cap backwards. He gets up and starts pacing back and forth.

"A bullet don't care how old you are," I say, getting up, fists clenched, a vein popping in my forehead.

"Bro, you're tripping. Nazmul just got out of jail, his boy's in a wheelchair after getting shot in the spine, and you remember Keerthigan? Dude that got shanked behind my building, died from a punctured lung? This ain't no joke."

My phone vibrates. There's a message from Yousuf.

YOUSUF: He didn't make it.

"Arif, they fucking killed Abshir. You want to do nothing?"

I wanna chuck my phone out the window. We're out the door in no time. There are still remnants of bloodstains on the street.

An old lady is walking her dog on the other side of the street like nothing happened.

We're standing in front of Yousuf's door. The wailing from inside is like straight out of a horror flick. I don't know if I'm ready for this.

Arif presses my shoulder with one hand. I knock. No answer. I knock again. A man Yousuf once introduced to us as his uncle opens the door.

The living room is crowded with Somali men. In the center is Yousuf's father, weeping and being consoled. On the steps sits Yousuf, looking lost and defeated. We greet most of the men before finally walking over to him.

I hug his cold, almost dead body. His head rests on my shoulder and I wish I'd come earlier. Arif hugs him next. The three of us are crying. Last night really happened. Abshir's gone. For good.

Diet Coke and mango juice are being served, along with some biscuits. I can hear women crying upstairs. I think of my mother and what she would do if she ever lost me.

"This is fucked, man," I say, pulling myself together. "We gon' fuck up whoever did this."

"Fawad, I'm telling you, chill the fuck out. Now's not the time," says Arif. "What's wrong with you, bro?"

Yousuf just nods.

"Salatul Janazah will be tomorrow in Pickering," says Yousuf, wiping his tears.

The last time I was at a funeral prayer was for my dad.

"We'll be there," says Arif.

We give his shoulder another squeeze. Fatima, his older sister, asks him to come to the kitchen and help serve some refreshments. He gets up wearily, but we sit him back down.

51

"Here, we got this," I say. "Just take it easy."

Arif and I pitch in, looking after guests, many of whom speak only broken English. Nothing we're not used to. I've recognized a handful of words from Tamil, Bengali, Somali, Amharic, Mandarin, and Vietnamese. Regent Park ain't no less than no United Nations.

A few minutes later, Imam Aziz and Omar walk through the door. My skin crawls around Omar. I nearly flip the tray of drinks. Everyone stands to greet Imam Aziz. He cuts through and hugs Yousuf's dad. Everyone gives them some space, and they exchange some words in private.

It's time for the afternoon prayer. All the men get up and start forming rows behind the Imam, facing east. Arif and I help move a massive coffee table into the kitchen to make room. I see Omar chatting with Yousuf out of the corner of my eye. I can't help but feel uneasy.

The four of us make up the last row. We finish the prayer with a special dua for Abshir so that he may be granted entry into heaven.

After prayer, it's the four of us now hanging by the steps.

"So you know who done it?" says Omar, in a quiet tone.

Yousuf shakes his head.

"What do you know?" I say.

"None of your business," he says, scoffing.

Yousuf is a statue. His face grave and solemn.

"He was as much a brother to me as him, aight?" I say, puffing my chest out.

Omar laughs. "What you punks gon' do anyway?"

He finishes his juice and heads over to chat with some of the older dudes, friends of Abshir's.

I shut up. What *were* we going to do?

"Need anything else, big guy?" Arif asks Yousuf.

A few seconds go by with the two of us staring at Yousuf, waiting for a response.

"I'll be fine. Think I'm going to go crash in my room for a bit," he says, getting up. "I'll see you guys at the funeral tomorrow."

We nod and give him another hug before he heads up the stairs. I wanna stick around and see if I can fish something out of Omar or some of Abshir's friends, but Arif's adamant about heading out.

Arif and I hug Yousuf's dad again. We say goodbye to the Imam and a few of the other men we know from mosque before making our way out.

The sun shines brightly.

I stare up at the sky and feel its rays on my skin. It feels like a warm shower after sweating it out on the court for several hours. I think of Yousuf and how he could use being outdoors right now, away from the heaviness inside him.

"Where to?" says Arif, staring at the concrete in front of us, both of us inspecting the caution tape. "Back to yours?"

"I can't be inside right now. Let's hit up Riverdale."

"I'm down, let's go."

Riverdale Park is a few blocks north of Gerrard Street right beside Cabbagetown. Right next to it is Riverdale Farm, where the scent of cow dung stirs up nostalgia in my mom for the village life she left behind whenever we walk past it.

We cross the street and that invisible forcefield that divides the haves from the have-nots, and walk past beautiful Victorian homes. The front lawns are perfectly manicured. Some have more effort put into them than others.

A family pulls up in a minivan. From inside hop out two little white kids, who start running and screaming at each other as their mom chases after them. Do they have any idea what just happened a few blocks away? Like, any fucking clue at all? Nope. They're in their own little bubble. It's as if we don't even exist.

Finally, the mother grabs hold of both their hands while the father unloads grocery bags and they go into their home. Like I said, what happens to us on the other side of Gerrard, it's all invisible to these folks.

It gets quieter and quieter as we continue walking, with the odd car passing us by. On the left-hand side is the baseball diamond for Sprucecourt Public School. That's where I first went before transferring to Lord Dufferin for middle school. So many memories in that field.

Once, Yousuf, Arif, and I got our hands on some BB guns and were playing around when someone called the cops on us twelve-year-olds. We were surrounded in no time, told to throw down our weapons, knees to the ground, hands behind the backs of our heads. They scuffed us up but let us off the hook. One officer said we were lucky they were letting us go, lucky there was still sunlight, because if it had been dark, we'd have been leaving with toe tags. I was shook. Didn't know what a toe tag was. Had to google it when I got home.

We reach the parking lot for the park. We walk on it and head toward the hill overlooking several baseball diamonds down below. There's also a bridge out in the distance that leads to a huge track where Arif and I go running sometimes.

At last, we find our bench. So much time spent just goofing off here.

I'm still taking in the scene of the paramedics loading Abshir's body into the ambulance. It all feels too raw to process. My stomach is churning. Arif takes out a box of cigarettes.

"Where'd you get those?" I say.

"Nazmul," he says, lighting one up and holding the pack toward me.

"He'd help us," I say, taking one. I give it a few puffs before letting out a cough.

"Fawad, promise me, dude—just chill out," he says. "You ain't hung with these older dudes. Some of 'em fresh out of jail. I've heard their stories. We don't want to end up there. And that's better than being dead."

"Bro, your best friend's brother just got shot and you acting so nonchalant. What's up with you?"

"What's up with me? You in there trying to rile Yousuf to take revenge. Are you fucking out of your mind? What you gon' do? Get a gun and shoot whoever shot Abshir? You can't even leave your home at night to watch a movie, and you thinking you hard all of a sudden."

We both get up, glaring. I tense up. Something comes over me. I shove him. "Fuck you."

He comes at me and I barely dodge him. We're at each other's throats. Next thing I know we're rolling down Riverdale hill. We get off one another, huffing and puffing. Think he knocked out one of my ribs. His lip's bleeding. I stagger over to the bench before I start breaking down again.

"I don't know what to do," I say, throwing my hands in the air.

Arif sucks the blood off his lip and comes to sit next to me. Not the first time we've gotten into a tussle.

"Sometimes you just gotta ride shit out, do nothin'," he says, brushing grass from his arm. "It's hard, but we got no choice."

"We ever gon' get out of this shithole?" I say, sniffling and wiping snot away with my shirt.

"We got no choice," he says, getting up and offering me a hand.

I take it and he catapults me to my feet. I'm not thinking straight.

Amen to that. *You hear that, Dad? I'm going to get out of this garbage heap you left me in. No thanks to you.*

. . .

The next day, Nazmul drove us to the funeral, and it left us unhinged. We saw Abshir's face, lifeless, without blood, and I broke down. Everyone did. At least it was still a little recognizable.

I remember when Mom, Jamila, and I landed in Pakistan and rushed to the village for Dad's funeral. They showed his face. I swear, for a moment I wanted to say they had the wrong guy.

The most touching part of Abshir's funeral was the heartfelt messages from his classmates, his crew in Regent, and, of course, Yousuf. He's always been a poet at heart. I catch him scribbling shit in his notebooks, but he never wants anyone to find out. Once, and only once, Arif and I got him to read some of his work out loud to us. I kid you not, it got us both shook. I've heard spoken word before, but his words took us somewhere else. At the end of the procession, the Imam made dua, praying for Abshir to find peace wherever he is.

Arif and I didn't visit Yousuf and his family for a bit, to give them some space. Now, a few days later, we come back, and I stare at Yousuf sitting on the edge of his bed, wondering where his head's at. All he's been doing for the last couple of days is smoking up. Hasn't left his home. Says he's too paranoid to step out, like every time a car passes by, he thinks whoever shot Abshir gon' get out and get him next.

I don't say anything more yet about getting back at whoever did this or about me and Arif getting into a fight. I want to lighten the mood a little.

"Remember the time Abshir taught us his little fadeaway?" I say, reenacting it, wanting to break the silence. "They had to kick us out of the rec center because of how badly we wanted to nail it. He was so patient, too, when we kept messing up."

"I just remember that year he was serious about putting out a mixtape," says Arif, smiling. He pretends to be Abshir and raps, "I got big dreams that come loose at the seams, stitching 'em up like my mom does my jeans."

Finally, we get a reaction out of Yousuf. He's still just sitting at the foot of his bed, black T-shirt, sweats, his 'fro going all over the place. "Yeah, that was a dope verse."

"But what you read us that one day," I say, sitting next to him, putting my arm around him, "that's powerful—like real, raw talent. I think you should put more of your stuff out. God knows kids need to hear it."

"Abshir used to say that too," he says, reaching under his bed and picking up his notebooks.

"Let's put your stuff up on Insta," says Arif, taking one and passing another to me. "I'm not saying I follow poets and shit on there, but I'd follow you."

I'm looking at Yousuf, still lifeless. I don't know what's running through his head. But all of a sudden I'm feeling restless. I can't pretend that nothing happened anymore. I close my eyes and those shots from a few nights ago jolt me awake. Images of Abshir's limp body being carried away by the paramedics. My muscles are quivering, but I get a handle on myself.

I clear my throat and grit my teeth.

"Man, I just want to get out of this neighborhood," I say. "I lost count how many people we know who've been shot at."

"Now I bet someone gon' try to get back at whoever did this," says Arif, shaking his head.

"You're probably right," says Yousuf, shrugging, his face still wearing a blank expression. "Abshir's boys already know who did it, they already plotting when to hit back. Asked me if I wanted in. They gon' do it when that son of a bitch goes out to pick up his daughter from school. Only time dude gets out of the house. I didn't want anything to do with it. It's not what Abshir would've wanted."

I imagine stray bullets flying near kids playing in a playground. Bullets don't have a conscience; they don't distinguish between targets, decide who deserves what. They just tear through flesh and leave wounds.

The image makes me drop onto the bed. My chest feels tight, almost as if I've forgotten how to breathe. I open my mouth but no words come out.

Arif crouches down into a squat to try and meet Yousuf's eyes. "Listen, man, I won't pretend to act like I know what you're going through, but I lost a cousin last year, and that shit hurts and stays with you. You take your time but you hit us up whenever. It's times like these you can't wall yourself off. Otherwise, that heaviness eats you alive."

I get up and pick up my backpack. "I'm literally a minute away. Just say the word, and I'm here."

"Thanks," says Yousuf. Arif stands up too, and Yousuf stretches out to lie on his bed, just staring at the ceiling. "Can one of you grab the light on your way out?"

I switch it off. It's dark out and all I can make out now are shadows. I close the door and look at Arif. He doesn't say anything. We say salaam to Yousuf's mom, who just finished prayers and is rolling up her prayer mat. It's as if grief's been etched into her face.

Outside, the first thing Arif says to me is, "We gotta keep tabs on him."

I nod. He's right. Yousuf's in a tricky spot. He's saying he doesn't want any part of no revenge or nothing, but who knows when that might change? I know I wouldn't be able to keep shit together if anything happened to Jamila. I'm going to ask Mom to start praying for him too.

"Also, Nermin messaged saying she wanted to hang, but I let her know things are a little busy," he says.

"Yeah, she messaged me too. Told her the same. We'll catch her at school."

We dab fists and part ways to head home.

6

It's been two weeks since the shooting. Can't believe it's September already. I'm up extra early for the first day of school. It's my second year at Northern Secondary and I don't want to be late on account of Jamila hogging the bathroom.

Yousuf's been barely responding to my texts, and even when he does, his responses are short and not helpful in letting me know how he's holding up. I checked with Arif and the same is true on his end. I've been hesitating to just go over unannounced like I usually would. Instead, I'm thinking I'll go to No Frills after school, where his sister, Fatima, works as a cashier, and check in with her about how he's really doing.

For now, just gotta not be late for day one. Except as I make my way, I realize the door to the bathroom is already closed. I get closer. I can hear the shower. I bang once. I bang twice. I bang again. She's not supposed to be up so early.

"Fawad, I'm going kill you when I get out," she yells.

"You're not supposed to be up this early," I yell back.

"Well, I am, so deal with it."

"Agh, I hate you so much right now."

Obviously, I bang the door one more time for good measure. Not that it'll do me any good.

I go into her room. She's got canvases galore, with paint tubes and entire tubs of paint shoved into one corner. I went with her once to an art store and that shit is expensive. How does she afford it? Part-time retail gigs, I suppose.

Jamila is an artist. She's in her final year at some fancy artsy-fartsy high school that costs a lot of money but because of her "circumstances" and portfolio, she got a whole lot of scholarship funds to make it happen. Her latest work-in-progress on her easel is a woman decked out in traditional South Asian gold jewelry, struggling with putting on a sari. I think she told me she was going to call it *Not Sari*, which is so her.

My eyes move to the top of her IKEA dresser, where I spot a photo of us with Dad from five years back. Jamila looks like a straight-up nerd. I can hardly recognize her. We look happy. Then I think of all the shit we've been through since then. It makes me wonder if it's even possible to ever feel that way again.

"Get out of my room," shouts Jamila from behind me.

She's wearing a black tank top and high-waisted ripped jeggings, with a towel wrapped around her still-wet hair.

"I'll dry my hair here. You can thank me later. Loser." She brushes past me and starts shuffling through boxes of jewelry on her dressing table.

Not sure if she wants me to bow down and exalt her for such generosity. Instead, I just shrug and head to the washroom as she turns on her music. She plays loud hip-hop every morning while getting ready. Mom hates it, but it does make for a good listen on the toilet.

I shower and brush my teeth at the same time (it really is the best life hack), then put on my black tee, black Puma hoodie, and black jeans—my go-to outfit that I'm going to rock with my white Air Force 1s, which I'm maniacal about cleaning. Finishing touches are making sure Jamila's in the kitchen having breakfast, sneaking the hair dryer out of her room, and then using some hair product to get my hair just right. Gotta look fly on day one.

In the kitchen, Mom's doing her thing by the stove. It runs on gas and is barely functional. She usually struggles to turn the elements on with the knobs before resorting to using an ignitor, which sets off the flame in a burst as it makes contact with the gas. I'm no safety expert, but that shit just looks dangerous. I don't like cooking because of it. Part of me feels like my head is going to get blown off.

After taking a seat at the table, I notice Jamila's already halfway through a paratha. There's not a lot of space in the kitchen, but we've got a full-sized dining table, which Dad bought when we first immigrated. There's only three of us now, so it's pushed up to the wall, which really needs a paint job.

Even though my mom cleans all the time, it still looks like grime city in the corners. What really bugs me, though, pun not intended, is the cockroach infestation. I see one crawling up the side of the stove and it's gross.

Mom looks Jamila up and down as she plops another paratha in the communal paratha bin. "I can see your thighs with those jeans, Jamila," she says.

"They're jeggings, not jeans, Ammi, and that's the point. Jeez."

I knew the ripped jeans wouldn't go over well. If anyone's got the guts to not give a shit about Mom's opinion, well, between the two of us, it's Jamila.

I clear my throat, hoping they don't get into a full-blown argument this early. "Hey, Ammi, these are delicious today, by the way."

Mom puts a fresh paratha on my plate, along with some scrambled eggs.

"Just today? Oof, Allah, ungrateful brats, the both of you."

"I don't see why you still care about how I dress," says Jamila, nonchalantly dipping a torn piece of paratha into her chai. "I'm not a two-year-old, you know."

They give each other the stare-down. Luckily, Mom has to flip the paratha before it burns.

"This is how I brought you up to talk to me?" says Mom, putting another finished paratha on my plate. "Do you even know how hard it's been for me after your father passed? Of course not. All you can do is think about yourself."

"Here we go again, everyone hop on the guilt train," says Jamila, rolling her eyes and pushing her chair back to get up and leave.

"Guys, can you please stop? It's too early for all this," I say.

"You stay out of this," they both say at the same time.

At least they both agree on something.

Jamila decides she isn't quite done eating, scoots back in, and takes some more yogurt out of the container. She's staring at me as I lick my fingers, which are dripping with oil from the mango achar.

"What? It's not like you don't eat with your hands."

"Forget it. Bet you don't do that in front of your white friends at Northern."

I shrug and smile. "It's so much more efficient than all that fork and knife business."

"Don't listen to her, there's nothing wrong with eating with your hands, beta," Mom says, flattening out a ball of dough with her rolling pin.

"Also, why are you always wearing that hoodie?" says Jamila, pinching the garment on my arm and then acting like it's diseased or something. "I told you to buy some new clothes instead of splurging on those stupid sneakers, didn't I?"

"No one cares, jeez," I say. "Besides, what's wrong with it?"

"Everything," she says, thrusting her chair back and heading to her room. She reemerges with her backpack and waves at the two of us. "I gotta run, Ammi. Bye, loser. Stay out of trouble." She leaves.

Now I'm self-conscious about what I'm wearing. I don't have a ton of options. Guess I should've picked up some other things after all.

I glance over at the clock and realize I don't have time to look through my closet.

"I gotta run too," I say, hugging my mom. "Love you."

She never responds with "Love you, too," just nods.

TV shows and movies depicting parents saying "I love you" to their kids are either all false or just not made for Pakistani families. Either way, I know even though she never says it, her round parathas scream it for her.

"Fawad, don't be late," she says, just as I've got the door open.

"I won't, I won't, Ammi. I'm just going to school."

"Allah hafiz. Wait, come here."

Here we go again. She recites Ayat al-Kursi under her breath and blows air around my head to protect me. Don't ask.

. . .

64

Northern is situated north of the city. Surprise, surprise. To get there, I take the streetcar to College subway station. Then I have to take Line 1 north to Eglinton station. It's about a ten-minute walk from there.

The corner of Yonge and Eglinton is mad hectic in the mornings. There's a ton of construction with new condo buildings going up, and having lanes of traffic closed doesn't help. I squeeze through the crowd like a salmon trying to swim upstream. There's other kids I recognize heading my way. I'm not great at making friends, so I act like I'm in a rush.

Even as I'm pretending not to notice, my stomach's churning as I look at the outfits on some of these kids. Supreme and Anti Social Social Club hoodies galore. One kid's even rocking an army fatigue Bape tee I've had my eyes on since forever. Then there's those Yeezys that cost three bills easy. True Religion branded jeans folded at the ankles. Apple AirPods plugged in and new iPhones gleaming as they swipe through ad-free Spotify accounts, no doubt. Meanwhile, I got me a hand-me-down Android from Jamila.

One day, I swear to myself, I'm going to be able to afford all that and more. I'm going to make it to the NBA. That's right: Fawad Chaudhry will be the world's first Pakistani to go pro. I mean, I know I gotta make the school team first. Actually, I gotta convince my mom to let me try out for the team first, but it can be done. At least, theoretically.

I didn't bother trying out last year because, frankly, I wasn't good enough. Not to mention I was short. This year is different, I can feel it. I busted my balls all summer, sweating and running drills with Jerome—preparing for tryouts.

I catch the main Northern building standing tall, towering over the trees in the front courtyard. It's an eyesore compared to what North Toronto's campus looks like just a few blocks down. But we did build a new football field a few years back for a whopping million and change.

Outside the main entrance, I catch Arif chilling with Nermin. They spot me too. Seeing them light up makes *me* light up. We're like a string of Christmas lights we admire during winter . . . even though we don't technically celebrate the holiday.

Nermin's looking dope in her black Adidas track jacket, black jeans, and a blue hijab. She's looking like a straight-up diva. She's Arabic—her family immigrated from the UAE a couple years back—and, uh . . . cute, especially with those big brown eyes. I'd be into her but she's my only best friend who's a girl. The last thing I'd want is for things to get awkward between us.

We met when Arif and I volunteered at this Islamic conference the summer before high school. Turned out she was going to Northern too. Ninth grade was basically us cheering her on at her soccer games and all three of us being holed up in a library on weekends, studying.

Arif's got a light-blue denim jacket on with a white tee, black jeans, and white Converse. Dude's growing out his hair with the intention of having a man bun, but really he's just on the prowl. I think the only girl who doesn't give in to those dimples of his has to be Nermin, at least as far as I can tell.

I breathe a sigh of relief around them. My body loosens up. It hits me how tense I've been this entire morning on my way over. Probably first-day jitters.

"Yo, guy, it's been a minute," says Arif as we do our shake.

"Still haven't heard from Yousuf, have you?" I say.

Arif shakes his head. "Nah, not yet. You still down to hit up No Frills after school to chat with Fatima?"

"Yup."

Nermin clears her throat. We do a side-hug. She usually doesn't hug dudes, but Arif and I aren't regular dudes—we're her best friends. I think that's why she makes an exception.

"How come you're late?" she says, giving me a jab on the shoulder.

"Whoa, it's just day one," I say, giving her a little shove back.

"Hey, you're not supposed to do that to a girl." She's got her hands on her hips now, pretending to look pissed.

"Nermin, you're a star forward on the soccer team. I think you can handle it."

Her snake eyes are the best, bar none.

"Whoa, easy there. I'm just kidding."

Arif takes out a piece of paper from his bag. "Yo, let's see what classes we got together."

Nermin and I take out our sheets and we all scan through.

"What?!? This is wack, guy," he says, crumpling up his sheet. "Well, at least we got gym class together, Fawad. Oh, and all three of us are in math, which is perf, cuz, well . . . I could use the help."

Nermin and I have science together too. That's a shitty percentage of classes to have your best friends in. I'm no math nerd (okay, maybe just a little), but three-eights is, like, 37.5 percent—which is actually a pretty average field goal percentage in the NBA.

I take in the football field to the left. Not to mention the little gargoyles perched up on top of the main building looking all angry while staring down on us. I wonder why they look so constipated.

"Earth to Fawad," says Nermin, cupping her hands and holding them as if they were a megaphone near my left ear. "Captain, we got a space cadet orbiting the atmosphere. Permission to retrieve."

She and Arif mime walkie-talkies.

"Roger that," says Arif. He gives me a smack on the side of my head.

"Hey, I was just looking at the building. I think brown brick buildings love me," I say, laughing.

Arif cracks up too, catching my reference to Regent. Nermin looks confused. She lives in a proper home in a proper neighborhood near the school. Her parents both managed to crack into their professions after immigrating here: her dad's an engineer and her mom's a university professor. Not too shabby at all.

I was pretty embarrassed when she asked me what my folks did. I couldn't look her in the eye when I told her Dad used to be a cab driver and Mom was basically a housewife. She didn't judge, though; in fact, she got upset at me for being ashamed in the first place.

"We got an assembly to catch," says Nermin.

"Lead the way," says Arif.

"You coming or what?" says Nermin.

I nod yes and follow behind.

The auditorium is massive. We take our seats. The lights dim, then there's a spotlight. The principal, Mrs. Stone—a short, white lady with a bob cut—walks in.

She welcomes us, and we stand for the national anthem. There's a band and a choir up onstage, and I join in for the last verse: "We stand on guard for thee."

I briefly catch the eyes of a girl sitting farther down the row. She's slim, hair tied back in a bun, tight top that lets me see the contours of her breasts. I gotta rein myself in. I don't want to be that guy on day one. That's just not cool.

Arif looks like he's having a field day. Last year, he went through five girlfriends. Now, he's looking around like he's making a mental checklist of which girl to hit on first. I don't know how he has the confidence. I hate him for it and wish I could do the same.

After the assembly lets out, there's a crowd in the hallway. The three of us are trying to figure out where our first classes are located.

"Whoa. Yo, let's go say what up to Paul," says Arif.

I look over at a group of dudes from the football team. Among the deluge of white faces, I spot a Black dude, Paul, who plays quarterback. Tall, well-built, and always sporting a clean fade and line-up, he's been at the top of the athletic food chain in Regent for as long as I can remember. In middle school, he was captain of the football, baseball, basketball, and rugby teams. The last kid to do that from the Park was King. Big shoes to fill.

In high school, though, Paul chose football over all the other sports. Said it gave him the most leverage, whatever that means.

Arif's pumped about seeing a familiar face. From the look on Paul's face, so is he. Nermin and I follow behind Arif.

"What's shaking, homie?" says Arif, cutting through the circle of jocks. He draws a mixed bag of reactions from the dudes.

"Oh, you know, holding it down," says Paul. "Where's Fawad at?"

Paul spots me and takes a few steps forward to say what up. Everyone's staring at me. I don't like it.

"You two should try out for the team this year," says Paul, putting his arms around the two of us.

His words draw a snicker from the crowd around us.

"Nah, man, track and field is more my jam," says Arif, flailing his arms because he can never stay still when he gets excited. "I like to sprint and be done with it. A whole game is just way too much work."

His hands do more talking than his lips sometimes. As he's breaking down why he's not interested in trying out, his left hand hits an iced coffee held by a dude beside him.

The dude reacts in time to avoid getting all of it spilled on him, but catches some on his white polo golf shirt. He's got a sharp jawline and long, wavy hair parted on the left.

The other kids around us burst into laughter as he stands there looking dumbfounded, staring at Arif like he's scum. Suddenly, he jumps at Arif, pushing him to a locker, and grabs his shirt. "What the fuck, man?" the guy says, cocking back his fist. Pin-drop silence and lots of eyes all on them.

"Whoa, calm down, homie," says Arif, trying to get out of the hold. "It was an accident."

"Yeah, just like you."

All right, that's just uncalled for. This privileged son of a bitch needs to loosen his tight ass. I can't stand seeing Arif being picked on. He'd never let that happen to me. My fist tightens. I jump in and shove the guy off Arif. "Lay off, douchebag. We all saw it was an accident."

"Who the fuck are you?" he says, straightening up.

"Whoa, whoa, easy, big guy," says Paul, jumping between us. "Adam, calm down, man. They're my boys from Regent."

Adam smirks. "Right. Shoulda guessed."

"Hey, dude, c'mon now," says Paul. "Let's start over, shall we? Fellas, this is Adam, the best damn running back in the city."

"Whatever, man. I gotta go wash this shit off," says Adam, breaking loose from Paul's grip and leaving with the rest of the jocks.

"Don't sweat him," says Paul. "Dude's got a little bit of a temper, but it's all for show. He ain't poppin' shit. Anyways, I gotta run too. I'll catch you fellas around."

"Thanks, bruh, same. We'll see you around," says Arif, shaking off the shove and fixing his hair.

I'm still angry as fuck. "What a prick."

"Whoa, bro. You gotta take it easy. It's just day one," says Arif, brushing off my shoulder.

It's true. Something is different this time. Maybe I'm just tired of taking it and letting things be.

"Honestly, what were you thinking, Fawad?" says Nermin. She's holding her temples like she's got a headache. "Both of you could've gotten hurt."

"Forget it. I don't know what came over me," I say, taking a few deep breaths to calm myself down before I face Arif. "But you know I got your back, right?"

"Boys," says Nermin, shaking her head. "Let's go. We got three classes before lunch. My stomach's already eating itself."

. . .

Arif and I take public transit home but get off a few stops early to go see Fatima at No Frills.

Parliament Street has become more and more gentrified ever since the Regent Park revitalization, with stores I grew up closing, fancy pizza and coffees shops opening up, and stores selling

71

made-to-order jewelry and home goods with hipster logos. But No Frills feels like the great equalizer. Who doesn't like to shop for groceries on the cheap?

We pass the Shoppers and right next to it catch a whiff of that two-for-one pizza and feel our stomachs grumble. At No Frills, we both pick up chocolate milks and wait in line for Fatima to cash us out.

"Salaam alaikum, Fatima," I say, and Arif greets her too.

"Wa-alaikum assalam, you two," she says, scanning the barcodes of our drinks. Luckily, there's no one behind us, so she's not in too much of a rush.

"How's he holding up?" says Arif.

"Yeah," I add. "He's not replying much. I mean, I know I could just barge into his room, but I also don't want him to flip out."

I pay for the chocolate milks and she prints out the receipt.

"Only Allah knows. He didn't go to school. He's holed up in his room, smoking joints my cousin smuggles in. He only eats when we bring food to him. So I don't know, to be honest. But if anyone can get through to him now, it's you two. Inshallah, this dark cloud leaves our family soon."

We nod. "Thanks, Fatima. We'll keep trying."

This sucks. Like, this really sucks. We say goodbye and walk out. Thinking about Yousuf makes me think about Abshir. Thinking about Abshir and how he's gone makes me think about how no one really knows how much time anyone has. There was so much I wanted to thank him for and now he's gone, just like that.

"You okay?" says Arif.

I shrug. "Hanging in there."

"What we gon' do about Yousuf?"

"You'll be the first to know as soon as I think of something."

We spend the rest of the walk home in silence. I really don't know what else is left to say.

7

Gym class is the only time I forget about trying to fit in and make friends. I wish I could have gym class all day on a loop. Like a Kendrick Lamar track when I'm hyping myself up to play ball.

My infatuation might have something to do with basketball being the first "unit." Better yet, the gym teacher is brown, like me.

Mr. Singh's got a beard and rocks a matching turban to go along with his tracksuit. It looks fly as hell.

It doesn't matter he's got a bit of a belly . . . put a ball in his hand and it's like watching a spoon thread through soup. What I mean to say is, he's smooth as silk, smooth as Arif when he gets going with his flirting, and lastly, smooth as a baby's butt, because that's, like, the smoothest thing out there.

Apparently, he played college ball at the University of Ottawa. I didn't know brown dudes hooped back then, but it gives me a little glimmer of hope. If he could do it, maybe I can too. I mean, I'm five foot eleven—I'm sure I could still shoot up a few inches.

Steph Curry was probably my height when he was in grade ten. He's six foot three now. Maybe if I drink enough milk like my mom tells me to, I could match that. Back in Pakistan, I've got some crazy-tall cousins. It's gotta be in our genes somewhere. I don't know what my dad's actual height was, but I always thought he was mad tall. Fingers crossed. Toes crossed.

Mr. Singh blows his whistle. After running us through some drills, he's giving us time to play some pickup. Oh man, bring it on.

We're doing half-court runs so that there can be two games running in parallel. Arif and I are on one team. There's a bunch of other white dudes in the class we now know and are cool with.

Some of them look like they can ball. Others look like they only play football or hockey. The dudes in the latter category are the ones to look out for, since they run at me like they want to tackle me or body check me into some imaginary boards.

I'm doing some crossovers. Making my defenders stutter left to right, right to left, right to right, left to left. Ooooh, did that dude just fall down? Ouch, I would not want to be him right now. I make matters worse by pulling up for a jump shot that's almost at mid-court and nailing it like I wasn't even trying.

Arif's chest-bumping me and going crazy. I have a grin that's a mile wide. I'm guarding this white dude who looks intimidating . . . He tries a move, I poke the ball out from under him. I lob it to Arif, who gets the easy lay-in. Piece of cake. A vanilla cake, that is.

A few minutes later, my opponents are pissed. We're up 10-3. The game's up to 11. There are four of them guarding me now when I have the ball in my hand. I mean, I don't want them to lose *that* badly in front of the whole class. Everyone else seems to have stopped playing, and the people watching from the bleachers have gone quiet. They're watching me merk these dudes like I'm eating my mom's parathas.

To put on a little show, I dribble the ball through one dude's legs, catch it on the other side, and do a behind-the-back to get past another dude. The other two give up chasing me. There's only one other guy guarding my four remaining teammates. I look at him straight in the eye. He knows I'm going to shoot. He charges at me. Even though four of my teammates are wide open a few feet from the rim, I jack up a shot just for fun. Nothing but net.

Ooooh, baby! I'm getting jiggy with it, doing the Curry shake. Hitting my chest like a gorilla that just got crowned king of the jungle. I shake hands with the losing crew and high-five my teammates. Could I come to school and just play ball all day? Oh man, how great would that be?

Everyone's headed to the locker room. Mr. Singh's standing by his office, arms crossed, looking a little unimpressed even after I put on a spectacle. I want to poke his belly and ask him what's up.

As I'm walking with Arif, I spot a couple of girls heading toward us. Both of them smiling. I have no clue what to do or say, so I'm going to let Arif do all the talking.

"That was quite the game," the hotter of the two girls says. "You guys play often?"

"Fawad here pretty much eats and shits basketballs," says Arif, his voice changing into the smooth FM-DJ voice he likes to put on for girls. He thinks it puts them in a bit of a trance. Cue eye roll.

"What he's trying to say is, yeah, I play quite a bit," I say in staccato, not buttery smooth as I intended. "I basically go to bed with a basketball."

She giggles. Oh man, that's never happened before.

"I hope you're joking, but that's kinda funny. I'm Kate, by the way," she says. "This is Lindsey."

"Arif," he says, before I can even open my mouth.

"Fawad," I say.

They look at me like they're constipated.

"Faad?" says Lindsey.

Oh boy. This again. Why did my parents think it was okay to decide to immigrate here but not change my name to Fred or something?

I let out a nervous chuckle like it's the first time I've heard that one.

"Close, but its Fa-wad."

They don't repeat it back, but they nod their heads.

"Aren't you in my science class?" says Arif to Kate. "You're the girl the teacher's always coming down on for being on your phone."

Kate blushes. "Yeah, my Insta's always blowing up."

I don't blame the app. She's definitely a ten.

"Oh yeah? Show me," says Arif. Before I blink, he's got his arm around Kate. They're on their phones like they've known each other for ages.

Meanwhile, Lindsey's standing there staring at me like I'm supposed to know what to say.

"Do you watch the Raptors?" I say.

"More of a Leafs fan."

"Cool."

You son of a bitch, get me out of this are the telepathic vibrations I'm shooting in Arif's direction. Surprisingly, they work. He walks Kate back to where we are, arm around her shoulder. How is he that smooth?

"The four of us should totally hang out," says Kate, playing with her hair before weaving an arm through Lindsey's and dragging her off.

"Sounds great," says Arif, speaking for me as per usual.

They wave goodbye. I'm giving Arif that look. He's gotta be out of his mind.

"You can go to lunch with both of them," I say, tossing the ball in my hands away. "No way I'm spending time with Lindsey while you get Kate."

"Bro, do it for me," he says. "Or are you not interested because you got a girl on lock back home? Don't tell me you feel guilty over Nusrat?"

He said her name again. I want to strangle him. Maybe hang him upside down from a basketball rim. He runs into the change-room before I can get my hands on him. Then I hear Mr. Singh clear his throat.

"Hey, kid, you trying out for the school team?" he says, dribbling a ball as he walks toward me. "Tryouts are in a couple of weeks."

"Um, yeah, I was planning on it," I say, blushing. "The thing is, I still need to ask my mom." I feel like the world's biggest loser. But if there's any coach that understands my pain, it's Mr. Singh.

"Oh, I see," he says. "Is it grades? You got some academic challenges or something?"

"No way, Mr. Singh. I've got an eighty-five percent average."

He nods. "So then, what's her concern? Are you a trouble-maker?"

"No. No, sir, she's just . . . paranoid. Doesn't like me home late and all that. You know how they are."

"Follow me," he says, walking into his office. "See this stack here? That's all the varsity athlete scholarships kids going on to postsecondary can apply for."

He takes a seat behind the desk, and I pull back a chair across from him and look through the stack of papers.

"Your folks got an RESP set aside for you?"

"R-E-what?"

"Do you know how much university is going to cost you?" he says, leaning in and interlacing his hands like he's onto something.

I shake my head. He smiles and then leans back.

"Forty thousand minimum."

My eyes widen. That's a lot of money.

"Exactly. So I recommend you keep your grades up and work on your game, and if things work out, maybe a school will like what they see. They might even give you some money to go play there for them."

"You really think I could get a sports scholarship?"

"Right now? Not a chance. But with a little bit of polish, I'd say you've got some potential," he says. "See that photo over there? That's me playing OUA basketball at the University of Ottawa on a fully paid scholarship."

I stare at the picture. It's easy to spot the lanky brown dude with a beard and hair bunched up in a bun.

"At least talk it over with your parents. No harm in trying," he says, getting up. Talking to my dad won't be a problem. Mom on the other hand . . . yeah, that'll be something.

I nod. "Yeah, I can do that."

"Okay, now get outta here before my next class comes in."

I get up and shake his hand. I'm standing outside his office staring at the school gym, taking it all in. I finally feel at home.

Then I remember Arif teasing me about Nusrat. I rush into the locker room to whip his sorry ass with a towel, and get him in a headlock.

"Swear you'll never say her name again. Swear on your mom," I shout in his ear. The rest of the kids around us can't tell whether we're playing or serious. Arif pries himself loose. That bastard is like an Energizer bunny.

"Nusrat, Nusrat, Nusrat," he yells before running out of the locker room. I really gotta work on my conditioning. I'm exhausted.

One of my white classmates walks over and asks, "Who's Nusrat?"

"Long story," I say, gathering my bag and smelly gym clothes while plotting my revenge on my so-called best friend.

. . .

Ball. B-ball. Basketball. Hoops. So many ways to refer to the same sport. I'm scheming, strategizing, planning, or rather *calculating* how to convince my mother to let me try out for the school team. The whole commute home I've been on autopilot, imagining one scenario after another. I need to anticipate her reasons for saying no.

The most obvious reason is she wants me to focus on school. My parents always wanted me to be a lawyer, so I get Mom wanting that now that Dad is gone.

Another reason is she wouldn't want me out too late. The after-school practices would probably drive her worrying instincts mad. Regent after dark isn't the safest, I'll give her that much.

Having a paranoid brown mother is like having a leash around your neck. I feel like I've earned her trust enough to have it hang loose, not have her tighten it.

I'm a pretty good kid, comparatively speaking, for someone growing up in the hood. I got friends or know friends of friends who don't just act like gangsters . . . they *are* gangsters. Bandanas, turf, and heat. I don't really go near any of that. Never been into it.

It helps that I'm one of, like, five Pakistani dudes in Regent, so it's not like we could just pull our weight against the dudes from Bangladesh, Sri Lanka, Somalia, Ethiopia, Jamaica, Vietnam, and China. People think I'm talking some United Nations crap when I explain to them all these crews we deal with. Not to mention what it takes to be a neutral party and be on friendly terms with all of 'em.

Call me a diplomat, because I mind my own business. I know when to cross the street and when to say "what up" to someone.

I'm almost home and don't have my arguments down pat. Maybe I should just tell Mom the truth. Bare my heart. Like a Bollywood hero trying to convince the girl's dad to let them be together.

I reach to yank open the building's front door. Denied. Looks like the superintendent is on top of shit. That was quick. I'm feeling around my pockets for my fob, but I ain't got my keys. Oh right, they're in the pocket of the jeans that I wore yesterday. Yikes, that means I didn't lock the door this morning. I tug at the door. It seems firm.

I hate to do this, but I don't have many options. I rub my hands together, grab the handle, put one foot on the wall, and pull. My face tightens. I catch a glimpse of my reflection in the glass pane and want to laugh. I kick the door before mustering up strength to give it one more tug. Success. I'm in. The building's safety is compromised. Meh.

From outside our apartment door, I can hear my mother talking to someone on the phone. I have a good idea who it might be. I wait a few moments, since it sounds like the conversation's winding down. I knock. Nothing. I knock again. Finally, my mom comes and opens the door.

"Okay, call me after the wedding," she says before hanging up. The word "wedding" puts me on guard. I don't like it coming out of her mouth, to be honest.

"Where are your keys?"

"I forgot them at home."

She gives me a quick slap to the back side of my head. It doesn't hurt, but still: Why? I try not to look her straight in the eyes, preferring to look at the floor instead. "Sorry."

"Sorry, ka bacha."

I put my things away and start unwinding on the couch. She scoots me to the side.

"Here, get up, let me show you something." She pulls out her phone and starts swiping to find WhatsApp.

"Ammi, I'm tired."

She gives me a stern look and says, "I should slap you again. I said *get up*."

That will do it every time. I straighten up immediately. My mother's hands are like bricks. I think they got that way from kneading all that dough. I don't want them to hit me again either way.

"One of your cousins got married."

Big whoop. Like they have anything better to do back there. "Oh, who?"

"Farzana."

"I have no idea who that is."

Another slap to the back of my head doesn't help rattle my memory. "Your khala's daughter."

"Oh yeah." I still have no clue who she's referring to.

She taps on her chat with Nusrat, whose last message contains more than thirty photos. She clicks on one of them and takes me through the slideshow.

"That's your mamu," she says. "That's the bride. Oh, look at her dress."

Mamu is my mother's older brother. My uncle is a bulky, short man with a paunch and a mean-looking mustache. He's greeting the groom's party, the baarat, who've come to take his daughter away to a home three blocks down.

"Why does she have all that makeup on? Looks gross."

Another slap to the head. Okay, so maybe she doesn't look so gross. She seems pretty happy. It's cute.

"I mean, she looks pretty. Who's the groom?"

"Your choti khala's son. Look here. He's riding in on a horse."

The groom looks handsome and thin, and he has thick, curly hair poking out from under his turban. Dressed in a sherwani that's black with gold trimmings, he has a serious look throughout the photos. Don't know what it is with my family and smiling in pictures. So weird.

"Oh, so they're like . . ." I say, feeling my stomach turn upside down.

"Cousins," Mom says, like it's no big deal, continuing to scroll through the photos.

"Yeah, but Ammi, that's, like, first cousins," I say, turning to face her and hoping she feels the gravity of my words. Nope. She just continues scrolling.

"So?"

I hold her shoulders so that she has no choice but to face me. This is my chance to make my point.

"Remember that time I told you about that news article talking about all those risks with cousin marriages? It's not good for the kids. There's a high risk for birth defects."

"That's rubbish. We've only ever done cousin marriages."

I smack my forehead and shake my head in dismay. "I just think if Abbu was still around, he'd side with me. Especially if he knew about the risks and whatnot."

"Well, too bad for you, he isn't. Now you listen . . ." she says, wagging her finger and ready to launch into her own defense of the whole thing. There's no winning with her on this. I have bigger fish to fry, so I play it cool.

"Forget it. I'm hungry . . . can we cook?"

"There's okra in the fridge. Wash and cut it. I'll make it quickly."

"Okra? What about seekh kababs?"

Another slap to my head. That's, like, five. I've lost count. Ow.

"Fine. Fine. Jeez."

As I finish up slicing and dicing, I realize that while she's cooking up the tarka and distracted, I should talk to her about *the thing*.

I toss the ends of the okra and wash the knife and a few dishes still in the sink.

"Ammi, do you know how much university costs in Canada now?"

"No." She doesn't even look back.

"Forty thousand dollars."

She almost drops the wooden spoon.

"Haye, Allah, that much?" she says, one hand on her hip. I've got her attention now. Time to milk it.

"I know, right?" I say, exaggerating my own disbelief. "You know what, though? There are student loans available, and a teacher was telling me there's lots of scholarship money out there."

"See, that's why I tell you. High school is very important. You need all As," she says, going back to mixing the tarka and throwing the diced okra in. "Irfana's girl got accepted to U of T on a full scholarship. She had a ninety-eight percent average."

I gulp. Ninety-eight percent?!?! Those stupid hyper-smart brown kids make the rest of us pretty-smart brown kids look dumb.

"Um, yeah, sure, grades are important," I say, drying the dishes. "But schools also look at what you do outside of the classroom too."

"Like what?"

"Like, you know, extracurricular activities."

"Extra-what?" she says, stopping her stirring and turning to face me.

"Like clubs, sports. You know, like how Jamila is student council president."

"Yes, yes, so do something like that, then." She's right back to cooking. Her attention span is worse than a goldfish's. Okay, here goes.

"I thought maybe I'd try out for the basketball team."

"You and that stupid sport are not a good match. How do you expect to concentrate on school if you spend so much time playing?"

I put away the dish towel and stand right next to her. "Ammi, I have an eighty-five percent average."

"Yes, but your father wanted you to go to law school. It's not easy to get in," she says. "Gulnaz's daughter's been trying for the last two years. You need much higher marks."

Goddamn Irfana and Gulnaz aunties and their daughters. I want to scream. I start pacing back and forth.

"Yeah, but Ammi, you do realize undergrad will cost forty thousand bucks. If I play basketball, I have a shot at getting a sports scholarship."

"Oof, Allah. They have OSUP or something from the government. No basketball. Pick anything else."

"*OSAP*, Ammi, but that's student loans I have to pay back. You do realize that, right?"

She dashes a bunch of spices and a whole ton of salt into the pot before putting a lid on it to let it simmer. Then she moves swiftly to the fridge, taking out a container with kneaded dough for rotis.

Her motions are smooth and effortless. She's already rolling a ball of dough and sprinkling it with additional flour before she stretches it and massages it into something she can go at with her rolling pin.

I'm losing steam and she's losing interest. I need to think fast.

"Abbu would've let me try out," I say. She loses a little color from her face. I've struck a nerve. Second time I've used the Dad card today. This time, it just might work.

"Well, too bad for you that he's dead and can't give you permission from his grave, then, isn't it?"

Ouch. She's putting in extra elbow grease with that rolling pin.

"Ammi, okay, wait—how about I average ninety percent this year? Could I at least try out then? I don't even know if I'm going to make it."

Silence. I'm on the edge of my seat. C'mon. There's a heart in there somewhere. There's gotta be.

"No." She puts the flattened dough on the pan. It starts rising as she moves it around with her fingers. Doesn't matter how hot it gets, she refuses to use tongs.

My final shot was swatted into the crowd. I can't get past her. I should just head back into the locker room. Hang up the jersey for good.

We hear the apartment door rattle. Jamila unzips her knee-high black heeled boots and sets them aside. Next, she chucks her backpack onto the couch. She's got shiny leather pants on with a hot-pink top. Only she could pull this outfit off and make it look normal.

"Hey, kiddo. Hi, Ammi," she says, heading straight to the kitchen sink and pouring herself a glass of water.

Mom doesn't pay much attention to either of us. "You're late."

Jamila gulps down her water and sets the glass on the counter with a loud thud. "So?"

Silence. I wish I could talk back to Mom like her. Where does she get it from? I have to pull out the wild card. It could go either way. I have to try. It's down to the wire. Wait . . . maybe, just maybe, she could help me.

"Jamila, tell Ammi to let me try out for the basketball team."

She gives me a cocky look but decides to play along. She's got her arms crossed and is now ready to spout some sass. "Why can't he play on the team?"

Mom continues juggling and flipping the roti on the stove, and prepping the dough for more. "Who's going to study? That stupid sport won't help him earn any marks."

Jamila walks over to the dining table and plops a few grapes into her mouth. She tries to hand a few to me. I can't eat right now. There's too much hanging in the balance, so I refuse.

"Ammi, he's a smart kid. Universities don't just look at grades. I think it'll be good for him."

Did. She. Just. Stand. Up. For. *Me?* I'm doing everything I can to keep my jaw in place.

"Besides, we don't even know if he'll make it," she says, looking at me and winking.

Ouch.

"Okay, fine," Mom says. "The two of you are impossible. Just stop talking about it now and eat. You're giving me a headache."

Fine? Does that mean, yes? Why was it so easy when Jamila asked? Not that it matters. Just when I think I'm in the clear, and I pour myself some okra and take one of those scrumptious rotis, Mom turns and looks at me while still flipping an uncooked roti in her hands.

"But Fawad Afzal Chaudhry, if your grades slip below ninety, I'll personally come to grab you by the hair and drag you out of that school gym."

"Deal," I yell. I put my plate down and rush toward Jamila to give her a hug. She stops me with a hand out that holds my head and keeps me an arm's length away.

"Some other time. I gotta change and leave. Ray's waiting outside," says Jamila, messing up my hair. "You're welcome."

"That stupid boy again," says Mom, sighing.

"Ammi, he's not stupid. He's my boyfriend and we've been dating for two years now."

"Dating is haram."

"Fine, I guess I'm going to hell."

These two just don't know when to quit. They're staring each other down like in some goddamn Western. Instead of bullets, they're conjuring up words to draw blood.

Guess someone's gotta be the good guy around here.

"Tell Ray we say hi," I offer, all smiles. "Oh, and thanks, Jamila."

That sort of defuses the tension. My mother's grinding her teeth and muttering something to herself under her breath.

The two of them won't talk for a week. My mom says, "Oof, mere Khudaya," and goes back to making sure the roti on the pan doesn't burn.

"Just make the team," says Jamila before turning her back.

"Oh, don't you worry about that," I say. I don't think she hears me or really cares. I know who will care. I quickly grab my phone and text Yousuf and Arif.

ME: Guess who's trying out for the ball team?

Arif responds right away with a gif of Steph Curry sinking a three from half-court. Yousuf doesn't reply at all. *C'mon, man, where are you?*

I'm sitting on the couch while Mom watches *Bigg Boss*, the Indian edition, hosted by Salman Khan. I like to sit out here at least for a little bit after eating because I feel like if I'm just holed up in my room like Jamila, who does Mom have to keep her company? But for the sake of not getting worked up about these ridiculous would-be Bollywood starlets and whatnot, I bury my head in my phone. So are we actually spending quality time together? Maybe not. But at a certain point I tap out and with my face still glued to my phone, I head over to my room.

I haven't posted on Insta in a minute, so I'm scrolling through photos and videos I could put in my Stories. Mostly, I just post me playing ball and follow accounts showing how to get a higher vertical jump, good home workouts, that type of stuff . . . and okay, I follow the occasional girl here and there. But I find a video I took of Yousuf playing this song he wrote on his guitar for me and Arif in his room.

He's fingerpicking and crooning out the words:

There ain't that much time
to think how we might rewind
these minutes that turn to hours
and all these memories time devours.

We think we invincible.
We think there's no end in sight.
This roller coaster called life
starts out looking so bright.

But then those gray clouds
come and never leave,
and all we're left with
is sorrows and memories.

There's gotta be a meaning.
There's gotta be more.
Even if there isn't
we just gotta stay the course.

How does he write this stuff? His voice is not what you'd expect to come out of his mouth. It's like a raspy blues tone. I only ever heard it on a Michael Kiwanuka track, and to be honest, it's hard not to have it send shivers up your spine. That's what happens to me, anyway.

If it could do that for me, I wonder what it could do for others. Hell, I only have 124 followers. What's the worst that could happen?

I upload a thirty-second snippet to my Story. Caption it "Try not to feel something . . . my boy @_Yousuf_RP4LIFE doing his thing . . ." and it's off into the ether. I toss my phone away. He's got something special. Abshir always used to say if Yousuf wanted to, he could record and release an independent EP. He'd even put up the cash to make it happen. Yousuf was always too shy, though; never wanted to perform for no one. Wonder what it would take to change that?

I grab my basketball before turning off the light, and pull my blanket up over me. I still can't believe I can try out for the school team.

Yes, I sleep with a basketball clutched in my hands. It's for luck. What's so lucky about it? Nothing much, really. My dad gave it to me for my eleventh birthday. Up till then, I'd had to rely on Yousuf's crusty ball—you know, one of the really cheap ones from Canadian Tire? If there were days he couldn't play, I wouldn't be able to either.

Dad was never much of a talker, but for some reason this one day, he told me about all these crazy dreams he had for me and Jamila. That I'd either be prime minister or a Supreme Court judge or that Jamila would be a heart surgeon and yada yada yada.

He promised to get me whatever I wanted as long as I kept my grades up, said that education was all that mattered. It was why he and my mom had packed up everything back home and come here, apparently. Lastly, that I could play basketball to my heart's content, but that him giving me that ball was conditional on my never taking school lightly.

I wonder how he'd feel if I told him I'd rather be a pro basketball player than a lawyer any day. I feel like he'd understand. At the very least, he'd want to come see me play. Not like Mom.

Mom and Jamila think it's weird that I sleep with a basketball. My mom says it'll get the bedsheets dirty, and Jamila believes it's probably mad uncomfortable.

I've tried telling them that it just rolls out of my hands when I pass out.

What I can't really explain is how putting it between my palms and feeling all the grooves where the leather sinks and rises, and the lines in between, calms me down.

I'm pretty nervous about making the team. If I don't make it, I don't know if I'll continue playing. I watched the junior team play from the stands last year, when I thought I didn't have what it took. Now, it's a different story.

It'd be the biggest disgrace for a kid from Regent, who spent a summer training with Jerome, to not make the team at a school like Northern, where most of the dudes playing will be white.

Not that white dudes can't ball. I mean, the NBA logo is Jerry West. Plus, I've seen my share of videos of Larry Bird merkin' dudes. It's just that I can already imagine Omar giving me shit for it. "Fuckwad can't even play ball with white kids," he'd say. Guess I'll find out soon enough.

8

I end up snoozing and wake up late, scrambling to get out the door. Luckily, Mom prepped a paratha roll stuffed with leftovers the night before.

I'm tapping my foot, waiting for the streetcar, taking big bites of my breakfast and feeling my insides get warm even though it's starting to get a little chilly outside.

Mr. Singh doesn't seem like the type of coach that would be okay with latecomers. He might not even let me try out. That would kill me too.

Finally, the damn red-and-white electric beast appears. I get on and reach into my pocket for a student ticket. Fuck. I left my tickets at home. I'm giving the driver my best puppy-dog look. It doesn't matter. There's no way I'll be able to go back home, get my tickets, and make it in time for tryouts.

"Sir, I . . ."

"Listen, kid—no ticket, no ride," he says before I even make my case.

Well, that's all she wrote for my very brief basketball career. Fawad Chaudhry forgot his student tickets at home and dragged his sorry ass back to bed, never to play ball again.

As I'm about to step off the streetcar, an older Somalian girl dressed in a black abaya and hijab gets out of her seat. She drops in a ticket for me, and I can't really believe it. Life. Saver. She's cute, but probably three or four grades too old for me to have a chance. She might even be in university.

The driver shrugs and gets the streetcar moving.

"Um, thanks," I say to the girl.

"Don't worry about it," she says, sitting back down. "You're Yousuf's friend, right? I'm friends with Fatima. I feel like I've seen you at their home before."

"Yeah, I haven't seen him in some time, though," I say, in reality wanting to tell her the truth about how worried I am about him.

"Oh, I'm sure he's still processing," she says, plugging in her earbuds. "It's never easy."

"I think so too. Anyways, thanks again. Really appreciate it."

She smiles and I head toward the back of the streetcar to take a seat.

I'll thank her again when I get drafted for the NBA. Right after my mom, because let's be real, it's her parathas fueling the whole dream in the first place. Oh, and my dad. He got me a ball when I could still barely make a layup.

Still got to make the team, I remind myself.

Arriving an hour and a half before school starts is a little spooky. There's no one around until I get to the gym. I can hear the sound of basketballs being dribbled, shot, and hitting the rim, and sneakers squeaking up against the hardwood. They make a sound so sublime that I don't think any DJ could come close to matching it. I'm not late, thank God. Allah, I mean. Same thing.

I hit up the changeroom and come out ready to ball. First, I scout out who else is here. There are at least twenty dudes here, but a couple of guys I recognize from having watched last year's team in action. (I had done my homework and made my own scout reports.)

Luke and Scott are the twin towers on the team—who are also actually twins; they play small and power forward, respectively. They also remind me of the Winklevoss brothers from the *Social Network* movie. Except they're redheads and have freckles.

They're playing one-on-one to warm up. Luke has the better jump shot, while Scott can jump high enough to touch the edge of the rim. That means he is imminently close to dunking. Hot dang.

Next, there's this kid named Andrew. Pale or damn near translucent skin, blond, and busy practicing his handles. He's my main competition for starting point guard.

Last year, he averaged 8.8 points per game and 6.2 assists. This year, he's definitely had a growth spurt, but I'm still taller. Muscle-composition-wise, I need to work out to compete. He seems faster too.

Closing out my picks for starting five are Spence and Isiah. The two Black dudes on the team who obviously have everyone's number.

Spence is the equivalent of Klay Thompson, at the shooting guard position. He's mixed, light-skinned, and sports an Afro. Isiah is like Toronto's very own Serge Ibaka, at the center position.

So really, I just have to prove I'm better than that Andrew kid and Coach will put me in as a starter. No big deal. *Gulp.*

Gotta make the team first, I keep reminding myself.

Ball in hand, I start dribbling, doing some drills, running, and then I line myself up for a shot behind the three-point line.

My shot makes a loud splash. Spence notices and passes the ball back. "Shoot it again."

Can't say no to that, so I put it up. Again, nothing but swish.

"One more," says Spence.

Swish.

Luke and Scott stop their game and watch Spence passing me the ball and me draining those long balls like, well, Curry.

"What's the big deal?" says Andrew, stepping back and putting up a shot. *Clank.*

Spence starts cracking up. Andrew looks a little pissed, but before he has a chance to get another shot up, Mr. Singh appears from the shadows and blows his whistle. He's got a green Adidas tracksuit on, along with a green turban.

"All right, gather around," he says, waving us in. "There's twenty-five of you, and I got spots for twelve. I'm going to let you boys do the math. We're going to start by running around the gym and waiting for one of you to drop." He blows the whistle. "Go."

Shitters. My stamina is a weak point. I'm looking around at the other guys. Luckily, there's a couple of dudes who look like they could shed a few pounds that I can probably beat out. I breathe out, keep my head down, and start jogging.

Twenty laps in, a kid finally gives up.

My calves are killing me. I'm seconds away from collapsing, and I feel like a zombie. Thank you, random white boy. I owe you one.

Coach blows the whistle. He thanks the kid for his time. After we watch him limp to the changeroom, we're running drills up and down the court.

Three of us at a time are weaving, throwing, and passing the ball until one of us lays it in or pulls up for a jumper. I keep up but miss a pass, and even more embarrassing, miss a layup on one trip. Can't do that again.

I see Andrew smirking and whispering something to Scott while still looking my way. Mr. Singh just shakes his head. "Keep pushing, kid. C'mon now, c'mon now."

On one run, I slip and my knee skids on the hardwood. Some skin comes off, but I bounce back before anyone has a chance to come help.

I. Got. This.

During the last fifteen minutes, we're playing a full-court game. Andrew and I are on opposite teams. I get cocky bringing the ball up. I attempt to step past him into the clear, he knocks the ball loose, and I'm too winded to chase after him, so he gets an easy bucket.

"Chaudhry, who's going to run back?" Coach yells.

I tap my chest and acknowledge the mistake. Fuuuck me.

Luke throws the ball in, and I'm off. This time I spot Isiah in the post. He's double-teamed. He kicks it back out to me for a wide-open three. I feel some redemption as soon as the ball hits the bottom of the net.

Andrew's already pushing the ball up. I'm trailing behind him. I'll be real, guarding this dude is not easy. He leaves me in his dust and pulls up for an easy floater across the lane.

"Stay with him, Chaudhry. My grandpa could run faster than that," Coach shouts from the sidelines. He's shaking his head and holding his temples like he's got a migraine.

I nod again. There are some chuckles from the other kids. My heart and lungs are exploding. I'm getting shown up by this white kid who I thought I could school with one hand tied behind my back. Jeez.

Finally, Mr. Singh blows the whistle. I'm barely able to keep myself standing. My entire body feels wobbly. Andrew's joking around with Scott and Luke. I see him walking toward me.

"Good run," he says, holding out his hand. "You'll make a great number two."

I don't know how to respond. I don't leave him hanging, but in my head, the words "Go fuck yourself" come to mind. I don't say that, obviously. Instead I just mutter, "Thanks."

We bump fists, then he leaves.

"We have another tryout next Tuesday," Mr. Singh yells as the boys head to the changeroom. "I'll post the roster outside my office Thursday morning. Good work, boys."

I feel like the "good work" part was intended for everyone but me. The scowl on Mr. Singh's face reminds me so much of Dad, it's not even funny.

In all fairness, Andrew did kick my ass the entire time. So much for starting point guard. At least I'm good at keeping the bench nice and warm. Sigh.

. . .

I march into the guidance counselor's office right after practice. There's still some time before first period starts. I'm there because I need to switch out of art.

The teacher is bonkers. Plus, I can't mix colors to save my life. It was pretty easy in ninth grade, so I just stuck with it. This year, though, it's a lot tougher than I expected. I'm hoping to switch into dramatic arts so I can have another class with Arif. He's the biggest goof, so I'm promised some good laughs. Plus, Dad always wanted to see me act in a Bollywood movie, on top of being a lawyer, so this would be a pretty good start. *No pressure, Dad, really.*

I don't get much flack from the counselor. It's done pretty quickly, and I head to my locker, where I hope to catch Arif so we can head to drama together. He's there, chilling as usual. Except I spy with my little eye that girl from gym class, Kate. They're way too touchy. Okay, fine, I'm a little jealous. What a bastard.

"Eh yo, what's poppin'?" he says when he notices me coming. "You already know Kate."

She raises her hand to wave. Damn, she's pretty. Don't even get me started on her smile.

"Hey," I say to her before turning to Arif. "I'm doing good. Had ball practice and whatnot. Just thought I'd let you know I finally did it."

His eyes light up and he leans away from the locker to say, "Bro, not so loud. Besides, is Nusrat still going to want to marry you if you're not a virgin anymore?"

Did he just put Nusrat and my virginity together in the same sentence? In front of Kate?

I look at him like I'm about to rip his head off.

"Who's Nusrat?" says Kate, twirling a strand of her beautiful silky hair in one hand.

Before Arif can answer, I put my hand on his lips, pin him to the locker, and give him my hardest stare. Kate's startled, so I ease off, but as soon as I see he's about to open his mouth again, I punch him in the stomach.

Kate is in shock and not pleased. I smile at her to no avail.

"Yo, I was just kidding," says Arif, gathering himself. He's a little winded and wincing, but I'm surprised he isn't retaliating. Maybe having Kate around isn't such a bad thing.

"Are you okay?" says Kate, putting a hand on Arif's shoulder.

"He's just playing around," says Arif, smiling.

"I switched into drama, is what I was trying to say," I tell him.

"Say word? Oh shit, that's this period," he says, checking his watch.

"Yeah, you wanna head together?"

"Sorry, bro, I'm gonna walk Kate to geography first."

"Right, okay, I'll see you guys around," I say.

"One sec, before I head off—that clip you posted of Yousuf playing guitar, you know that shit's going viral, right?"

"What? It is? But I only got, like, 124 followers," I say, pulling out my phone to look at the Story. It's got ten-thousand-plus views, and I've got DMs from at least a hundred folks reacting with the fire emoji and clapping emoji and whatnot. Then I go to Yousuf's Insta profile and he's picked up 2,500 new followers. Damn. That was fast. Hope he doesn't hate me. I take a screenshot and text it to him with the mind-blown emoji and the words "You a star . . ."

"That's nuts," I say, eyes still bulging at the numbers on the screen. "You think he's gon' be mad?"

"I don't know, bro," says Arif, slapping me on the back and walking away with Kate. "Shit's unpredictable at the moment, but if it was me, I'd be feeling pretty swell right now."

I put my phone away and plan out when I should drop by and pay him a visit. But first thing's first. Drama class.

I check the classroom number on the piece of paper I got from the guidance counselor. Drama's in the basement, so I start heading down the steps. Kids are rushing past me. It's too frantic for my liking. Rushing to places is not my thing, late slips be damned.

I'm hopping down the stairs like I'm doing a basketball drill. As I'm about to get to the second floor, I see a dude rush past a girl, knocking her binder out of her hands and sending her papers flying. He races past me, and before I can give him a piece of my mind, he's gone.

Me being me, I scramble to help. I pick up the pieces of paper, and when I've got them in a nice and tidy pile, I walk toward her to hand them over so I can be on my way.

She's still gathering some papers from the ground when I tap her on her left shoulder. She turns, and it's like I got hit by a truck. Not a small truck either. I'm talking one of those big eighteen-wheelers lugging shit from one end of Canada to the other that you avoid driving next to on the highway . . . that type of truck.

I mean, someone pinch me. I've only seen someone's hair blow like that in Bollywood films.

I'm taking her in. Black tee with the front tucked in, skintight light-blue jeans, nose ring. She's mixed—half-white and half-Asian—with black hair tied back in a bun. She's got black eyes and oh man, those lips. They're really pink. No, red. No, some color in the middle. I said I was terrible at mixing colors, didn't I? But I think the beauty mark on her left cheek is what gets me.

She's waving one hand in front of me to see if I'm there. I snap out of my daze.

"Thanks, I can take those now," she says, tugging at the papers I've crumpled because I'm holding them too tight. There are sweat marks on them now. Worst of all, I'm ready to vomit because of how nervous I'm feeling.

"Oh, sorry. Here you go," I say, letting go and putting my hands in my pockets. What else would I even do with them?

She puts the papers back into her binder and zips up her bag.

"I'm Ashley. What's your name?" she says.

I hate my parents right now.

"Fawad," I say, mouthing out the syllables to make sure there's no miscommunication.

"Fahd?"

Put me out of my misery already.

"Like a-wad with an *F*."

"Oh, Fawad. I like it. I've never heard that name before," she says, smiling and holding the straps of her bag.

"Yeah, I get that a lot," I say, trying to play it off as no big deal.

"I'm just headed to the basement for class. Are you going that way?" she says, pointing down the stairs.

"Uh, yeah. I, um . . . am," I say, wiping my sweaty hands on my pants.

"So, shall we?" she says.

"Uh, yeah, let's shall."

Who the hell says that? I take a deep breath in and think about what Arif would say.

He'd play it cool. He'd make fun of her. He'd make her laugh some way, somehow.

"Your handwriting looks like chicken scratch."

"Excuse me?" She stops and looks at me with raised eyebrows.

Mayday, Mayday! I'm sinking fast.

"Oh, it just reminded me of my doctor's writing when she writes my mom a prescription."

She smiles. Sweet relief.

"Yeah, my mom tells me that all the time." We get to her classroom door. She looks at me and says, "See you around, Fawad."

Before she can turn the door handle, I say, "Hey, wait! Are you on Snap?"

She lets go of the door and walks back toward me. I take out my crusty Android phone.

Ashley takes it, adds herself to my Snap, and just like that I have a way to get in touch with her.

Before she enters her class, she looks back and smiles.

I'm also hella late for class and will probably have to go all the way back up to the office to get a late slip. Worth it.

Just before I duck into drama, I look her up on Insta—luckily her handle's the same—and scroll through her feed. I mean, I already know she's pretty, but damn, the girl is balling too.

There are vacation pics. Photos of her with friends in her backyard. It looks as big as the courtyard of my entire apartment building.

Plus there's a bunch of white and Asian dudes: Aarons, Michaels, Adams, and Ryans, no doubt. One of them's got his arms around her in one photo. They seem like they're really into each other. Well, doubt anyone of 'em can shoot a three like me, so I got *something* going for me. Let's see how it goes.

...

After school, instead of heading straight home from the street-car stop, I stand outside Yousuf's townhome. I can see lights from his TV—he's probably playing *Call of Duty* or something. Should I head in or maybe . . . I spot a little rock in his tiny-ass front lawn and chuck it up toward his window. *Clank.* No response. This is how I'd get him to come play ball before we got phones. Old-school, but effective. I pick up another rock and before I chuck it, he pushes open his window.

"You scared the shit out of me," he says, shaking his head. "Why you gotta be throwing rocks at my window like we back in fifth grade?"

"Sorry, man, I . . . I don't know what I was thinking," I say, hanging my head. "Can I come up?"

"Yeah."

I knock on the front door and his mom opens it.

"Salaam, Aunty," I say. She welcomes me in, her expression solemn. She's never spoken much English, but we've gotten by with some basics. Sidee tahay is "How are you" in Somali. It's not much but it's something. I can say it in Bangla too: it's "apni kemon achen?"

She smiles and nods. On the TV stand are photos of Abshir, Fatima, and Yousuf graduating from middle school. Abshir was so close to graduating high school. I take a deep breath. Seeing his photo takes me back to him coming home with random gifts for Yousuf, me, and Arif. If he got his little brother some Yu-Gi-Oh! cards, you'd better believe he got a pack for us too.

She calls for Yousuf. He doesn't come out, and she shakes her head and stares at the ground before calling for him one more time. I save her the effort, quickly kicking off my shoes and gesturing to her that I'll just go up instead.

It's been a couple weeks since I've been here, which is kinda weird considering we're always cycling between my, Yousuf's, and Arif's places. I open the door to his room. He puts away his video game controller. He was definitely smoking a joint. He opens the window to clear the smell out.

I walk up to him, hand raised, and we do a little hug. Don't want to admit it but I missed the guy. His 'fro is disheveled and his little scruffy beard-in-the-works is an interesting look, though he should really shave it off.

"How you doing, bro?" I say, as he sits on a beanie chair and I sit on the edge of his bed.

"It's going, I don't know . . . Life's okay, parents aren't too worked up about all the school I'm missing and shit," he says, before retrieving a little box. "Got enough joints to keep me occupied. Just been playing games and sleeping, really."

"You wanna come out and play ball sometime?"

"Nah, man. Haven't left the house since the funeral. Just feel like something's going to happen. That rock you threw at the window had me shook. I know I'm just being paranoid but . . ."

His voice starts breaking and he's sniffing, wiping at his nose. "Yeah, just miss him, you know?"

My shoulders droop and I stare at the palms of my hands, thinking back to Abshir showing me how to hold the ball before shooting. Everything starts aching and suddenly it's as if it's all happening again.

"I miss him too," I say, tearing up. I grab a tissue and wipe my eyes.

"It just doesn't go away," he says, his tone flat.

"It's hard, bro. I know I was in a slump for half a year after Dad died, and it still hits me sometimes when Mom makes extra biryani, and I think he's going to come home from work and have some."

"I remember that," says Yousuf with a sigh.

"You know what, though?" I say, crying and smiling at the same time. "They're not really gone. I still talk to my dad sometimes."

"You do?"

"Yeah. Not out loud, but here and there. And I know it sounds crazy, but I swear it's as if he can hear me."

Yousuf smiles. "You think Abshir can hear us?"

"Of course. We more than our bodies, you know that. And if he could see us, I don't think he'd want you to waste away here. He always wanted us to make something of ourselves, remember?"

Yousuf nods.

I take out my phone, remembering why I decided to drop by in the first place. "Check this," I say, showing him the little snippet I posted of him, and how many views it got, and all the followers he now had.

"When'd you take that video? I don't even remember singing," says Yousuf, scratching his head. "Guess that's why my damn phone's been buzzing all day. Had to switch it off. Haven't wanted to go near it, for some reason."

"You got a gift, man," I say. "I think when you're blessed, it's only right to share it. Right?"

"I don't know. It's just one thirty-second clip. You know how many dudes trying to make it in the industry. It's not easy."

"Forget making it, just do you."

"I'll think about it. I appreciate you dropping by, fam. It's no fun being holed up in here playing *COD* with randos."

"I got you. Also, I know it's not easy but I think your mom could really use a hug whenever you do go down."

Yousuf smiles. "All right, all right."

I glance up to check the time and remember I didn't tell my own mom that I was going to be late. Going to hear it now. We do our shake, and I'm feeling that heaviness lifting when I head down with Yousuf and see him embrace his mother. They start crying. I quietly say salaam and gently close the door, looking up and thinking, they're really there—just have to believe it.

9

Every day since I bumped into Ashley, I've been thinking about her. She never followed me back on Insta. Northern's too big a school to predictably run into her. I could send her a Snap, but of what?

I'm glad the week's over and it's the weekend. Wish I could sleep in, but nope. Gotta go to a 10:00 a.m. Quran class.

I remember when it was cartoons I woke up for. Since Mom enrolled me in these classes, there's no more of that. Except when I'm sick, which I try to be often.

Mom stopped buying it after a while. She made it pretty clear there is no getting out of reciting the Holy book from start to finish. I want to impress her, commit it to memory, but does she even realize how *long* the Quran is?

I stayed up late last night watching Netflix. I can barely keep my eyes open as I brush my teeth, and I think I might have used shampoo instead of bodywash but whatevs. Part of being brown means having enough body hair to warrant shampoo. Sad, but true.

I notice a cockroach crawling up one wall. Last year, I went to the doctor for ear pain. After giving it a thorough look, the doctor took a syringe and flushed my ear with water. A few moments later, there was a dead cockroach in the tray. These suckers can get in anywhere.

I'm out and the crisp October air makes me wince. I texted Yousuf to see if he was coming, but he responded that he had to help out at home, so next stop is Arif's.

He lives a few blocks south. The garbage and recycling bins behind my building are overflowing, and I catch a whiff that I wish I hadn't.

I pass through the parking lot and cut through narrow alleys until I hit the area that's currently under construction. Fences, bulldozers, and signs telling people to stay out are littered everywhere. A building was just demolished and its remains are still here.

A few steps down is a huge park next to a brand-new aquatics center. There are also new townhouses and newly minted condo buildings.

In a matter of years, the neighborhood went from low-income to mixed income. Now we have refugee families on welfare living next door to young couples that just bought their first condo and walk their dog twice a day. Crazy, right?

Outside Arif's building, I message the fool to come down. He appears in a white thobe with a topi, a skullcap, on his head. Like he's an angel or something.

"Damn, I don't know why I gotta wear this when you don't," he says, tugging at his robes.

I shrug and we man-hug. "What you talking about? Girls love a dude dressed like a ghost. It's also a Halloween favorite. But yeah, guess my dad never really wore one, so my mom doesn't make me either."

He cracks up. "Yo, I don't care what no one says, I look fly in this right here." His hair is slicked back under his topi. He does look pretty dope, but obviously, I'm not going to tell him that. He's already got enough of his head up his own ass.

"How's homie?" says Arif.

"I think he's doing better. Caught up with him yesterday."

"We should try to get him to get out of his room. I'd go crazy staying home all the time."

"He's a little paranoid about something happening. To be honest, I think he needs help. Just don't know who to ask."

"Help? Like therapy and shit?" says Arif.

"Yeah."

"You think that stuff works? It's just talking, isn't it? He could do that with us."

I chuckle. "Shrinks go to school for years to do that. Think it's gotta be a little different."

Arif shrugs.

We walk toward Parliament Street and then head south. There are two Bangladeshi stores hawking groceries, meat, and those prepaid phone cards to make long-distance calls, with a dive bar called Tony's Tonic in between them.

It gets grimy as soon as we get to Dundas Street. The storefronts get increasingly more rundown. To the east are more cafés, pizza shops, and places that sell hair extensions, each looking dilapidated and like they could go out of business at any minute.

Right at the corner is the Council Fire. We've started learning a little bit of history around Canada's Indigenous population in school. I don't think the curriculum paints the whole picture, though. White people have a way of covering up their tracks.

I watched the movie *Gandhi* over the summer and had no idea about all the shit brown folk had to go through to gain independence. In 1947, India and Pakistan were created after the partition. In 1971, India helped East Pakistan gain independence and Bangladesh was born. Blows my mind.

Arif and I pass by the barbershop where we get our hair cut. Good ol' Mary-Jo. Saturday mornings are prime time for men to get their fades and line-ups touched up. Wait times can sometimes push three hours.

I didn't eat breakfast, so when we pass the Afghan spot, my stomach roars like it's Questlove banging on his drums. All I can think about is having some chicken shawarma after the lesson.

"So, what happened with that girl?" says Arif.

I shake my head. "Nah, forget it, man."

"You know you gon' end up with your first cousin if you don't grow some balls, right?"

Again with Nusrat. I wanna throw him in a headlock when I catch sight of a bunch of dudes up ahead. It's easy to tell by the laughing that it's Omar and his gang. Arif smacks me across the arm.

Up ahead, we hear Omar. "Yo, swear on my life, dawg, I got head from Noelle. She got some sharp teeth, though."

"Say Wallahi," says Gibril, another one of his cronies. Omar laughs and then turns and spots us, narrowing his eyes at me.

"Knew I sniffed some curry. What's up, dumbshits?" he says. He's got on a backwards Jordan jersey, from his Chicago Bulls days, and matching cap tucked over a red sweatband.

"Man, it's too early for your bullshit," says Arif, raising his brow. We cut past them.

"Eh, Fuckwad, how's that pussy friend of yours? Come out of hiding in his room yet?"

Laughter erupts. He didn't . . .

I turn around to look him straight in the eye, flaring my nostrils. "Say that again."

"So, did he?" Omar says, his crew still laughing.

I get ready to charge at him when Arif clutches my arm. "It's not worth it."

"Your boyfriend keeping you outta trouble, eh?"

That last bit is enough for Arif. He turns around and shoves Omar.

"You got a problem, homie?"

Gibril and his dudes jump in and grab Arif.

"Whoa, easy boys. Not here," says Omar, waving them off. An older Somali man walks out of the mosque and stares us up and down before crossing the street. Probably knows Omar's dad, which is why Omar straightens up and acts like we all chums now.

"You lucky you Naz's cousin, homie," mutters Omar, face-to-face with Arif, towering over him. "Otherwise, these Timbs would've been halfway up your ass by now."

"Keep talking, we'll see who's lucky," says Arif. I can see his veins popping. I know he's ready to pounce, even if it'll be two on six.

The dudes let me and Arif walk up ahead, remaining behind, pissed and fuming. The worst is we'll all be in the same class shortly. Shawarma doesn't sound all that good anymore. Probably best to head straight home after the lesson.

. . .

We take off our shoes and put them side by side on the racks.

"Can't believe that dude," says Arif, shaking his head. "What a little bitch."

"I swear if he says one more thing about Yousuf . . ." I say, "I'm going to lose it."

"He wants you to. You gotta keep your head straight."

It's true. It's not like I'm Nazmul's cousin and could have him and his boys chasing after Omar if shit hit the fan. I don't have no backup, no crew, no Abshir.

We head into the carpeted area of the mosque and enter the main hall. The walls are lined with shelves containing the Holy book.

Before we can touch one, we first have to do ablutions. That means going down to the washing area, where there are stools for us to sit on, and getting ourselves cleaned up. Mouth, eyes, nose, ears, hands, arms, feet, and we're done.

I take out a topi from my pocket and put it on. Staring in the mirror with my hair tucked tightly under it, I examine my reflection. I like the little scruff that's growing. It kinda draws attention away from my nose. That's a big plus, in my opinion.

"All right, princess, let's keep it moving," says Arif, even though he spent just as long fixing his hair.

I just smile and follow him. We retrieve a Quran each, along with a stand to put it on, from the shelves.

With Arif, I practice the surah that I'm supposed to have memorized. Believe it or not, he's way ahead of me when it comes to Arabic. Don't get me started on how well he nails the recitation. It's like me and math, where I just *get* it.

Imam Aziz finally walks in. We all greet him. He always has a grim look on his face. Dressed in a black thobe, he's very skinny, with a protruding gut and a beard that's orange from having henna applied to it.

There are always prayer beads in his hands. I don't think I've ever seen him without them. He probably thinks about Allah all the time.

Imam Aziz settles down just as Omar, Gibril, and the rest of the dudes emerge from the washing area to take their seats.

One by one, we go up and get our past week's homework checked and then receive our homework for the next week.

My heart is racing when it's my turn because I didn't practice all week. I blame it on Ashley because she won't get out of my head. Obviously, I can't tell him that. Pretty sure that's a bona-fide sin.

We flip to the page I'm supposed to recite from. Some of the last-minute practice with Arif pays off.

"Very well done, Fawad," the Imam says, a big grin on his face. "We have a Quran recitation competition coming up next month. You should participate."

"Thank you, Imam Saab. I'll, uh, have to check with my . . . mom."

He reaches over to his side and picks up a flyer printed on neon green paper advertising the event, which is happening at Madina Masjid. It's a huge mosque located on the Danforth. I smile, fold the paper, and tuck it away in my pocket.

"Very good. Now for this week's homework . . ."

He and I practice new verses in a call-and-response manner until he's happy with my pronunciation of each syllable. Then he taps my shoulder. "That's enough for now. Tell Arif to come next."

Whew. I blow out a deep breath, leaving the Imam, and signal to Arif that it's his turn. I catch Omar's eyes as I head to my seat. Not good.

Imam Aziz loves Arif. It doesn't take long before he's done. Arif walks back to sit next to me, all smiles. It's Omar's turn next. As soon as he walks up to sit across from the Imam, his dad, Imam Aziz's face goes stone-cold.

He points at where he wants his son to start. Omar begins but is quickly cut off. Imam Aziz smacks his own forehead out of frustration. He's speaking in Somali but I can tell he's lecturing Omar on how he's doing it all wrong.

I'm trying my hardest to not pay attention. Except I can't help feeling a bit of pleasure watching the whole thing go down. It's the same story week after week for as long as I've been living in Regent.

Omar starts again. This time, his dad raises his voice and shouts, "Again, how many times do I have to tell you? Stupid boy."

I grimace and jerk my head back. All the boys are looking now. At last, angry and frustrated, Imam Aziz dismisses Omar. "Go practice some more. Go now."

Omar gets up and walks back to his crew, flaring his nostrils, looking pissed. I look away, pretending like I'm deep into practicing the new lesson. My brain's plotting how best to avoid him after this.

Then I remember: he has to stay at the mosque for the afternoon prayer since his dad leads it. Maybe that shawarma plan might just pan out after all. My stomach growls so loud everyone turns to look at me.

Gotta stop thinking about food and focus on the Scriptures. Feed the soul, I tell myself. Man, am I hungry, though . . .

10

I'm in much better form for the second tryout. I'm not letting Andrew get by me like I'm a sitting duck. *Quack, quack.* I get a steal, and I hit this crazy step-back three right in his face.

On another possession, I do such a badass crossover that he nearly falls to the floor. You can hear *ooohs* from the other dudes.

He comes back harder, drives the ball in more, and plays tighter defense. He even hits a few jumpers with my hand right in his face. Then come a few turnovers from me. One possession, he strips the ball right from my hands. On another, he intercepts my pass. Then he blocks my shot. You get the picture. Bastard. On one turnover, I stop running after him. Mr. Singh blows his whistle and singles me out.

"Who's going to run back, kid?" he yells, pointing at the other side of the court. "How many times do I have to say it?"

I'm winded. I need to increase my stamina. I see Coach making some notes. My stomach churns. He's going to cut me, I know it.

I want to just pack up and leave, but I decide to stick it out.

We finish running the scrimmage game and Coach gathers us in a huddle.

"All right, I think I've seen all that I need to see," he says, continuing to make notes on his clipboard, then looking up. "Boys, Northern hasn't won a championship in eight years. I think this might be our time. No one wins games on fancy step-backs or crossovers. Games are won with fierce determination. That's what I'll be looking for when I make the cuts and post the list on Thursday."

Gulp. Was Coach looking at me when he said those things about fancy this or that? Jeez. He's the one who wanted me to try out in the first place. I shake my head. I should've never given it a shot.

. . .

I catch up with Arif and Nermin afterwards. They're waiting for me outside the gym.

"So, how'd you do?" says Nermin, giving me a punch on the arm. She doesn't know her own strength. It actually hurts, or I'm just really sore from practice.

I shrug. "I think he's going to cut me."

Arif puts his arm around me as I slump over. "Bro, c'mon, do you even know how sweet that jump shot of yours is?" he says. "Like, I get a hard-on watching you shoot."

TMI. "Dude, that makes me never want to shoot a basketball ever again."

"Whatever, I'd put my money on you," he says, giving me a slap on the back.

"So, Arif was telling me there's a girl you got your eyes on," says Nermin, clutching the straps of her backpack. "Is it true?"

I can't lie. Nermin has the ability to see right through me. I shrug. "It's nothing, really. I don't think it's going to go anywhere."

"Dude, *c'mon*. Do you really want to end up with Nusrat?" says Arif. I can't tell if he's joking or being serious.

"Not Nusrat again," I say through my teeth. "I've already had a rough morning. Can we ease off that?"

"But tell me the truth," he says, not backing off, and getting right up in my face. "Are you worried about your mom finding out? Cuz, bro, we're all in that same boat."

"A little, I guess," I say, shrugging. "Jamila's already dating and my mom wants me to be the good kid. The one who actually listens to her."

"Yeah, but what do you want?" says Nermin.

I stop and stare at the floor. To be honest, no one has ever asked me that. What do I want?

I think for a second. I want to spend all my time playing basketball. I want a girlfriend like any normal fifteen-year-old. I want to be able to say no to some preordained cousin marriage. But mostly, I just want to move out of Regent Park.

"Earth to Fawad," she says, again pretending to have a walkie-talkie in her hand. "Where do you just disappear off to?"

"Sorry, no one's ever asked me that. What I want, I mean," I say, feeling a little teary-eyed. I'm sad, but we're in the middle of the hallway and I need to keep my shit together.

Nermin senses it and changes the subject. "Show me her photo, at least?"

I take out my phone and pull up Ashley's Insta profile. Nermin gets close to get a better angle before grabbing the phone out of my hand.

"She's hot," says Nermin, scrolling through her feed.

"Yeah, I know," I say.

"My boy's got good taste," says Arif, winking at me.

She hands me my phone back. "So, like, why haven't you made a move?"

"Because she's too hot."

Nermin smacks her forehead. "Boys. Fawad, just ask her out. What's the worst that could happen?"

I imagine Ashley laughing maniacally right after I ask. I can see her forehead growing horns, dark-red clouds swirling behind her, and a trident in her right hand.

Then she pierces my chest with the trident and roasts me on a huge tribal fire. She takes my well-cooked heart out, gives it a good look, and throws it to the wolves.

"You don't understand," I say.

Kate walks up to us and says, "Hey, guys."

Nermin isn't overly fond of her, from what I can tell. At least by the way she barely waves and avoids looking in Kate's direction. I manage to get out a "Hey Kate," with a bit of a fake smile. I go back to showing Nermin Ashley's Insta.

Meanwhile, Arif starts play-wrestling with Kate with her back against a locker. It doesn't take long before the two of them start making out. You'd think they'd have a little more self-control.

Adam, Paul, and some other jocks from the football team are walking by us. Adam does a double-take and walks over to Arif, tapping him on the shoulder.

"Hey, dipshit, that's my sister," he says.

Of course she is. Why wouldn't Kate be related to the biggest douchebag in the school?

Arif turns to face him with a sly smile on his face. "Small world," he says.

"Adam, seriously, I'm not in kindergarten," says Kate, coming out from behind Arif.

Adam's face tightens. "You stay out of this," he says.

He shoves Arif against the lockers; Arif lunges right back at him. They're at each other's throats. Their bodies lock, and both of them try to free up an arm to take the first swing.

"C'mon, man, don't be that guy," says Paul, pulling Adam away and holding him back.

Adam struggles but finally frees himself from Paul's grip. He straightens out his bomber jacket. "Just remember, he isn't always going to be around to save your ass."

"Fine by me," says Arif, his chest out and shoulders back.

As Paul, Adam, and the other dudes walk away, I watch Arif regain his composure and pretend like nothing happened.

"We'll see you guys around," says Arif, grabbing Kate's hand and walking off.

"So Arif's going to get his ass kicked," says Nermin, crossing her arms as we watch them round the corner.

"Yup. Pretty much."

. . .

It's Thursday morning and Mr. Singh is supposed to post the list outside his office today. I don't want to get out of bed. I think I'm going to call in sick. Maybe get Arif to check for me and text me the bad news. It's 7:30 a.m. when my door swings open and standing there is Jamila.

"Hey, loser, Mom's asking why you haven't gotten up yet," she says.

I don't respond. Instead, I pull the covers over my face, hoping she'll go away. Of course, she doesn't. She rips the duvet off my bed. I cling to a corner.

"Leave me alone. I'm sick."

119

"Aww, poor baby, what's wrong?"

Her sarcasm kills me. Why can't we ever talk to each other like normal people?

"I told you, I'm sick," I yell.

She lets go of the duvet and sits on the side of the bed. "No, seriously, what's up?"

I don't want to tell her, but I also don't want to keep it bottled up inside. It takes a few seconds before I finally say, "I think I got cut from the basketball team."

She looks at me like I'm a moron. "So what's the big deal?"

I sit up and grab the basketball from the floor. It's far more comforting than having this conversation. "I really wanted to make it," I say, hugging the ball and slouching over it.

She scoots closer. "There's always next year. You know that. Besides, it's just basketball."

I hate those three words. "It's not *just* basketball. That's like me telling you not to worry about your portfolio for getting into that animation program. That it's *just* art."

Her hand ruffles my hair. "Hey, sorry. Didn't know it meant that much to you, that's all. In that case, you're going to make it. I just know it."

I feel a little reassured. I want a hug but I can't remember the last time we hugged. Definitely before Dad passed away.

She nudges me on the shoulder. "C'mon, Mom's made stuffed aloo keema parathas. Your favorite."

I lie back down. "Tell her I'm not hungry."

"All right, spill the beans. You not wanting to eat aloo keema parathas is weird. That's like Dad not eating a whole pot of biryani by himself, then asking if there's more for the kids."

I smile but my lips are stapled together. Biryani was definitely Dad's favorite. Mom had to hide plates for us just so he wouldn't eat it all.

I scoot back up into a sitting position and the two of us are just looking at each other.

She breaks out in a laugh. "It's a girl, isn't it?"

I nod and blurt out, "I just don't know what to say to her."

"At this point, start with anything."

I giggle nervously. "What if she doesn't respond?"

"That's kind of a response too. Here, let me have a look. What does she look like?"

I show her Ashley's Insta on my phone.

"Oh, she's cute," she says, taking one look. "But you're a looker too. Have you checked the mirror lately? Puberty is doing you some good."

I'm stunned by the compliment. Can't remember the last time I heard one from her.

"Just say something funny," she says, putting a hand on my shoulder. "Then once you have her laughing, ask her out. The worst thing that can happen is she says no. But at least you won't be sitting here wondering."

Damn. Sage wisdom.

She gives me a hard smack on the back. "All right, get up now. Mom's not going to let you skip school over basketball or a girl."

"Gotta go to law school," we say in unison, mimicking Mom, and crack up laughing.

"Thanks," I say.

"Anytime. Well, that's a lie. Sometimes. Whenever I'm in the mood. Holler."

"Wait," I say, just as she's about to get up.

"What now?"

"This whole Nusrat thing," I say. "Mom's not serious, is she?"

"Even if she is, what does it matter?" she says. "You know no one can force you to make that decision."

"Thanks, Jamila," I say. Something inside me really needed to hear that.

"Now hurry and get up," she says.

I nod, jump out of bed, rush to the washroom, and quickly shower and get dressed. Mom's already left for work by the time I'm chowing down on the parathas. They're still so good cold.

To be honest, I'm not enticed by weed, cigarettes, or even booze. I'm straight-up addicted to these bad boys. Nom nom.

...

I make it to school a few minutes late to first period. I'm 110 percent sure I didn't make the team. I still go to the gym and check the list posted on the board outside Mr. Singh's office anyway.

The usual suspects are there: Luke Feldman, Scott Feldman, Andrew McQuillen, Spencer Denvers, Isiah Abebe. A few names later, I see Fawad Chaudhry. Wait, that's me.

Oh my God. Oh my God. I made the team. *Ahhhhhhhhhhhhh.*

The halls are empty. I'm pumping my fist like I've won some Olympic medal or some shit. I can't wait to tell Arif. I can't wait to tell Nermin. And I know Yousuf's going to be over the moon for me. Oh man. I can't wait . . . to warm the bench. But who cares? At least I made the team. I just gotta level up my game. That's right: I got a secret plan hatching in my head right now. Poor little Andrew McQuillen won't know what's coming for him. Fawad Chaudhry is going to show him what he's made of.

I'm doing a crossover with a make-believe ball. Then I do a spin move. I attempt a jump shot aiming at the garbage can and I hear nothing but swish. I've got my arms in the air the way Curry does when he's loving the energy from the crowd.

Then I realize that the halls aren't as empty as I thought they were. Fuck.

Ashley, of all people? Agh. I'm so embarrassed. I want to go back home, crawl back into bed, and never come out again.

My face feels hot and my hands start sweating. I see she sees me. I see her too, and I wave. She walks toward me. Where the hell is Arif when you need him? I'm going down.

"Hey, what was all that about?" she says, binder clutched in front of her chest.

"Uh, I, uh . . . made the team."

"Ohhhhhhh," she says. I wish time would freeze, so I could watch her lips make that *ohhh* sound forever. "Congrats!"

"Thanks," I say as I rub the back of my head like I got lice or some shit. I should stop that ASAP. I straighten up, trying to get my limbs to cooperate, but I'm like jelly.

"Wanna walk me to class?"

"Uh, sure." Then, out of nowhere, I blurt out, "You should come out to a game. I mean, I won't be starting. If you like basketball, that is. I know not everyone does. Like, my mom doesn't like it at all."

Did I forget how to form sentences? What am I blabbering on about? Why am I not dead yet? Can someone hear me up there? Hello? Dad?

Ashley's blushing. She flicks her hair back. "Sure, I'd be up for that. I'm on the volleyball team. We're already mid-season. My mom doesn't like it either, but my dad's a huge sports buff, so yeah. If you want to come to a game. Thought I'd just mention it."

She's actually *blushing*? And did she just say what I think she said?

I think I'm nodding my head way too many times.

"Uh, yeah, I'd love to. I'll be in the bleachers next game."

"This is me," she says, pointing at the classroom door we're standing outside. "See ya."

I wave as she opens the door, turns around, smiles, and closes the door behind her. I press my forehead to the wall beside her classroom. I made the ball team *and* Ashley wants to see me play *and* she invited me out to a game. I mean, it's not a date, but it's something. I'm not dreaming, but I pinch myself just to make sure.

11

If I am going to have a shot at getting playing time or proving myself to Mr. Singh, I am going to need a secret weapon—and mine is Coach Jerome.

Hailing from Regent Park, originally an immigrant from Jamaica, he got himself an NCAA scholarship to a Division II school as a small forward. He was poised to enter the NBA draft when he got hurt trying to dunk over a seven-foot dude.

Luckily, he finished his undergrad degree. With his hoop dreams slashed, he moved back to Toronto, got his teaching degree, and has been teaching elementary classes at Lord Dufferin and coaching basketball ever since.

Kids in his class still don't believe him when he tells them that he's from Regent. I know I didn't. First day of class, he got up there and said, "Welcome, everyone. My name's Jerome. Some of you may want to call me Mr. Williams, but friends don't call friends by their last names or use titles like *Mr.* or *Miss.* I grew up right here in this very neighborhood . . ."

Gasps. Then laughter. One kid said, "No, you didn't . . . you're a teacher."

Jerome also helps kids he thinks have a shot at the big league with some private coaching. It's a competitive market with all these training camps and whatnot, so he's always been hell-bent on trying to level the playing field.

I head to the fancy-ass new community center in Regent after school. Crazy how I don't get that same I'm-going-to-get-the-shit-beaten-out-of-me feeling walking down there now that the new condos are up.

When I enter the center, I spot Alicia at the front desk. We're cool. Like, one time she closed the gym a few minutes late because I really wanted to practice my jump shot. I don't think she'd do that for a lot of other kids.

"Hey, Alicia, is Mr. Williams . . . I mean, is Jerome in?"

"You know it. He'd sleep here if he could," she says. "He's in the gym with Kingsley."

I rush in. Kingsley's got a weighted vest on. He's running up and down the court with sweat pouring out of him. He's shirtless, and underneath the vest his muscles are literally bulging in and out. Straight-up beast mode.

My eyes zoom in on his new sneakers, the KD 11 iDs. They're pretty sweet. Then I see Jerome sitting on the bench with a whistle around his neck. He's yelling at Kingsley to pick up the pace. I'm getting dizzy just watching him maneuver around the pylons set up on the court.

"Well, well, look at who we got here," says Jerome, getting up from the bench. He blows his whistle and tells Kingsley to take a breather. He meets me halfway with a big smile on his face.

Kingsley reaches the other end of the court and crashes. He hits the pads on the walls with his back and slides down into a sitting position, savoring the break and leaving a huge sweat patch behind him.

Jerome puts his right hand on my shoulder, and man, is it heavy. He gives it a squeeze and shakes me like he can't believe I'm standing in front of him.

"Hey, Jerome," I say, waving at him. "I got some good news. Guess who made the school team?"

"C'mon, I knew you were going to make the team. You starting?"

"Uh, not exactly."

"That's a yes or no type of question, Fawad. You know better than that."

"Okay, in that case, no. I got beat out by this white kid," I say. "Think he went to some fancy ball camp over the summer or some shit."

"Some fancy ball camp, eh? Also, how many times do I have to tell you not to judge people by the color of their skin? You're doing it to them, they're doing it to you. What's Mahatma Gandhi say?"

"'An eye for an eye makes the whole world blind.'" It's hard not to be a quotes encyclopedia after taking a class with him. "You're right."

"I think you've got almost everything, but you're missing one key ingredient."

"I know, I'm scrawny. But I got a plan for that. Starting tomorrow, I'm going to have four eggs instead of the regular two. Mom already knows. We even bought extra groceries."

"No," he says, smacking his forehead. "I'm talking about this right here."

He taps the left side of my chest with his index finger.

"Pecs? But I've been doing push-ups, Coach. Honest."

"Heart, Fawad. When you came here this past summer wanting to play on my squad, you were already making the same excuses."

"I was?"

"Not tall enough. Not strong enough. Probably thinking you weren't Black enough. Now, not rich enough or white enough to go to some fancy camp. You were training with me all summer. You think I worked you guys any less? It's the same when you were in my class—never believing in yourself. You're going to need a little bit more heart when you get out into the real world. And you gotta stop assuming things about people. This is about more than basketball, you realize that?"

I shake my head and feel my stomach drop like a brick.

"Most importantly, you gotta learn to stop making excuses. You gotta learn to do whatever it takes to get the job done. Make sense?"

I nod. The only problem is, what if I don't have the "whatever it takes" part? How do I get that?

"That's kinda why I came, actually," I say. "I was wondering if you could train me. You know, like King over there?"

"You mean Kingsley?" he says, bursting into a loud laugh that echoes throughout the gym.

Right. Kingsley, not King.

"Hey, Kingsley. Fawad here is volunteering to put himself through hell. Any words of advice for him?"

"Don't do it, kid," yells Kingsley, still panting and wagging his finger.

"C'mon, Jerome. I swear I'll do whatever it takes."

He looks me up and down. "All right, you got five minutes to get changed and get to baseline for suicides. We'll start there. But hold up one sec . . . How's Yousuf doing? I heard about his brother."

"Oh yeah. To be honest, I don't think he's doing that great. He's been in his room for the last month, paranoid, and smoking way too much weed, which probably isn't making the paranoia any better. I threw a rock at his window and he was telling me how that had him shook. Reminded him of the bullets outside his home . . ."

"I think it'd be good for him to talk to someone. Has he been seeing a counselor?"

"Don't think so. But I think that would do him some real good right about now."

"Listen, I've got a friend at SickKids Centre for Community Mental Health. They've got free services for kids dealing with grief. He should go talk to someone there."

"SickKids? Like the hospital?"

"Yeah, they have ads up everywhere."

"Is it safe? Like, to talk about stuff with people there?"

"That's what they're there for. It's confidential. He doesn't have to worry about anything leaking to the police or nothing."

"And he just talks to a counselor?"

"It's more than talking, Fawad—it's therapy. Losing a brother to gang violence isn't something you can just walk away from like nothing happened. He's angry, scared, and God knows what else. It's important to sit with someone to work all of that out."

"You're right. Okay, I'll pass that on."

"Oh, and I had a kid in my class watching that video you posted of him. He's good with that guitar."

"Right? I think so too."

"Tell you what. I'm organizing a conference for young men in a few weeks called Dream Big, where I invite some of my friends to come mentor and give talks. I've got a couple of slots open for performances. He should play. And you and Arif need to come out too. I got athletes, lawyers, musicians, CEOs . . . all brown and Black men coming in to talk."

"He's really shy, but if I tell him you want him to perform, I'm sure he'd be down."

Jerome checks the time on his watch. "All right, now. Shall we?"

He blows his whistle and sets a timer on his phone. Oh shit, he meant like *now* now. I grab my gear out of the duffel bag, whip my shoes off, put on my shorts and sneakers, and make it just in time.

I'm beat after one suicide. On top of that, I'm starved without my usual post-school snack, but I push through it. After suicides, Jerome continues putting me through the wringer.

"Can you guard this Andrew kid?" he says, hands on his hips, sizing me up.

"Sort of," I say, panting and bent over, clutching my knees.

"Fawad, what did I tell you about yes or no questions?"

I stand up straight and look him in the eyes. "No, my footwork is terrible."

He whistles and motions Kingsley over. At six foot seven, he's a bit intimidating.

"Eh yo, I know you, dude. From the championship game, right?"

He holds out his fist to dab me. I'm still trying not to let my jaw drop over the fact that he remembers me.

"So, here's what we're going to do now," says Jerome, sticking the basketball in Kingsley's hands. "Fawad here is going to play defense and try to stop you from getting a bucket. Every time you score, he's going to give us fifteen push-ups. Got it?"

Me play defense on Kingsley? He could step over me en route to the rim. This is going to hurt.

"Sure, I can do that," I say, shaking but trying to be nonchalant.

On our first go-round, I get low and up close to Kingsley. Got my hands up. I'm feeling my inner Kawhi take over. Call me "The Claw," baby. I can't wait to swipe the ball and show them what I'm made of.

I don't even blink and Kingsley throws the ball between my legs, catches it behind me, and dunks it with ease. I didn't know humans could move that fast or jump that high. This is going to be a long afternoon.

Jerome blows his whistle from the bench. "That's fifteen. Hurry up."

I'm straining at fourteen but do the last on my knees, hoping Jerome doesn't mind.

The next possession, I ease off Kingsley so I can stay with him if he chooses to drive. He just pulls up for a jump shot. Nothing but net. Another fifteen. Fuck. My. Life.

This continues until it's 11–0. I realize that my defense is shit.

"All right, that's good for now," says Jerome. "Kingsley, finish up with a hundred free throws. And you, Fawad . . . I want to see you in here twice a week after school. Deal?"

I'm still on the floor, unable to get up from my last set of fifteen. The best I can do is stick out my arm and do a thumbs-up.

This sends both Jerome and Kingsley into a fit of laughter. I roll to my side and start getting myself up as slowly as possible. My arms are pulsating with pain. I'm ready to pass out.

I drink, like, a whole tank of water afterwards. Once I've changed into my regular clothes, I drag my feet back up to North Regent. I'm starving and thinking about what Mom might be cooking.

She'd said she needed to cook the eggplant in the fridge before it went bad. The only thing is, Jamila and I, and even Dad when he was around, hate eggplant. We have a theory that she cooks it to torture us. There's gotta be worse things, I guess. But seriously, who likes eggplant?

...

Even though I am tired as fuck, I take my ball out of my duffel bag and dribble it all the way back to my apartment building, thinking about all the homework that's been creeping up on me. On top of that, Arif's been begging me to walk him through a math assignment.

When my basketball is in my hands, I feel like I'm on top of the world, like there's no amount of things I can't juggle. Rotating it and getting a feel for the grip. Dribbling it and doing a fake in one direction only to cross over and go the other way. It feels so good. I also love shooting it to practice my follow-through, using street signs as nets.

I do that with a stop sign at the corner of Parliament and Dundas. After the ball ricochets, I catch it just in time before it hits a parked car—that's definitely happened before.

I look at the mural on the back of my building, opposite the parking lot, as I dribble the ball on the faces of the kids painted in black-and-white. I head up the steps to use the back entrance.

My stomach is growling. Yup, I'm starved. Please, God, don't let it be eggplant. Anything but eggplant. Maybe it'll be minced chicken kababs.

The back door is painted green, just like the balconies, with the building number and street name on it. It's hefty, and to the left is the keyhole to open it. The fob doesn't work here.

I can't see through the little glass panel on account of it being so old and scratched up. I unlock the door and pull it open, but then I stop dead in my tracks.

Sitting on the steps going to the second floor are Omar, Johnny, and Steven. A few steps higher is a girl I don't know. They're passing around a blunt. I see Omar's eyes narrow in on me.

If I dash now, he won't let me live it down. If I push through, there will be trouble for sure. I swallow my spit, straighten up my posture, and walk in as if they're not even there.

"Ha, if it ain't Fuckwad," says Omar, getting up from the step and staring me down. My breath quickens and I can feel my heart palpitating. This is a bad idea. I turn to slip back out the door, but Omar dashes over and pulls it shut.

He's only a few inches away from me now and he stinks of weed. I push against the door, but his grip is stronger. I turn to shove him back and he pins me to the door. His elbow is against my windpipe and his bloodshot eyes look at me crazily.

"Where do you think you're going?"

"I'm just headed home," I say, struggling to breathe. "I live here."

He loosens his hold. I gasp and try to reorient myself.

"All right," he says. "I could be okay with that, but first, give me that ball of yours."

Fuck him. Over my dead body. "Nah, c'mon, man. It's not like you ain't got one. Just let me go already."

"Yeah, but I ain't got *that* one," he says, trying to snatch it from me. I put up a fight and hold on for as long as I can. From the corner of my eye, I catch Johnny and Steven getting up. It's a losing battle.

"Don't be dumb, Fuckwad," says Johnny, getting closer.

"C'mon, be dumb. I ain't seen shit go down in a minute," says Steven. His eyes are glazed. He's definitely high as a kite.

"Leave the kid alone," says the girl.

"You stay out of this," yells Omar.

After trying everything in my power to not give up the ball, I finally lose it—Omar snatches it out of my hands.

"I like it already," he says, spinning it on his index finger. "Now run along before you piss your pants."

I want to go down fighting, but something inside me tells me to swallow my pride. That it's not worth it. Not like this.

I keep my gaze low and dash toward the door on the other side of the hall. Johnny trips me and I nearly go flying. I regain my balance and listen to them chuckle.

What about any of this is funny? You'd have to be sick in the head to find this amusing. I reach out for the door handle.

"Hey, Fuckwad," says Omar, doing a hard dribble.

Before I can turn, he's whipped the ball, and it hits me on the back of my head. My forehead crashes into the door. Fuck. More laughter. More taunting.

Everything is spinning and I feel my head ache. I finally grab the door handle, swing it open, and run down the hallway to my apartment, just wanting to tune them out.

I hear Omar yell "pussy" before I'm finally at my door. Still can't cry. Mom would probably call the cops. Then they'd really never let me live it down. Hell, they'd probably do worse shit to me next time around.

I take a deep breath in, wipe a tear away, and grip my fists as tight as I can. *I'm bigger than this*, I tell myself. It's the least I can do. I just gotta play it cool for the first two minutes, rush to the washroom, turn on the tap, and then I'll be clear to cry.

I open the door. Luckily, Mom's still in the kitchen. "Fawad, is that you?" she says.

"Yeah, Ammi. I've gotta go to the bathroom. I'll be right back."

I kick off my shoes, throw my duffel bag in my room, and dash to the washroom. Jamila steps out of it as I near the door.

I can't even right now. I try not to make eye contact and wish I could disappear. Be invisible. Dead even. I'd take that.

She stares at me, places her hands on my shoulders, and says, "Fawad, what's wrong?"

I break. I can't be strong anymore. I cry.

Omar's face and laugh continue to haunt me. I feel weak. Powerless. A piece of shit that just got shat on.

Jamila's arms are around me, then she leads me to sit down. My mom rushes over, and I tell them what happened. I don't want them to go out there or call the cops.

"Who are these boys?" Mom asks.

"Forget it, Ammi, trust me. Just leave it. It won't help," I say, sobbing.

"This is bullshit," says Jamila.

My mom has a broom in her hands, waves it like a club, and is ready to give those boys a beating. It makes me crack a slight smile as I blow my nose and wipe my eyes.

I make them swear not to get involved. Then I go to my room. I crawl into bed and curl up underneath my covers. Jamila turns the light off and shuts the door.

My body is convulsing. I want to strangle Omar and rip his head off so he can never bother me again. I hate him. I hate Regent.

I hate that we're poor and have no choice but to live here. If we didn't live here, I wouldn't have to worry about which entrance to go through just to come home. I hate that Dad just left us here. I hate Dad. A lot.

Fuck everything. It's all pointless and rotten. If Abshir was around, Omar would never have had the nerve.

I want to message Arif, but I know he'd escalate it, maybe even get Nazmul involved. I've had enough trouble for the day.

When I wake up, I realize I still haven't eaten anything. My stomach is in knots from hunger. I walk into the kitchen and check out what Mom made. I just go with it, because even eggplant can taste okay on days like this.

12

Omar snatching my ball replays through my mind way too many times for me to get any semblance of a good night's sleep. I wake up feeling like my entire face is puffy. Mom and Jamila let me sleep in, so I'm running late for first period. I drag my feet out the door, remembering how I ran across the hallway yesterday with my tail between my legs. Oh well, not the first time, and if I'm being real, probably not the last time either. On top of that, the workout with Jerome makes it hard to move and not feel pain.

Fatima's waiting at the streetcar stop when I get there. She's wearing her usual black abaya. We both hop on the streetcar together. She goes to George Brown College for their Early Childhood Education program—wants to run her own daycare one day.

"Salaam, Fatima," I say. The two of us manage to find seats side by side. That's the one benefit of leaving a bit later: avoiding the early morning rush. Most students don't even take off their backpacks, so they end up using twice the space they should. It's nice to be able to have leg room.

"Everything okay? You look tired," she says.

I feel like anytime someone says that you look "tired," that's just polite for "terrible," but I nod and recount the episode with Omar. She's cool—another older sis like Jamila who's seen it all, and probably heard it all too.

"I'm sorry to hear about your ball. I know how much it must mean to you," she says.

I try not to say too much more because I remember she's friends with Omar's older sister, Yasmin. Last thing I want Omar thinking is I snitched.

Jerome's words from yesterday come to mind, and I realize if there's anyone Yousuf might listen to about getting help, it'd be Fatima (and definitely not me).

"Has Yousuf gone back to school?"

"Not yet. Inshallah, soon. He's been playing his guitar more. I told my parents to let him be for a little longer."

"I was thinking . . . Jerome told me about how SickKids has a mental health center, and they have counselors who might be able to help Yousuf work through—what did he call it?—his grief."

"Oh, I didn't think about that," she says. "Therapy is expensive. Do you know much they charge?"

"I think he said it was free."

"Maybe it would be good to look into that for him. Might be just what he needs. You're a good friend, Fawad. I'm really grateful that he has you and Arif."

I blush. "I really hope he agrees to it. Can't wait to start dragging him out for basketball again."

Fatima laughs. "Some selfish motives, but yes. Jazakallah, I'll do my best to get him an appointment, even if I have to go with him. This is my stop. Salaam."

"Oh, I'm getting off too."

We reach College subway station and we take opposite trains. All of a sudden, the day feels like it's gotten better. Sure, I'm out a basketball, but it feels like I might be closer to getting a friend back. Fingers crossed.

Right before reaching school, I text Yousuf about Jerome praising his singing, and how he wants him to perform at the Dream Big conference. He's always looked up to him, so it's a good way to start seeding the idea.

. . .

After school, I drag Arif with me to Ashley's volleyball game. It honestly didn't take a lot of convincing. Girls wearing high-cut shorts, jumping around . . . I don't even think I have to finish my sentence. Nermin's got soccer practice, but we've got a few minutes beforehand where we're just hanging by our lockers.

"Okay, but how long does this actually take you?" I say to her, pointing to something she posted on Insta recently. Apparently, over the summer she started taking Arabic calligraphy classes. I don't know how someone gets this good so fast but, oh my God, she's good.

"A couple of hours. There's a lot of preparatory sketching before I do the ink," she says casually.

But that's just the half of it. She's also got some English hand-lettering, and those swirls and curves around quotes like "Indeed we belong to Allah, and indeed to Him shall we return" are stunning.

"I could do that," says Arif, taking out a piece of paper and scribbling his name on it. "See? Pretty darn close."

Nermin and I both sigh. The thing is, part of me thinks he actually believes half the shit that leaves his mouth. "All right, all right, maybe you just quit while you're ahead," I tell him, grabbing his piece of paper, scrunching it up, and shooting it into the trash. *Swish.*

"Nermin." I put my hands on her shoulders and shake her. "I just had a brilliant idea. My mom's birthday's coming up. Could you do a piece with the Ayat al-Kursi? I swear she recites it literally every night for me and Jamila. She'd love it."

"I don't think I've ever done anything that elaborate," she says, taking out her bag and closing her locker. "But sure, don't see why not. For now, I gotta run . . . literally."

We crack up and she's out. "Hey, my mom's birthday just passed. Could I get a print too?" says Arif.

She turns, shakes her head, and smacks her forehead.

"I think that's a yes," says Arif. "Good thinking."

"Thanks," I say, rolling my eyes. We head toward the gym.

"Also, Jerome told me to tell you about this conference he's organizing," I say. "He wants Yousuf to do a little performance at it."

"Oh yeah? What's it about?"

"Think it's called Dream Big or something."

"Sounds lame."

I give him a backhand slap. "Jerome's organizing it. He's got a crazy network—I think it'll be dope. Besides, there's free food."

"I'm in."

"You're the easiest person to drag anywhere," I say.

"Hey, free food is free food."

"Uh-huh."

We grab a spot on the bleachers and the game's just about to begin. It's not crazy packed. Cliques are sitting together. There are some students from North Toronto too. Heated rivalry alert.

Northern better knock 'em back to that fancy-ass campus they got a few blocks away, make them wish they never showed up. Okay, so I'm a little competitive.

Ashley's on the court and they're just about to get started. I kinda want to call out her name, but I also don't want to draw any attention to myself. Luckily, as she's tying her hair back, she turns and our eyes meet. I smile and she smiles, then I even get a wave before she gets her game face on and stares across the net, ball in hand, getting ready to serve. The referee blows the whistle and the first set kicks off.

Now I've never thought much of volleyball, but I see her throw the ball up and explode into action to serve it across the net, and all I can think about is what I would do to have a vertical jump that incredible. Oh man, I'd be able to tap the backboard and, maybe if I get a few more inches before high school finishes, dunk (okay, touch the rim—don't want to get too crazy here).

What ensues next is nuts. The other team sets and then drives a spike to our team, and then back and forth, back and forth, and honestly, I'm not really following the ball as much I'm just following Ashley.

The second set wraps, and I check my phone and realize there's, like, a million text messages from my mom wondering where I am. Oops. I text back saying I was finishing some homework assignment (kinda was), and that I'll be home in the next half hour.

"Hey," I whisper to Arif, who's really into the game, especially as the competition is stiff (no team's led by more than three points). "I gotta go. Mom's going to kill me."

"Ah man, it was just getting good."

I decide it's best to leave just as the third set starts so that Ashley doesn't notice I had to split early. And I drag Arif along with me. He's bummed, but all that's running through my mind is how high Ashley can get above the net.

After sitting through my mom's lecture of how I never tell her what time I'm going to be home, and eating dinner, I go to my room and open up Insta to see Ashley's Stories. Nice—Northern won the game.

And she followed me. I need to dial down how fast my heart's pumping. I click the icon to DM her. What do I say? Where's Arif when you need him?

"Hey, that was a sick game. Thanks for the invite.
Any chance you could teach me to jump that high?
Think my basketball career might be on the line. ;)"

I hit Send. Ah. Why'd I hit Send? I'm so stupid. Who writes that? She's going to block me. She's never going to talk to me again. My life's ruined . . . and then I see that damn indication that she's read my message. I can't breathe. Literally can't. I'm frozen stiff.

Then I see "Hey! Thanks for coming out today. :)" and I let out a sigh of relief. Whew.

And she's typing more. Never been more happy to see those " . . ." in my whole life. All right, I think I'm getting the hang of this.

13

After school I'll be playing the first game of the season, and it's all hitting me. Team practices. Training with Jerome. Nightmares of Kingsley scoring on me. The horror of Andrew showing me up. Mr. Singh stroking his mustache and yelling, "What the hell was that, Chaudhry?" every time I mess up.

Also, homework. Assignments. Quizzes. Tests. Gotta keep the average at 90 percent. On top of that, Ashley's taking up a whole lot of space in my head rent-free.

We've been texting back and forth for a couple of days now. It started with her sending me a bunch of YouTube videos with workouts for improving your vertical jump and then progressed to us sending photos of what we're eating to each other. We're both foodies, so that's definitely a win. I discover she's half-Chinese. Her mom's from Hong Kong and she's fluent in Cantonese and French—because why not?—and whips up a mean chow mein when her parents come home late from work.

Her dad's a lawyer, and her mom owns a yoga studio. Though apparently she used to work in something called private equity. I have no idea what that is, so I ask her and find out that her firm used to buy up companies that weren't doing so hot, turn them around, and flip them. Pretty stressful, she says.

At first, I just imagine parathas being flipped, but once I figure out what it really is, the job sounds kind of neat, and hardcore. Turns out her mom was also an immigrant and came to study as an international student, met Ashley's dad, and, well, the rest is history. I tell her about my parents, or *parent*, rather, and then we do a video call one evening and next thing I know, we've got lunch plans.

But right now, I gotta focus. Especially since it's an away game. On the bus ride over, the fellas are bumping Migos, Post Malone, and a little Drake. Scott's got a pretty sick Bluetooth Beats speaker. It's only been a handful of practices, but I'm starting to realize that I was wrong to judge 'em and their ball skills just based on their being rich or white—that I was just doing to them what I've been used to dealing with my whole life: being stereotyped based on where I was from and what my parents earned. It sucks both ways. They're pretty chill.

Nothing like seeing a bunch of white kids bopping their heads to hip-hop, though. Spence is the DJ, and for that extra kicker, mostly to suck up to Mr. Singh, he puts on the Panjabi MC and Jay-Z track "Beware of the Boys," and the bus is in a frenzy. You'd think we were off to a championship game or something.

Once we get there, we make our way to the gym of Oakwood Collegiate, passing by the cafeteria on the way. I peep Kingsley of all people hanging with his crew. I'd forgotten he went to this school. He notices me too and raises his hand to say what up.

Spence leans over and says, "You know King? Dude's like the next LeBron."

"Yeah, we're both from Regent. We play together here and there."

"What?! Damn, son. That's cray. Hit your boy up next time. I'd love to do a run with him."

"I gotchu."

We dab. In the changeroom, Coach hypes us up. Even though I'm going to be coming off the bench, I'm just as excited as ever. Walking into the gym gives me goosebumps. The stands are packed with students, teachers, and parents.

As we make our way to the rack of balls, I'm looking over at the other team warming up. I realize we're going up against Darius . . . the same Darius that lit us up in the summer league. There's also this other kid I've heard lots about, Ben Jerkins.

Apparently, he's on some Steve Nash–level shit. When I heard that, I was, like, "Nah, *Andrew's* on some Steve Nash–level shit." But as I watch him sink his shots and see how quick his handles are, I get a little worried.

Isiah wins the tip-off for Northern.

Darius's handles are something else as he dribbles between two of our guys and jumps up for a floater. *Swish.* He and Ben are a two-man wrecking crew.

Luckily, Spence is keeping us in the game. He's not the tallest, but boy, can he jump. He hits two threes. Whatever he misses, Isiah scoops up and puts back in. Scott is struggling and looks a little shaky. Andrew finds Luke for a mid-range jumper that finds its way to the bottom of the net.

We're still down by ten with two minutes to go in the first quarter when Coach subs me in for Andrew. He slaps my shoulder and wishes me luck. No pressure. I got this.

I'm guarding Ben. He tries to lose me with a crossover, and I thrust out my hands and knock the ball loose. I dive for it, hitting my chin on the floor and landing out of bounds.

The Northern bench is all over it. Even Mr. Singh yells, "Atta boy, that's the kind of hustle I wanna see!"

When I bring up the ball next, Isiah comes up to set a pick, standing firm so that my defender can't keep up, which forces a switch. I throw the ball back to him as he rolls and gets into the paint. He gets doubled and kicks it back out. I line up for a three-pointer. *Swish.*

I get back on defense, with Ben making a push and handing it off to Darius. He loses me and gets an easy lay-in.

"C'mon, Fawad, that was too easy," Coach yells. He's biting his nails. Never a good sign.

I raise my hand to acknowledge the mistake and keep hustling. The first quarter wraps up. We're still down seven. It's a tough one.

I start the second, and turn it up a notch. My handles are smooth like butter. I move without the ball like a butter knife. My buckets are wet like yogurt. I might also just be really hungry.

We're down by five when Spence spots me open in the corner and fires the ball over. I catch and shoot. Bucket.

The bench is on its feet hollering, and Mr. Singh's clapping. I sit for the last four minutes as Andrew jumps back in, but it's obvious he's having serious trouble keeping up with Ben. I don't say anything, but I'm antsy on the bench. Oakwood's lead climbs to twelve by the time the second quarter finishes. Shit.

I'm still on the bench when the third quarter starts. Me and my butt on the wooden bench are getting frustrated with the play on the court. I keep glancing over at Coach. He's not looking my way.

We're now down by fifteen. Mr. Singh's had enough. He calls a time-out.

"Spence, I want you to guard Darius," he says. "Fawad, you're going back in."

I nod, trying to conceal my excitement and keep calm. I high-five Andrew, who looks winded. He whispers, "Good luck. You'll need it."

Just the kick I was hoping for. I'm ready to get it. Step-back jumper. Money. Finding an open Isiah on a steal. Money. Getting a steal from Ben as the third quarter winds down and lobbing it to Luke for an open three. Money. I'm making it rain, baby. We're back to being down by eight. I keep it up in the fourth quarter, but we're still down by two with a minute left. Darius's got the ball.

Ben sets him a pick at the top of the key, forcing me to switch with Spence and guard him. I need to get this stop. Every ounce of my attention is focused on what he might do next.

He's dribbling to waste time as I get low with my hands up. Darius makes a move, fakes, crosses over, and I'm with him. He's slashing, and instead of going in all the way, he squares up for a shot. My arm stretches high as I leap with him. He puts up a shot. My fingers catch a portion of the ball and send it flying short of the net.

Everyone's in disbelief and on their feet. The Northern bench is hooting and hollering as Coach yells for Isiah, who has the ball, to pass it. I catch the pass and, with Darius still stunned, race toward the other side of the court.

As I drive in, I draw two defenders, who think I'm going for the clutch shot. Suckers. Spence is open behind the three-point line in the corner, and I pass the ball to him. He lines it up. Count it. We're up by one.

Darius is pissed. He's calling for the ball. We're double-teaming him and pressing the backcourt, waiting for the clock to wind down. Frustrated, he passes it to Ben, who's still in the back-court. Three. Two. One.

He gets a half-court miracle shot off, and it's an air ball. We win with a capital *W*. We're high-fiving, chest-bumping, and straight-up grooving over the comeback.

After we shake hands with Oakwood, we start heading to the locker room. Coach and I hang back. He's all wide-eyed and giddy. I think he's proud of me. That's what I'd imagine my dad to be looking at me like if he was in the stands.

"Keep playing like that and I might have to reconsider that starting lineup," he says.

I'm looking around to see where Andrew is and hoping he didn't hear that. Don't want any bad blood. If I'm going to start, it'll be because I earned it, not just in Coach's eyes but in the eyes of the whole team.

14

The next day, I need to shake off the win because today is special: I'm taking Ashley out to lunch.

I've changed outfits about twenty times. I don't want to look like a poor brown kid from the projects.

No loungewear, sportswear, casual wear . . . damn, where is my formal wear? I need "take-a-girl-out-for-lunch-and-not-look-poor" wear. The contents of my closet are all over my room . . . and then I see the birthday gift Jamila gave me earlier in the year that I had forgotten about, still in the bag. I pull it out of the closet and unfold a half-sleeved shirt with a floral print and beige chinos.

Now I remember why I never bothered taking them out of the bag. I like things loose, baggy in some respect. Maybe, though, just maybe they'd work for today?

I put on the pants and look in the mirror. I've never seen the contours of my ass look so great in pants before.

I put on the shirt next. I mean, damn, the combo is hot, but it's *so* not my style. My insides are squirming. This makes me feel like I got a target on my back for someone to kick me down a flight of stairs.

Ashley. Do it for Ashley. I walk into the kitchen like nothing's the matter.

"Someone's gotta date," says Jamila, dipping a cumin biscuit into a cup of chai. Chai in the morning is her thing.

"Hush, don't say such things," says Mom, giving her a scolding look. "He's too young to be thinking about dating."

Jamila cracks a smile. "So, is it the same girl?"

"No girls and no dating," Mom yells, putting her hands on her hips, which is never a good sign. "Am I making myself clear, Fawad?"

I want to crawl down my chair and hide underneath the dining table.

"Ammi, relax. I'm not into any of that stuff," I say while doing a slicing-my-throat gesture so Jamila will shut up.

Jamila leans in and whispers, "Good for you. She was cute."

I nod silently, avoiding eye contact. I focus on the two parathas with carrot pickles, yogurt with sugar, and cup of chai on the table.

"About time you wore my gift too," she says. "I knew it'd suit you."

Then she bursts into singing "Tenu Suit Suit Karda." As much as I hate her sometimes, I also sometimes love her. I join in. We're doing bhangra—specifically, the shoulder pump.

Mom looks unamused. She used to smile and joke a lot more when Dad was around. She shouts, "Chup—you're not supposed to sing while eating."

Jamila and I crack up. Before she heads out, she says, "Ammi, I'll be home late. It's Ray's birthday. We're going to go out."

"Oof, mere Khudaya," says my mother, slapping her forehead with the back of her hand. "What am I going to do with this stupid girl? Ray, ki aisi ki taisi."

I start smirking because I love it when my mom busts out the Urdu and rhymes things. Jamila shrugs and leaves. She *so* doesn't care. It's amazing.

"You better have more sense than her," Mom says, taking a seat at the table. She places the final paratha on her own place and tears off a piece to dip in her chai.

I nod as I stand up, kiss her on her forehead, and give her a hug. None of which she reciprocates before I head out.

Just before I leave the kitchen, my mom says, "She was joking, right? You don't have no date shate, right?

"Yes, Ammi," I say, shaking my head in disbelief. "I mean, no. I mean, she was joking. Anyways, Khuda hafiz."

"Good" is the last thing I hear before I'm out the door. One day, I'll channel my inner Jamila and tell her the truth. For now, I don't have it in me.

. . .

"Damn, someone's looking fresh," says Nermin, dusting off my shoulder. "What's the song by Jay-Z again?"

I start beatboxing the beat of "Dirt Off Your Shoulder." Drake's cool and all, but I don't think anybody comes close to Hov.

"Um, bro, did you wake up on the wrong side of the bed or something?" says Arif, looking me over and pretending to check my temperature. "Like, those pants are way too tight. I ain't never seen your ass look like that."

Nermin slaps him across the arm. "Arif!"

She puts her arm in mine and we walk to our lockers. Arif's got his arm around my shoulder on my other side. The three of us are taking up our fair share of the hallway, joined at the hip. We reach our spot.

"So, where you taking her, bro?" says Arif.

"Some sushi spot she suggested."

"You got enough to pay for both of you?" says Nermin, eyeing me up and down.

"Uh, I think so," I say, patting my pants and taking out my wallet. I inspect what I have in there. "I guess I didn't think that far out . . . only have a twenty-dollar bill. I might have something in my checking, though."

I pull out my phone and open my banking app. It takes forever to load on the stupid Android device. I see my balance and Nermin catches the look on my face.

She opens her bag, takes out her wallet, and puts twenty-five dollars in my hand.

"That should cover it," she says. "She might want to split the bill, but tell her she can grab the next one. That way at least you'll get her thinking about a second date."

"Wow, thanks, Nermin," I say, reaching over to give her a hug. "You're a lifesaver."

"Hey, how come I don't get no allowance for my dates?" says Arif, throwing up his arms.

"Well for one thing, you'd never pay me back, and also, you always have girls paying for your sorry ass." Nermin sticks her tongue out at him.

"Whoa, whoa," says Arif. "Just because they want to, not because I'm not balling."

The three of us laugh. Mostly because we all know that Arif is definitely not balling. He's got some serious looks going for him, and I'd milk them too if I were him.

"You goofs also need to show up for my soccer game," says Nermin, stomping her foot. "We're headed into the playoffs."

"Say what?!" says Arif. "Yo, I'd be down for watching some girls running around in shorts. Girls that play soccer always have the best legs."

Nermin gives him another smack across the chest. "Do you ever think about anything else? Like, ever?"

"Well," says Arif, looking deep in thought. "I guess not . . ."

We laugh, because that's probably the most accurate thing that's ever come out of his horny-ass mouth.

"I'll be there, Nermin," I say, taking the textbooks I need for the morning out of my locker. "Yo, Arif, maybe we could make a sign or something."

"No, definitely do not do that," says Nermin, turning pale. "Otherwise, your sorry asses will be uninvited ASAP."

"Um, not to change subjects, but which one of you is going to help me study for that math test coming up?" says Arif, flipping through notes in a binder. "Don't raise your hands all at once now."

"It's your turn," says Nermin, poking me with a finger. "I spent all of last week helping him study for science."

"Fine," I say, taking Arif's binder and inspecting his notes. "Dude, what the hell is this?"

Nermin peers over and validates my concern. "You write like a two-year-old."

"Whatever. Friends don't let friends fail math. Remember?" says Arif, looking offended and taking his binder back. "How about after mosque on Saturday?"

"Yeah, yeah, that works," I say. "But first, I need some help figuring out what to talk about with Ashley."

"Bro, don't even worry," says Arif, getting excited. "I got you."

"If only there were a class on getting laid," says Nermin, rolling her eyes.

"It's true, I've never seen him this excited about anything else. Like, ever. So, what's the game plan for my date?" I say.

"Just be yourself," says Nermin, putting a hand on my shoulder.

"Only girls believe in that," says Arif. He puts an arm around me and leads me away from Nermin. "Sorry, Nermin, this is for his ears only. I'll catch you at lunch. I gotta impart some wisdom."

Nermin shakes her head and starts walking away. She stops, turns, and says, "Don't listen to him, Fawad. She'll like you for you."

"Another thing only a girl will tell you," says Arif, shaking his head and waving her off.

We part ways, and the two of us find a corner to ourselves. Luckily, there's still some time before class.

Arif is waxing poetic on how to keep a girl interested when talking to her. I'm taking serious notes. Why doesn't he teach a class on this? Other guys would kill to hear the knowledge he's dropping. Everyone's a genius at something. I learned that line from Jay-Z too.

The bell rings. Game time in T-minus two hours.

. . .

By the time the lunch bell rings, my stomach is in knots. I'm playing out what I'm going to say in my head, and none of what I'm imagining is going well. In fact, Ashley's face is motionless, emotionless, and disinterested.

I walk to my locker, drop off my bag, and go to meet Ashley outside the school on the front steps. I'm worried she's not going to show up, that she was just joking when I asked her out. That there's no way she would want to be with a guy like me.

I've got my hands in my pockets, and I'm trying to play it cool as I wait, opening up Insta and checking our messages to see if she bailed last minute. Every time the door swings open, I get hit with a whiff of hope. Then I realize that the person walking through is not Ashley.

I get a WhatsApp notification.

NUSRAT: Did you talk to aunty yet???

She's going to kill me.

ME: Soon. Promise. G'night.

NUSRAT: Do it pls. Abbu was talking with her again about us!

ME: Sigh. On it. Sorry, gotta go.

I put my phone away and sweep what she just messaged me under some imaginary rug. I can honestly just think about one thing right now.

I'm so damn nervous, excited, afraid, happy . . . Why the hell can't my body make up its mind? Like, if there was a dial, why can't it just stay on one setting?

Two minutes pass. No Ashley. Three minutes pass. No Ashley. I'm ready to throw in the towel. If a girl likes you, she wouldn't be four minutes late, right? I feel like a fool.

The door opens again, and it's her. She's saying goodbye to some of her friends, her hair is being blown by some imaginary wind machine, and I finally get why a woman's entrance in a Bollywood movie is so hyped.

She smiles and waves at me. I'm digging her beret, floaty white top, black pants, and Vans sneakers. Très belle. I'm impressed I remember something from French class.

"Hi," she says. "Hope I didn't keep you waiting long."

I play it cool. "Nah, just got here myself."

"I like your shirt," she says, touching my bicep to feel the fabric.

Step-back three-pointer. *Swish.* Jamila with the assist.

I'm having trouble thinking straight. I blurt out, "Thanks. Um . . . how was class?"

The announcer in my head is giving me shit for asking such a lame-ass question. *Chaudhry with a stutter step. He takes a shot and . . . get that shit outta here. His shot is blocked hard. The ball is sent flying into the crowd.*

"Meh, I don't want to talk about school," she says as we start walking. "How was your first game? Too bad it was an away game, otherwise I would totally have come. I heard you won, though!"

"Yeah, went better than expected," I say. "Mr. Singh thinks we have a pretty good shot at winning it all. Oh, and I started showing up to practice a few minutes early to do those exercises from those videos you sent me. My calves were literally on fire afterwards."

She smiles. "That's so good to hear. Maybe we can play sometime? I'm not great, but I can shoot pretty decent."

And she wants to play basketball? That feels like a blindfolded half-court shot hitting the bottom of the net.

As we walk, our hands graze a few times. Each time, it shoots an electric pulse through my body. I notice the beauty mark on her left cheek. I can't stop staring at it . . . it's beautiful.

"Is that real?" I ask, pointing at it.

At first, she gives me a confused look, then she lets out a laugh. "You think I'd dot that on every morning?"

I let out a nervous laugh. "Maybe not every morning. More like every other day. You know, to keep things interesting."

She smiles again. Score.

When we reach the sushi spot, I open the door for her.

The server seats us and hands us two menus to look over. She points to all her favorites. Items I've never had and can't pronounce. I nod as if I know what she's talking about.

"Do you like chicken teriyaki?" she says, pointing to a photo.

I inspect it and say, "Uh, can't do. Fish is cool, but any other meat stuff has to be halal."

She takes back the menu. "Oh yeah, that's kinda like kosher, right?"

"Yeah, they're both super similar. It's all got to do with the meat being prepared with all these crazy specific guidelines. And pork's a big no-no."

"Okay, noted," she says, continuing to flip through the menu. "Do you know what you want to order?"

I hesitate because I don't know. What the hell is a "maki"? I'm angry at my dad for only having taken us to eat out at Indian and Pakistani spots, even though that's literally the only type of food Mom makes at home. What a weirdo, now that I think about it.

"I can order for us. We can share a few things," she says.

"Dope, let's do that," I say, closing my menu and setting it aside.

I make a note to dial back the slang. I don't think it's doing me any favors.

The server comes and gives us some hot tea to start. Then he takes our order, and in a matter of minutes, the food starts appearing.

There's miso soup and salad. Then yam and avocado rolls, sushi pizza with avocado on top, and finally some salmon teri-yaki. I like this girl's appetite.

I look over at the sushi chefs doing all the prep behind the counter. They're going at a dizzying speed and putting up order after order for the servers to take to the customers' tables. There aren't many empty tables left.

"Do you live in the area?" she says, putting some of the salmon teriyaki on a side plate for herself.

I almost choke on the salmon I'm eating. "Uh, actually, I commute up. You?"

She's slicing and dicing the salmon with her knife and fork before picking up her chopsticks. "Same. Well, sort of. My dad drops me off. We live in Cabbagetown."

Gulp. "Cool," I say, with beads of sweat forming behind my neck. No big deal. She's just from *the other side* of Gerrard Street.

"What about you?" she says.

"Not too far from there, actually." I clear my throat.

Moment of truth. Do I tell her? Do I not? Usually, I would pretend I'm from Cabbagetown, since technically it's kind of in the same area. With Ashley, I don't think that's a good idea.

"Regent," I say at last.

Her eyes widen for a moment. "Oh. Like, Regent Park?"

"Yup," I say.

"The new condos are nice down by Dundas."

"They're okay," I say.

The server brings out the California roll—it's got little orange eggs on it. "Oh, you'll like this. It's my favorite roll."

Yes, let's talk about food. I can do that, though my chopstick game is weak. I struggle but finally pick up a piece of sushi.

"Here, it's easier if you do this," she says, showing me how she's holding hers. She's a pretty good teacher. Also, I don't mind our hands touching.

The raw salmon is slimy, but I can dig it with everything else in the roll.

We chat about music, Netflix shows, teachers we love, teachers we loathe, and funnily enough, our moms.

"Oh my God, you too? I also can't let my grades slip if I want to keep playing volleyball," she says, laughing. "I thought I was the only one I knew whose mom made that type of deal with them. Though to be honest, she's way more relaxed now than she used to be."

"I think it's the opposite with my mom," I say. "She used to be a lot more chill when Dad was around, but after he passed away, I guess she had a lot more to deal with."

"Really sorry to hear about your dad," she says. "Was it sudden?"

"Yeah, but I don't want to get into it right now," I say, feeling my chest cramp up.

"I understand. I think for my mom, a lot changed after she got breast cancer. She did a complete one-eighty, quit her finance job, got into yoga, started eating healthy, and yeah, she's a lot happier than I remember her from when I was younger."

"Shit, that sounds pretty crazy."

"Yeah, chemo is . . . well, chemo, but I think it also helped her realize there's a little bit more to life than her daughter getting straight As, playing Chopin, and being a varsity athlete. If anything, I think I'm way harder on myself now than she ever was."

"Sounds like a crazy journey."

When the bill comes, I bust out the "I got this."

"Are you sure?"

I nod. "You can grab the next one."

She smiles. "Deal."

Swish. Assist to Nermin. Second date confirmed. The crowd is going wild.

I take out the forty-five dollars, pass them to the server, and tell him to keep the change. We scoop up the candies and leave the restaurant. The walk back to school is way too short. Agh.

When we get close to her locker, I see her friends waiting for her. I look at her, she looks at me, and she says three words that put me on a spaceship and blast me straight to Neptune.

"Lunch again tomorrow?"

I nod. "Uh . . . sure."

She gives me a hug, smiles, and waves goodbye before heading off to join her friends. I watch her walk away and wonder if I've ever passed her home while strolling through Cabbagetown. What a small world.

A kid bumps into me, and shit, I realize I'm late for science. I rush to class. We're studying chemistry, and I can't help but think about how Ashley might be the oxygen to my hydrogen.

I've got an imaginary ball in my hand. I put it behind my back and shoot it into the garbage bin. Count it. Bucket.

15

I'm on a high. Word of my last-minute block at Oakwood has got around school. I'm getting props and head nods of acknowledgment from older kids who normally wouldn't register my existence. Plus, I'm racking up nothing lower than 89 percent on my assignments and quizzes, which is really 90 percent, if you round up. It also doesn't hurt being with Ashley between classes and at lunch. I also wait with her after school until her father arrives in his Mercedes Benz and scoops her up.

I live the dream for a week before Arif turns me around and pins me against my locker before second period. Nermin stands next to him looking all pissed with her arms crossed. Her army fatigues, black Adidas track jacket, and matching hijab reflect her mood.

I wrestle myself out of Arif's grip.

"Yo, guy, you forgot all about us or something?" he says, poking me with his index finger. "Mr. Overnight Athlete Celebrity, or is that chick taking up all your time?"

"Yeah, Fawad, what the hell?" says Nermin, giving me a shove. "We were supposed to study for science at lunch yesterday. You didn't even give me a heads-up that you weren't going to show."

Oops and oops. "I'm sorry, it's just been crazy hectic. I was just going to text to see if we could do lunch together."

"Uh-huh," says Nermin, sucking her teeth. She's looking me up and down like I'm the biggest liar in the world.

"Honest," I say.

"What about Ashley? Were you going to invite her as well?" says Nermin.

"No, but now that you mention it, might be good for all of us to hang."

"Knew it," says Nermin, stomping her right foot. "Can't spend a lunch hour without her."

"What do you guys do, spending all your time together?" says Arif, giving me another shove. "You'd better be getting some booty. Otherwise, we done."

"Ugh . . ."

"Tell me you've at least kissed?" says Arif, puckering up his lips.

I shake my head. Negatory.

"What?! Bro, have I taught you nothing?" He takes off his baseball hat and throws it to the floor.

I shrug, pick up his hat, dust it off, and hand it back to him. "There's always someone around. She did ask me to walk her home today. Her dad's out of town for a meeting."

"Romantic," says Nermin, before kicking my shin. "What about my soccer game? Were you thinking of showing up for that, at least?"

"Ow." I bend over to rub my shin. "When is it again?"

"Tomorrow, dummy," she says, smacking her own forehead. Her glare is really scary.

"I'll be there—pinky swear."

Nermin squints at me and turns to Arif. "Also, you're one to talk, Arif. You and Kate can barely keep your tongues in your own mouths. Did you even notice I scored last game?"

He blushes before divulging, "Guys, you'll never guess what. She invited me over this weekend. Her parents and bro are out of town. You know what that means?"

It takes just the first playful elbow in the rib from Arif for me to register that they'll be having sex. Then he continues with the elbows. "Stop, stop, I get it. Jeez," I say, pushing him away.

"Arif, you're gross. That's hella haram," says Nermin, looking him up and down.

Arif and I both crack up. Hella haram is right.

"Nermin, you need to trademark that right now," I say. "Then put it on tees, caps, tote bags . . . there'd be such a big market for it."

She rolls her eyes at the suggestion. A group of girls who also rock hijabs walk by, and they give her a funny look as they pass.

"What's their problem?" I say, eyeing them right back.

"Probably jealous I get to hang with such cute guys," says Nermin, shrugging it off.

"I am pretty darn cute, I'll give 'em that much," says Arif, running a hand through his hair. "But that's straight-up rude, guy. I ought to . . ."

"I was talking about Fawad, dummy," she says, pinching my cheek.

I chalk one up for me.

"Always playing favorites. Anyways, we should head to class, guy," says Arif, punching me on the arm.

"When the hell did you guys get so physical?" I say, rubbing my arm.

"Just pent-up frustration," says Nermin, reaching over and giving me a hug. "It's all love, though."

"Hey, where's my hug?" says Arif, leaning over toward Nermin.

"Eww, no," says Nermin, putting a stiff arm between her and him. They're both ridiculous. "And Fawad, not that you deserve it after being the shitty friend you have been, but here—I've got something for you."

She opens her locker again and takes out a scroll, slowly unraveling it to reveal her exquisite Arabic calligraphic rendition of the Ayat al-Kursi.

"Nermin, my mom is going to love this. Wow, you have no idea."

Arif's jaw goes slack. "You did that?"

"Who else could it be, dummy?" I say to him, carefully inspecting her handiwork. I roll the scroll back up and put it away.

It's like Arif is trying to say something but his brain isn't processing what exactly he wants to express.

"Okay, okay, I'm glad you like it," says Nermin, pushing his jaw back up. "Now, can we get to class already?"

. . .

Ashley's waiting for me after school at our usual spot. We hug. I stare at her lips, wondering when would be a good time to kiss her.

She smiles. I wonder if she can read my mind. She's rocking a gray hoodie from A&F, black lululemons, and white Converse. Fly as hell.

"So, where'd your dad go?" I say as we hold hands and start walking.

"New York," she says. "His firm has an office there."

Damn. NYC.

"Dope. Well, you should've told him I'd get you home safe and sound on the subway."

She squeezes my hand and pulls me closer. "I've been on the subway before. Don't think I'm that sheltered."

"I'm just playing. I know you're a big girl."

For once, I'm glad the subway's got us packed in like sardines. Ashley and I are standing close. Like, I can feel her body against mine type of close. I wish we could be alone and this close without all these people around.

When we hop off at College Station and wait for the streetcar, I see she's cold. Her cheeks are turning red, and her hands are scrunched up in her oversized hoodie. I take her into the Tim Hortons and grab us both some French Vanillas.

"You're sweet. I could eat you," she says, taking a sip. I take one too, but it's mad hot, so I burn my lip and decide to wait before having more.

Back outside, we're cozying up. Her cheeks and nose are turning red. Her hair is being tossed around by the wind. I've got my arms around her and we're hugging real tight.

I'm on a whole other planet until I notice this aunty who also lives in Regent Park. She's one of my mom's close Pakistani friends. I feel panic kick in, since she could rat me out, and that might spell the end of me and us. We make brief eye contact. Agh, why'd I do that?

Aunties operate like the FBI. Word gets around so fast you'd think spreading intel was their full-time job. Gossiping about so-and-so's son hanging with so-and-so's daughter. It never ends.

I need to think and act fast. I awkwardly untangle myself from Ashley. Her smile disappears and she looks confused when she notices there's no streetcar here yet.

"Babe, we're gonna need to stand just a teeny bit apart," I say, keeping my voice down to a whisper.

If my mom finds out I was getting intimate with a girl out in the open where her friends could see, she'll put me on a one-way flight to Pakistan, get me married, and have me tilling the family farm for the rest of my life. I shudder.

"What's wrong?" says Ashley, her eyebrows furrowing out of concern. "Is everything okay?"

"Oh, nothing," I say, putting my hands in my pockets and trying to play off my dread. "Actually, so a few steps away is this aunty. She, uh, knows my mom and, well, it just wouldn't be a good thing if my mom found out about, uh, us."

Ashley takes a step back and her face scrunches up in disgust. "Why? That's so weird."

"I know . . . uh," I say, formulating the best way to explain the predicament. "So the thing is, these aunties like to talk behind everyone's back. And it would just be embarrassing for my mom. That's all."

Her mood goes sour. "I still think that's weird. But fine."

She turns her back to me, takes out her phone, and starts scrolling through Instagram. I take a few steps away and do the same. The silence and distance is killing me. Finally, the streetcar arrives. Ashley goes in and I follow right behind her, pretending like I don't know her. The aunty gets on and sits in the back. Luckily, it's crowded, so I lose sight of her until Parliament Street, and she finally gets off. The streetcar's cleared out a little.

I go over to where Ashley's sitting. I know she's pissed, but I had to save my ass.

"Hi. I'm sorry about that," I say, my chin dipping down.

She doesn't look up at me, just continues to like, comment on, and scroll through Insta.

"Ash, c'mon, don't be like that."

She looks up at me with disdain and repeats what I just said mockingly before saying, "Oh, now you want to talk to me?"

Sigh. She puts her phone away at last. "Fine, but first tell me what that was all about."

We get off the streetcar at Sumach Street. Regent is on the right side and Cabbagetown is on the left.

"The thing is, my mom doesn't want me to be dating right now," I say as we walk north toward her home. "If she found out, I'd get grounded and, well, maybe she'd even tell me to stop playing basketball."

"I get it. Sort of," she says. "I still think that was rude."

"I know, babe," I say, putting an arm around her. She's not pulling away. "I'm really sorry."

She uses her index finger to point to her cheek. I give her a peck and watch her smile. We're by the parking lot next to the top of the hill at Riverdale Park.

"Hey, you want to—"

"Yes, I was thinking the same thing," she says. "The view from the hill is so pretty. All the trees have changed color."

Maybe she can read my mind. Dangerous possibility.

The best thing about walking through Cabbagetown is that white people don't get as worked up as brown people when they see a boy and a girl holding hands. Any type of public affection is frowned on in Pakistani culture. Like, I don't even think

I ever saw my mom and dad sit on the same couch, ever. It's that extreme.

We get to the top of the hill at Riverdale. The view is incredible. The sun is setting. Even with all those pinks, oranges, and purples, I'd rather look at Ashley and that smile of hers.

"I really like you," she says, giving my hand a squeeze.

My heart jumps like Jordan when he won his sixth championship.

"I really like you too," I say. I think this is it.

I can sense she's waiting. I'm starting to feel a little sweaty underneath all my layers. I can feel my heart pound against my rib cage. I lean in and then get anxious about missing her lips on account of my nose getting in the way.

I course-correct, tilt my head slightly, and we make contact. Success. Fireworks.

Her lips taste like the French Vanilla I got her.

Our tongues touch. It's like they're dancing with one another. I'm so lost in her that I don't even realize we're blocking the path for a couple walking their dog. Ashley taps my chest gently and we awkwardly step to the side, blushing.

I'm staring at Ashley. She's staring at me. It's kinda like a blinking contest except even when one of us does blink after an extended period, no one loses. It's bizarre and awesome.

"We should go," she says, kissing my cheek. "My mom'll be worried."

"Ditto, I know all about that," I say as we hug. "Okay, let's go drop you home."

Her home is stunning. It's one of those beautiful, fully detached Victorian-style bay-and-gable houses with big windows. I can peek in and see a large painting hanging above a couch.

There's a few steps leading up to a green door; next to that is a porch with some outdoor furniture stripped of its cushioning. I have a weird thing for trees, and the one on their front lawn is majestic to say the least.

I can't help but daydream just a little about what it would be like to grow up here. My phone vibrates. Probably my mom checking up on my punk ass. Agh.

"Text me later. Maybe we can FaceTime," I say.

She nods, smiles, and gives me a hug.

We both reluctantly let go. She continues to look at me as she takes a few backwards steps before finally turning and opening the door. Once she's inside, I know she's safe and sound in her own world. Now it's time for me to go back to mine.

Walking home, I'm whistling, hopping, and doing a little skip. Then I get to Gerrard Street and look at the ugly brick exterior of my hood. I cross the street and leave dreamland.

Even so, I keep a little swag in my walk. I mean, I just had my first-ever kiss. Then I see the backs of Omar, Steven, and Johnny walking south. Fuck.

Omar's got my ball in his hands. He's spinning it around. I wait at the intersection to make sure they're far enough that if one of them does turn around, spot me, and maybe even chase me, I have a street-length head-start.

My heart is racing, but not like when I was with Ashley. This is the "live-to-see-another-day" type of beat. Luckily, nothing happens.

When I get home, I let out a sigh as I enter my apartment and lock the door behind me. Even if they'd followed me and attempted to break down the door, I'd have time to call the cops. I can't believe I have to think up shitty scenarios like that.

Inside, Mom's waiting for me, lips pursed, phone in hand, seated on the couch.

"Salaam, Ammi, what's up?" I say, putting down my bag.

"Arfa called," she says, taking a deep breath in. "She said she saw you with some girl."

Goddamn her. Why don't aunties just get a life? I think fast.

"Must've been someone else," I say, sitting down beside her. "I was at basketball practice, I swear."

She turns to look at me, still suspicious. "Swear on my life," she demands. "Jamila is bad enough. I don't need two rotten apples."

Oh man. Hell, here I come. "I swear on your life."

Fuck. I'm swallowed whole by guilt. It's dark. It's heavy. It's shameful. I lower my head and try not to make eye contact.

I see a slight look of relief on my mother's face as I drag myself toward my room. You don't swear on your mother's life if you're lying. She could die because of you.

I'm tempted to go out and take my words back, but it's too late—they're out in the ether. That little angel on my shoulder must've given me a failing grade for that one. Probably worth a million sins.

In Islam, heaven is underneath your mother's feet. I don't know if that means she gets the final say as to whether I'll be allowed into heaven, but it's possible? Also, how do Dads and the afterlife fit together? Would I get any brownie points if my dad thought better of me, to offset the shit I just got myself into? I'll ask Imam Aziz next time I'm at mosque. Maybe next Saturday.

In my room, as I put my shit away, Mom calls me to dinner. She and Jamila are already seated at the dining table when I get there. I like it when Mom eats with us instead of waiting for us to finish before eating herself.

It looks like she made all the rotis in advance. They're still warm when we dig into them, alongside some cauliflower and potato sabji.

Not my favorite dish in the world, but it's really good today. I push the guilt out of my mind by thinking about what it felt like to kiss a girl for the very first time. I think aloo keema parathas are now my second-favorite thing.

. . .

We're sitting and lazing about. *Indian Idol Junior* is running in the background, with these little kids belting out Bollywood tunes like they're nothing. I sing along with one of them and immediately get shut down by Jamila and my mom.

"Itni kojii awaz me na hi gao," says Mom. Basically telling me I need to keep my "ugly" voice to myself. Who needs internet trolls when your family is this supportive? Jamila agrees with her and just gives me a look.

But I don't really care. I continue belting out the tune anyway.

"Oof, Allah, Fawad, you're giving me such a massive headache. Go get me water, now."

"Fine," I say, getting up and fetching her a glass from the kitchen. At the sink, I get a text from Yousuf.

YOUSUF: Turn on CP24.

ME: ??? kk

"Ammi, can you turn on the news quickly?" I ask. There's a commercial break and an ad for some prepackaged rotis that taste homemade, showing a working daughter-in-law slipping them past her picky mother-in-law, who can't tell the difference. Yup, even in this day and age.

She flips to CP24. There's a news anchor standing outside the playground by Nelson Mandela Public School.

There's cops behind her, an ambulance, and the usual suspect, caution tape. Wonder what happened?

A brown-skinned woman holds a microphone close to her face.

THIS JUST IN: *A shooting in Regent Park leaves one man of Afghan origin in his mid-twenties dead and his six-year-old daughter in critical condition after yet another drive-by shooting.*

I have with me Constable Jacob Harrison.

ANCHOR: *Any leads on the suspect?*

CONSTABLE: *We're currently combing through* CCTV *footage and working with locals. We're asking any eyewitnesses on the scene to come forward.*

ANCHOR: *Is this connected to the shooting of Abshir Mohammed a few months ago?*

CONSTABLE: *It's hard to say at this point. Anything is possible. We just know that gang-related gun violence continues to be an issue for the city.*

The anchor thanks the constable for his time and continues reporting on the scene, interviewing several residents who can't believe someone would open fire with a playground in such close proximity. My stomach is about to turn upside down.

"Change it," I say, gesturing for my mom to flip back to the singing show. I sit down and take a few deep breaths.

"That's why I tell you to never leave when it's dark," my mom says.

"This was in broad daylight, Ammi. Just unbelievable," I say, shaking my head and texting Yousuf while heading to my room.

"Ammi, I think we really need to start looking for another apartment," says Jamila.

I can hear them debate the matter in the background, but their voices are inaudible once I close the door to my room.

ME: Fuck. Can't believe they actually did it. This neighborhood's gone mad. A little girl?! Agh, so sad dude.

YOUSUF: We just gon keep killin ourselves, nothin's going to change

ME: You all right?

YOUSUF: Just tired of seeing my community burn

ME: I hear you bro

I put away my phone and lie down. My head's feeling way too heavy right now. Who or what is to blame? There isn't an easy answer. Maybe there is no answer at all.

16

We'd won another game where I came off the bench and dropped a cool fifteen—no big deal. You know, just another day at the office. Hot shit coming through. My swag's, like, at an all-time high when I march into the South Regent community center.

I spot Jerome and Kingsley doing their thing. Kingsley's holding a weighted ball, he's got a weighted vest on, and he's doing drills with them. I think dudes in the military would have trouble completing what he does. I hope I don't have to do that.

Jerome doesn't look too pleased with how Kingsley's doing, though. He's blowing the whistle, yelling instructions, flailing his hands, showing how he wants Kingsley to do things when I walk up, feeling all fresh.

"Hey, Jerome," I say, gliding onto the court.

Jerome doesn't seem impressed. He blows his whistle, tells Kingsley to grab some water, and turns toward me. "Hey, Fawad. Why aren't you changed yet?"

"I wanted to tell you how I've been slaying men out on the court the past two games," I say, all animated and wilin' out. I'm even doing a little demo with an invisible ball. "You remember Darius? Guess who got a last-minute block on the dude? This guy."

Jerome shrugs. "Fawad, it's been two games," he says. "I really don't think you should be letting it go to your head. That's how you make mistakes."

I feel like a deflated ball someone just tried to dribble. "I just thought you'd be proud, that's all."

"Hey, listen to me, I *am* proud," he says, dribbling the ball in his hands before passing it to me. "But I don't want you to lose sight of the end goal. Also, you, Arif, and Yousuf are good for the conference, right? It's next weekend."

"Yup, we'll be there."

"And you told Yousuf I want him to do a little performance?"

"Yup, just gotta confirm he's down."

"Good. It'll be good for the community, especially after the last . . ."

"Yeah, it's been heavy."

"There's a lot of healing that needs to happen. It's gotta start at home, though. Anyway . . ."

He blows the whistle. "Let's get you changed and on the baseline."

I change out of my clothes like I'm Clark Kent in a phone booth about to become Superman. I'm at baseline. Best believe I'm hauling ass.

When I get to seventeen suicides, I'm feeling my lunch trying to catapult out of my stomach. Eighteen suicides, I'm gagging.

When I finish nineteen, I can't hold it in anymore. Whatever I ate is coming back up. I run to the nearest garbage can and vomit up two potato-stuffed paratha rolls and fall to my knees. They definitely don't taste the same the second time around. I think I might even cut out parathas for a bit after this. I'm sweating, gagging, and feeling like my eyeballs are going to fall right out of their sockets.

Jerome walks casually over to where I am, kneels, inspects me, and starts laughing. He catches a whiff of my vomit and plugs his nose. He quickly ties up the bag and takes it out of the gym. I'm winded. I crawl to a wall and catch my breath as I see him walk back in.

"Let's go, Fawad. You have to get tougher than that," he says, blowing his whistle. "Go get cleaned up and finish the last two. We have more drills to do."

"Last one, I did nineteen," I say in my defense. He shrugs. Ruthless. I get up, go the washroom, gargle, and clean the vomit marks on my ball shorts. I'm looking at my reflection and feeling like a mess.

Back in the gym, Jerome's smirking while holding another weighted ball. He puts it in my hands and fuck, it's heavy. I'm sinking.

"That's right, we're going to be using this today," he says, patting me on the back. I peep Kingsley on the other side of the gym nearly wiped out but still pushing.

"You're going to do all the ball-handling drills with this ball," says Jerome. He points. "You see the pylons? You're gonna start with a hard dribble on one side and do a crossover. Rinse and repeat. Let's move." He claps his hands and I hustle to the baseline.

This is like dribbling a legitimate rock or boulder. I'm sluggish, and Jerome's screaming to keep me on my toes. Fifteen minutes later and my hands feel like they're going to fall off.

Finally, Jerome blows the whistle. That oh-so-sweet sound. I drop the ball and pant like a mutt who is done playing fetch for the day.

I finish with my usual one-on-one game with Kingsley. I can't even think. I get low and my defensive stance makes me feel like a wall. It doesn't last long because as soon as I check him the ball, he's dribbling, calculating how he wants to destroy me. This time, when he drives, he doesn't leave me in his dust—I keep up all the way to the rim. That feels a little better. Still fifteen push-ups for me.

Five more buckets. Seventy-five more push-ups.

"All right, fellas. Let's make this a little more interesting," says Jerome, getting up from the bench with a grin. "Fawad, for every bucket you score, Kingsley's gotta do fifty push-ups."

My eyes widen. Me, score on Kingsley? Hah. I look over at Kingsley. He's just as *meh*. "C'mon, man, you know little man ain't gon' get no bucket. Why we even doing this again?"

"We're doing this to give you a break and help take this little man's game to the next level. Now, let's go."

He blows the whistle. I'm staring at Kingsley's stomach. That's what a good defender's supposed to do. All the other body parts move too damn fast. I'm tight up on him. He's trying to determine which way he wants to go.

This time I get a solid palm on the ball and mostly because he doesn't expect it, I do a hard swipe, miraculously rip it loose, and dive on top of it to get my first-ever offensive possession against him.

It feels weird switching roles. Kingsley's not bothering to get a hand up. He's standing two meters away just asking me to shoot.

I'm dribbling and plotting, dribbling and plotting, and dribbling some more until I'm, like, fuck it, I'm just going to shoot. The three of us are watching as my shot arcs up and then hits the inner right side of the rim, does a little bounce on the backboard, and rolls over to the left side of the rim before tumbling in. Bucket.

I look at Kingsley, then at Jerome, and they're both looking at each other like "did that just happen?" Jerome bursts out laughing. "You know what that means, Kingsley? Fifty push-ups."

Kingsley scoffs and does them without missing a beat. Telling you, he's on some military shit. He gets up and checks me the ball. As soon as I take one dribble, he takes it away and drives in like he's a locomotive.

I get out of the way and watch him fly past me and dunk the ball so hard the whole net's shaking. Damn. Fifteen push-ups for me. I don't get the ball after that. The game finishes 11–1.

My arms are dead after eight push-ups. Seven more. Kingsley walks over, kneels beside me, and says, "C'mon, little man, you got this."

I finish and then drop into what feels like a swimming pool of my own sweat. Kinda feels refreshing, to be honest. Better sweat than piss or vomit, while we're at it.

My arms feel like Jell-O. I don't know where my bones went. Jerome blows his whistle and tells me, "You did good, Fawad. That's a wrap for today."

I roll over, get in a sitting position, and notice the other side of the gym is packed with dudes running a pickup game. Then I realize it's Omar, Johnny, and Steven, of all people. There are some other kids from the Park too. On top of that, they're playing with my ball.

I grab my stuff to head into the changeroom, catching Omar's eyes and that smirk of his.

Fuck Omar. I'll get another ball. They can burn in hellfire for all I care.

I sulk all the way back home and take an icy shower. I make myself a protein shake to go with dinner. Mom made chapli kababs and rice. She's been super supportive of my goal to bulk up.

After dinner, I check myself out in the mirror in my room. The muscle definition is a new sight for me. I won't lie, I like it. I take a photo of my arm with me squeezing my biceps and message it to Ashley on Snap.

She responds with the emoji that has its tongue sticking out. For the next hour or so, I'm distracted by the Snaps she's sending me. I'm keeping her entertained too. Especially now that I've gone from three abs to five and a half. One of her pics shows her bra strap. I fall back on my bed. What wouldn't I do to see what's underneath.

Then I remember I still have homework to finish. Talk about a buzzkill.

...

I'm deep into finishing an English essay on *Lord of the Flies*. I'm doing a comparative piece on how the island could be a metaphor for the ghetto. I know that sounds a little out-there, but just think about it.

Where are the kids growing up in poor neighborhoods supposed to get the adult supervision to keep us from wanting to kill each other when every damn adult is either working three jobs or suffers from a debilitating addiction?

It's actually deeply satisfying to put these words to paper. My phone starts vibrating. It's an incoming video call from Yousuf. I pick up.

"Hey, man, what's up?"

"Nothin' much. Just wanted to say I started going to that therapy thing we was talking about. Fatima set up the appointment, and we were on the streetcar back from the first session, and she said it was your idea. I mean, I don't know if it's going to work, but it was good to get shit out."

"Bro, you have no idea how happy I am to hear that," I say, getting up and pacing around my room. "I feel like the entire hood could use some serious therapy after that last shooting. I was watching the news again and the girl survived."

"Yeah, shit's fucked on the real. I don't know, I guess I'm supposed to hate the dude, be happy he's six feet deep just like Abshir, but I don't. I just feel sad that there's men out there who don't feel nothin' shooting with kids in the background. That's just straight-up fucked."

I'm feeling my mouth grow dry and gut tighten just thinking about everything that's gone down in the last few months. "That's just Regent too—multiply that same shit across the GTA and yeah, there's a problem. Honestly, don't think more cops or whatever the mayor's thinking is the solution."

"You're right, man. I see you running for office one day. Think it'd do some city councillors some good to have a perspective like ours."

"Word."

"Also, check it. I, uh . . . took what I wrote for Abshir's funeral—just bits and pieces, to be honest—and turned it into something. Something I wanna . . . perform. At that conference."

Hearing that makes me loosen up and smile. "So, do I get to hear it first or what?"

"That's why I called, dummy," he says, setting his phone on a shelf and sitting a few feet away, grabbing his guitar. "Now, it's still pretty raw, so don't laugh, eh?"

"Bro, it's me. Let's hear it."

. . .

It's the weekend and Mom's birthday. Although she actually doesn't 100 percent know exactly when she was born. We've alternated a few dates before finally sticking to one, November 2, which is the last date she remembers her mom telling her.

Jamila pitched in for a frame and couldn't stop fawning over Nermin's handiwork. We wrapped it up and both pooled our lunch money to get her a cake and some samosas. We would've taken her out to Little India, but we both came to the same conclusion that it was a bit out of our budget.

One day, I won't have to think twice. I'd love to fly her all over the world. Instead, we cook at home, if you want to call it cooking. Jamila actually succeeds in following an online recipe for haleem, with me as sous-chef, because I'm really good at cutting things by now. Jamila in the kitchen is a bit like Jamila at her canvas in her room: messy. The clean-up duty isn't great, but we get everything done just in time before Mom comes home from her morning shift.

We act nonchalant—just chilling on the couch, watching TV when she walks in.

"Hi, Ammi," I say, not looking at her while she takes off her shoes.

"Hi, ka bacha. How many times do I have to tell you to say salaam, huh?"

I snicker. She can put ka bacha after literally anything. It means "the offspring of," translates really weird in English. Anyway, it's a desi mom thing, and it's funny.

"Why are you two just sitting here? Jamila, did you fold the laundry? Fawad, have you done the vacuum? Why did Allah give me such lazy children? Fawad, go get me some water."

She sits on the couch and stares at the TV. Jamila is watching Netflix and there's a run-up to a kissing scene. "Jamila, change it. What is this? You can't be watching such things with your little brother around."

I bring back the water, rolling my eyes. It's two white people on a bridge flirting with the idea of kissing in some dumb rom-com she's made me sit through way too many times.

Jamila stares up at Mom with her eyebrows raised. "You think this is too much for him? I think you'd be surprised what kids watch these days, Ammi."

She catches my eye and gives me a look. Fuck, did I delete my browser history that one time? Wait, ugh, I hate her so much right now. My cheeks turn red. "I don't know what she's talking about, but Ammi's right. Stop polluting my mind, Jamila."

"Right? Maybe I should show Mom all the righteous content you're into?"

"No . . . let's not," I say, feeling a lump in my throat. The thing with Jamila is it's hard to tell when she's joking and when she might actually do something. I think if she was hell-bent on giving Mom a heart attack, she might do it, but since it's her birthday, I'm going to assume she's joking. I laugh it off.

"Ammi, we got you something," I say, changing subjects and darting to my room to retrieve the wrapped frame.

"What is this?" she says, her look a mix of concern over how much it might've cost and joy at her kids getting her a present. Who doesn't like gifts?

"It's for you. Happy birthday," I say.

Jamila clears her throat.

"It's from both me *and* Jamila."

Mom carefully unwraps it and says, "Wow, mashallah, what a gift." She stares without blinking, her mouth falling open, just taking in all the tiny details and flourishes of Nermin's creation.

"My friend Nermin made it. It's the Ayat al-Kursi."

"We'll put it right up here," Mom says, pointing at an empty spot next to a clock on the wall. "Jamila must've picked the frame."

"Obviously, Ammi Jaan. Happy birthday. I know it doesn't always seem like it, but we love you," she says, wrapping her arms around Mom. I quickly grab my phone and take a photo. Who knows the next time these two'll be affectionate toward one another? I say, "Smile."

They smile, both beaming, Mom holding the gift in her hands.

"Okay, let's all do a selfie. Come on, Fawad," says Jamila, taking out her iPhone. We bunch up together and the three of us honestly look pretty great. I give Mom a kiss on the cheek.

"We also made your favorite—haleem," says Jamila, walking over to the kitchen and bringing out a tray with a plateful of our dish, plus garnishes—cilantro, lime, and freshly chopped ginger.

"You made haleem?"

"Ji, Ammi Jaan, I made haleem."

My turn to clear my throat. "Okay, the brat helped too."

We eat, and cut the cake, and both Jamila and I feed her a slice.

"Your father would be really happy right now," says Mom. "He loved cake. He loved anything he could eat. What an appetite that man had."

I chuckle. "Probably where I get it from."

The mention of Dad makes the room a little heavy. I have an idea. "Do you guys remember when Abbu used to belt out those really old ghazals?"

"Oh my God, yes," says Jamila, sitting cross-legged and putting one hand behind her ear like a proper classical Pakistani singer, pretending to play the harmonium with the other hand. Here we go. She starts busting out her best impression of Dad, her tone as baritone as she can get it to be.

Mom joins in.

Okay, fine, it's a classic. I can't help adding my voice to the mix, and now all three of us are belting out lyrics that honestly I don't really know the meaning to. But we sound good, that's all that matters.

"*Wah, wah, wah,*" I say.

The rest of the day is spent belting out more tunes, playing Antakshari, and watching a Bollywood classic that Mom loves called *Saudagar*. I know Dad's not here, but it kinda feels like he is. I know I don't always appreciate my family, but in this moment, I wouldn't trade them for anything—not even getting drafted into the NBA. Actually . . . okay, no. Even that doesn't come close.

17

The next couple of days, I've got that tune Yousuf played stuck in my head. Can't wait for the conference when I can watch him play it for a crowd. And that English essay comparing *Lord of the Flies* to the hood? Got a 92 percent—that's right, mic drop. Meanwhile, I'm still going strong with my training with Jerome and ball practice, though I swear I'm barely able to walk the next day.

Ashley doesn't seem to register this fact. We've been alternating between hanging with her friends and mine, even catching one of Nermin's games where she got a hat-trick, scoring three whole frikken goals. But today she's got me putting up posters for the winter formal that she's organizing.

Ever since volleyball season wrapped, it's become her latest obsession. She's really into extracurricular things, and damn, does she love checklists. The way her eyes light up after crossing something off is sort of like how I feel after sinking a shot.

The dance's theme is The Great Gatsby, which isn't super original, but after I showed her Nermin's Insta, she got really excited. So excited she commissioned Nermin to use her hand-lettering to create a poster that we're now plastering all over the school.

"I can't believe how beautiful these turned out," she says, taking a poster from the pile in my hands and stapling it to the bulletin board. "The yearbook committee asked me who designed it, and I think they're going to ask Nermin to do something for the cover. Isn't that exciting?"

"Yeah, that girl's in a different stratosphere. But yeah, the posters look great."

"Plus, I get to shop for a really pretty dress. I have one in mind. You're going to love it."

Each step is a struggle. My face is so tight, it probably looks like I can't breathe.

"Are you even listening, Fawad?" she says, turning to face me. I nod, and she strokes my cheek. Everything is right with the world momentarily. Then the pain kicks back in. "Another thing . . . I was thinking maybe your pocket square could match my dress," she says, doing a little twirl before turning to look at me with those big, beautiful eyes. "What do you think?"

"Uh, yeah, sure." Damn, Great Gatsby, eh? I'm playing through the book and movie in my head. It's going to mean getting a tux. Those are not cheap.

She puts up another poster and plants a kiss on my cheek. "You're really slow today. Can you keep up? We have the whole school to cover. We just finished the first floor."

Oh man, it's only the first floor. Damn. The stairs. The stairs. Fuck me.

"We can take a break if you'd like," she says with a twinkle in her eyes. She takes the massive stack of posters from my hands and sets them down before she hugs me. "Even if we've only covered, like, one hallway."

She laughs. I can't get enough of those pearly white teeth, those dimples, and that little beauty mark. I lean down and kiss her cheek.

"I swear I'll be fine in just a few minutes," I say, stretching out my legs and arms. That feels a little better. Then, with my back pressed against a locker, I inch down to sit on the floor. "Ball practice has been killing me."

"I know, babe. I'm glad our season just wrapped. But we'll probably be done in twenty minutes, tops."

She sits beside me and rests her head on my chest. I can feel my heart beating. I can't imagine what it must sound like to her.

"Do you want to come over and study sometime?" she says, poking her head up.

"Uh, won't your parents mind?" I say, feeling a gut reaction that screams *trouble*.

"No, they're cool. I've had boys over before," she says, stroking my cheek. "I mean, it's not like we'll be upstairs in my room or anything."

I calm down.

"Besides, I've already told them all about you," she says, squeezing me tight.

"Really? That's, uh . . . awesome," I say, not really knowing how to react.

She straightens up and looks me in the eyes. "Wait, you *have* told your mom and sister about me, right?"

I'm trying not to make eye contact. "Uh," I say. "Kinda."

"That was a yes or no question, Fawad."

Now she sounds like Jerome, and my muscles ache more than ever.

"It doesn't work that way with my family," I say, rubbing my arm. "My mom's not cool with the whole dating thing."

"You did say that."

She looks like she sort of understands, but doesn't really. I hold her hand and we interlace our fingers.

"What did you tell your folks about me?" I say.

She pokes my nose. "That you've got a big nose. Kidding. That you're cute, from Pakistan, play on the school team, and live in Regent."

It was all sounding good until those last three words. I feel like that place haunts me wherever I go. Why can't I just be a kid who goes to Northern? Or, I don't know, *anything* but that. Ugh.

"Ash, why would you tell them I'm from Regent?" I say. "They probably have a million ideas about what boys from Regent are like."

"Sorry, I didn't realize . . ."

Sometimes being poor is saltier than my mother's palak paneer.

"It's cool," I say, even though it really isn't. I look over at the pile of posters next to us. "Let's just finish putting these up."

I struggle to get up, and she pulls me back down. "We will, but in a bit."

She puts her arm around me, trying to get a smile, and when she realizes her efforts aren't paying off, she goes back to resting her head on my chest. I stroke her hair without even thinking about it. It must be what a musician feels like when they pick up a guitar.

I get a notification on my phone from WhatsApp. I hope it's not Mom trying to remind me to pick up milk on the way home again—I *told* her I'd grab it. Nope. It's a message from Nusrat.

NUSRAT: Abbu just asked me how I feel about you.
Ahmed is not happy. I'm stuck in the middle.
What are you waiting for?

It just never ends. She's right, obviously. I'm being a coward. I want to throw my phone across the hall. I'm gripping it so tight that my hand is turning red. "What the—?"

Ashley's looking at me, all confused. "Is everything okay?"

"Uh, yeah, just my mom," I say, trying to play it off as nothing.

I kiss Ashley's forehead, and she helps me up even though my thighs feel so sore that they're shaking.

Then I realize I can't bend back down to pick up the stack of posters on the ground. I point to them and, with a strained look on my face, say, "Could you get those for me?"

Ashley picks them up and puts them in my arms. We walk at a slow pace the rest of the lunch hour, which I'm super grateful for.

I've never been "in love" before, but when I look at her, I want to forget everything else. I wonder if that's what love is? Something we use to make pain fade away into the background?

...

On my way home, I'm feeling hurt. I can't believe Mom is taking things this far with the whole Nusrat situation. Now she's got her brother's buy-in; it's probably why he asked Nursat about me. How could she be so frickin' heartless? It's not like I've been hiding how I feel about the whole thing. Now here I am having to put an end to it before it blows up on both sides.

So yeah, I'm fuming. I'm planning on going berserk and losing it on my mom as soon as I get into the apartment.

Except when I open the door, there's Aunty Zubiya and her two little kids. Aunty's wearing a beige abaya, Maryam is rocking two unruly ponytails, and Abdul looks oddly more adorable now that all his teeth are gone.

I swear, if it weren't for them running up to me and giving me a hug, I'd flip the coffee table over. Hell, I'd turn into the Hulk if I could. A brown Hulk.

I tell the kids to calm down and give me two minutes to take off my shoes and jacket, and put away my bag.

"Salaam, Aunty," I say, putting on a fake smile. "Salaam, Ammi."

I try not to grit my teeth when I say "Ammi." Mom and Aunty Zubiya are casually sipping tea, and the kids show me a puzzle they want help with. It features characters from Pixar's Cars series.

"Did you hear Kiran's son Amir has a girlfriend?" says Aunty, while taking a sip of her chai. "Be careful with Fawad. Kids grow up too fast these days."

I look up at her and try not to scream that she should mind her own damn business.

"Fawad's not like other kids," my mom says, as if she even knows me that well. "Here, let me show you who I have in mind for him."

She starts showing her photos from her phone.

"That's your brother's daughter, right?" says Aunty, leaning in with great interest. "Best to keep things in the family. That's what I say."

Mom nods with a big smile on her face.

I almost snap a puzzle piece in two as I listen. The kids try to pry the piece loose when they realize what I'm doing. "Sorry," I whisper, and lodge it into the appropriate place.

We finish the puzzle just as Aunty Zubiya gestures to her kids that it's time to leave. They pack up and give me a big hug before heading out. Mom says goodbye to Aunty and disappears into her room.

I lock the door behind them, plotting how best to confront my mother. Instead, she comes out wearing a sweater and starts putting on her boots and jacket.

"Let's go to No Frills. It's going to close soon," she says, dragging an empty grocery cart with a cardboard box laid inside it out from the kitchen.

"But before that, I want to—"

"Hurry, we don't have much time," she says, patting me on the head. "Let's go, let's go. Put on your shoes."

I decide that I'll tell her on the walk over. Except as she's pushing the cart, she won't stop talking about gossip from our village in Pakistan.

"So, you know that stupid brother of mine?"

"Which one? You have two."

"Anwer, the younger one," she says.

"Oh, the one Abbu didn't used to like. Didn't they have—"

"Never mind. Mohsin's wife, Mehrin, was telling me he came to their home and asked Mohsin for Nusrat's hand for his own son. Can you believe his nerve?"

That wouldn't work for Nusrat either. "Was Nusrat asked how she felt about that?"

She doesn't register the question.

"I told Mehrin, 'Over my dead body.' She and Mohsin know I've had my eyes on Nusrat from the day she was born, just a few days after you. You two were made for each other."

I stop mid-stride and tug at her arm to do the same. She's surprised, and then I finally blurt out, "Ammi, how many times do I have to tell you? I'm never going to . . ."

Oh shit, is that Ashley up the street with her mom? What are they doing on Parliament?

"Here, let's go into the Bengali store before No Frills," I say, quickly hooking my mom's arm and leading her in, watching over my shoulder as Ashley and her mom go into the organic health food store nearby.

My mom's confused. We usually go to No Frills first, then the Bengali store on our way home.

"I just thought we'd cut through the inner streets on the way home," I say.

She shrugs. "Okay, I'm going to get some meat, then. We're out of lentils and okra, so you get those."

"Assalamu alaikum, sister," the man behind the counter says to my mom. He's got dark-brown skin and is wearing a topi to go with his green vest and gray T-shirt. His teeth look like they're bleeding, except his gums are red from chewing too much betel leaf. Either way, it's gross.

Since living in Regent, I've come to find out that this dude has a wife and daughter here *and* a wife and two sons back in Bangladesh. Player. His Canadian wife sits behind the till ringing customers up and bagging groceries while he chats up customers.

"Kya haal hai, baji," he says in his best Urdu accent, asking my mom how she is.

"Theek hai, theek hai," my mom replies, smiling at his attempt to speak the language.

Mom goes to the back of the store to order meat from the butcher. Seeing the butcher skin and grind the meat makes me queasy, so I stay put near the front.

I grab bags of red and black lentils. Then I bag some okra. Mom appears carrying bags of chicken breast and ground beef. We pay and bid the uncle behind the counter salaam.

I don't spot Ashley or her mom as I poke my head out. My heartbeat stops racing. I try to bring up Nusrat, but Mom's now talking about what she wants to cook tonight. Agh.

We're at No Frills a few minutes later and I decide that, rather than creating a scene here, I'll wait till the walk home. I know the aisles and their contents like the back of my hand. Eventually, we're ready to check out, and we go to the lane where Fatima, Yousuf's older sister, is working.

"Salaam, Aunty," she says to Mom. "Hey, Fawad."

"How's Yousuf?" says Mom, taking items out of the cart and putting them on the conveyor belt. "Fawad said he's doing better. I keep telling Fawad to tell him to drop by. I'll make his favorite seekh kababs sometime."

"He is doing better, Aunty," says Fatima. "And yes, I'll tell him. My mom mentioned to ask you to come some night for dinner too."

Mom had gone over to offer condolences after Abshir died, but the two of them hadn't seen each other since.

"Sure, beta, that would be good. And how are your studies coming along?"

"Subhanallah, Aunty, everything's going good," she says, smiling and turning the card reader toward her.

"Allah bless you and your family, beta."

We wave goodbye and she's on to the next customer.

The cart is overflowing; we have yellow bags hanging off the handles.

My mom tries to tell me she can get us home faster if *she* pushes the cart and I just carry some of the bags that are dangling off, but I insist. I'm not going to be walking through Regent with a bag of groceries while my mom pushes this big-ass cart around.

I'm getting my workout in as she continues to talk about Anwer's audacity to overstep her claim. So much for talking sense into her on our walk home. I can barely get a word in.

By the time we arrive back, I'm exhausted. I need a breather. I take the cart into the kitchen. Jamila will be home soon, and she can sort through and put the groceries in the fridge. She's mad OCD if I put things away and mix up which trays the veggies and milk go in.

I crash on the couch and watch my mom settle in as she starts scrolling through her phone. I think she's more addicted to her phone than I am. She's probably checking updates from Pakistan on WhatsApp. I must have fallen asleep because I wake up to the sounds of her sobbing.

Her hands are shaking and she's barely able to hold the phone to her ear. I rush to her side.

"Ammi, what's wrong?" I say, putting my arms around her.

She puts her hand up. I hear a voice on the other end of the line wailing too. Damn, what the hell happened?

I run to the kitchen to grab her a glass of water and set it down on the coffee table. Jamila comes home in this madness and is distraught by the sight of Mom. We're both confused as fuck.

Mom hangs up and takes a few heavy sighs. "Your mamu Mohsin, he—he—he has . . . cancer."

"Oh shit, what stage? Did they say anything else?" says Jamila.

"Stage four," says Mom, covering her face with her palms and continuing to sob.

Jamila bites her tongue and sits next to her, rubbing her arms to comfort her.

"How long does he have?" I say as I pace back and forth across the living room.

"A few months at most, bechara. Oof, Allah, kya qayammat hai."

I have a faint memory of him from Dad's funeral, the last and only time we were in Pakistan since immigrating.

"And poor Nusrat, oof—what's going to happen to her?" says Mom, through her hands.

Jamila looks over at me, seeing me getting worked up, and I can tell she just wants me to stay quiet.

What am I supposed to say? *Oh, don't worry, Mom, I'll agree to marry her because her dad is about to die.*

I swallow whatever is begging to come out, sit down on the other side of Mom, and press her arms to comfort her too.

"We'll figure it out," says Jamila, stroking Mom's hair now. "Don't worry, we'll sort it all out."

I have no idea what she means by all that. If she thinks I'm going to be a sacrificial lamb in all this, she has another thing coming.

It's not my fault Nusrat's dad has cancer, and it's not my fault I don't find the idea of marrying my first cousin appealing. On top of that, she doesn't even want to marry me. A shiver shoots up my spine. Then I look at Mom and see her anguish.

My sister continues to comfort her, but I bite my lip. I don't want to say anything stupid. Eventually, I'm going to have to tell Mom once and for all how I feel about Nusrat, and how she really feels about me. It won't be easy for her to swallow, but I'm running out of time and options.

I go to my room and message Nusrat.

ME: Sorry about your dad. We're all praying for him and we're here for you. I was also going to bring up the engagement thing but she got the phone call. As soon as things calm down, I swear, I'll make sure she knows and backs off. Tell Ahmed he doesn't need to worry.

I don't expect a reply anytime soon. She's got her hands full. Can't even imagine what I'd do if anything like that happened to Mom. I'm thinking back to when I was in Pakistan for Dad's funeral. After the mourning period, we had a few days remaining, and there was an evening our family was invited over for dawat at Uncle Mohsin's home. Nusrat, her younger sister, and her mom had cooked up a feast—hospitality is not taken lightly in that part of the world, I can say that much.

While we were winding down, Uncle Mohsin couldn't stop beaming about wanting Nusrat to be the first girl in the village to do her medical degree, and how she had the smarts to do it. He'd put aside a lot of his life savings from working abroad doing labor in the UAE just for his kids' education. Then they served dessert, some ras malai, and afterwards, we flipped through photos of us as kids, before my family moved to Canada, and I could not stop cracking up at how polite and meek Jamila looked. She took photos with her phone of some of those shots, and I kept thinking about how crazy life was—it was almost impossible to predict where a person would end up.

There were also photos of Nusrat and me, held in our respective mothers' laps and of us playing in the dirt courtyards. She'd just finished attending to and putting her grandma to sleep, and came to look with us. She had to do all the housework, study, cook, and so much more. I don't know how she did it—how she *does* it. It's the same feeling I have when I think of my mom: admiration.

But not I-want-to-get-married-to-her type of admiration. I wish Mom would get the difference.

18

The basketball court is the only place I can go to get away from the shit happening at home. Mom's been a mess ever since hearing the news about Mohsin Mamu.

On top of that, Ashley keeps stressing me out about the formal coming up. I love spending time with her, but I have not been digging her dragging me into helping out with organizing it. I'm like a surrogate member of the organizing committee.

On the hardwood floor of the gym, it feels like all is right with the world. When the ball bounces and comes back into my hands, it feels like magic, as corny as that sounds.

Every time I hit nothing but net, I feel some mysterious energy coursing through me. It puts me on this unexplainable high and makes me never want to come down.

I'm still coming off the bench for Northern, but I recently sunk eighteen points in a win against Danforth Tech—with three back-to-back three-pointers late in the third quarter, which helped put us *wayyyyy* out ahead.

And then against Jarvis, I came into the game and dropped twenty. Twenty whole points off the bench. That's, like, unheard of. Scott and Luke even hoisted me onto their shoulders after that game. Those dudes are legit tall. It was a little scary.

So I'm chilling on cloud nine, autopilot, cruise control, or whatever else they call it. Which is why in practice, I cheat just a little bit when finishing up the last suicide. I don't touch the baseline at the very end. I just kind of pretend I do, and stop short.

"Chaudhry, what the hell was that?" Coach yells after blowing his whistle. His get-up today is a purple turban alongside a purple tracksuit. I feel like it's inspired by the original Raptors uniform.

The hair on my back stands up. I'm looking around at the other guys like, *It wasn't me, I swear.* I shrug and try to do my puppy-dog face, hoping it'll get me off the hook. We're all sweating buckets.

"You don't think I saw that?" says Coach, walking up to me and pointing at the baseline. "Goddamn, everyone is busting their asses. You decide you're going to coast when it matters most?"

"It was just a suicide, Coach," I say, wiping my forehead.

"Did everyone hear that?" says Coach, looking around at the rest of my teammates. "He thinks copping out last minute on a drill is not a big deal. Well, guess what? He's wrong."

Here he goes, it's lecture time. He's pacing back and forth.

"If any of you boys think this is just about basketball, you're dead wrong, all of you," he starts. "How you do anything is how you do everything. You hear that?"

Damn. Straight-up dropping knowledge at 8:30 a.m.

"What Chaudhry did wasn't just cheating himself—it's cheating all of you," he says, wagging his index finger in the air.

"Coach, I—"

"Now, we're going to rectify this. You're going to run again."

Everyone moans, and there's an echo of grumbling throughout

the gym. I'm getting dirty looks left, right, and center. "You're a team. If one of you isn't all-in, none of you are. So, baseline, and this time, no cop-outs. You hear me?"

"Way to go, Chaudhry," Spence says, walking past me and giving me the cut-eye.

Everyone's running, panting, and ready to drop dead. It's the final stretch. I think I'm going to pass out mid-court when I rein it in. Things are going blurry, but I can't let Coach down, I can't let the team down, and hell, most importantly, I can't let myself down.

I can see from the corner of my eye that everyone is pushing as hard as possible. I'm not going to make it. It's the final run across the court. I'm going to fall, and fall hard. I just gotta protect my face. Actually, I'm going to throw up.

All right, there's only one thing left to do. I get a little past the free-throw line and dive headfirst, with my fingertips reaching for baseline. My arms and knees skid across the hardwood. I'm pretty sure some skin has come off. I make it.

Coach blows his whistle. Everyone gathers around to check and see if I'm dead. I raise a hand to confirm I am indeed not.

"Now that's what I'm talking about," says Coach, pumping his fist. "That's a wrap, boys."

I'm still on the hardwood. Seems to be a favorite spot of mine. Someone taps me on the shoulder. I turn to look. It's Scott.

"Fawad, we're finished," he says, holding out his hand to help me up.

I'm a little dizzy, to be honest. I reach out and grab hold. He pulls, and pretty soon I'm on my feet.

He chuckles. "There's some Band-Aids in the changeroom," he says, inspecting my elbow. "That doesn't look that great."

"Nah, I've had worse," I say, but I'm feeling my knees give out from under me. I wobble when I take one step. The gym is empty besides the two of us. I take it in. It's beautiful.

"Here," says Scott, putting one of my arms around his shoulder. Just thinking back to when I first stepped into the gym for the tryout, how I sized these dudes up, I can't help but realize: that was really messed up of me.

I'm so sore. I hobble alongside him and finally make it to the locker room. When we get there, everyone starts clapping and chanting, "Chaudhry, Chaudhry, Chaudhry."

Best. Fucking. Feeling. Ever.

. . .

I'm riding high that weekend when Jerome's Dream Big conference rolls around. He told us to wear collared shirts and to come with a big appetite—there was going to be a lot of pizza. Arif and I go together; Yousuf had to show up a little early to do a mic check. I just know everyone's jaws are going to drop when they hear what he's come up with. I'm singing the tune to myself already.

The venue is the new Daniels Spectrum building on Dundas Street, in Ada Slaight Hall, and it is packed with dudes I haven't seen in a long time. Older dudes too, but literally every nationality represented, all from Regent.

That's one thing that's hard not to love about the community: the diversity. Where else can you pass by one group and eavesdrop on some Somali and the next, some Vietnamese or Tamil? Omar and his crew are here too, but I'm not paying much attention. It's a big crowd, and the last thing I need is to be called "Fuckwad" right now.

Mr. Williams, a.k.a. Jerome, is suited up, looking sharp with those thick black glasses of his and a fresh fade. He's talking with older dudes, probably some of the guys he's invited to give talks.

"Ah, come here, Venkatesh. Let me introduce you to Fawad and Arif," he says, bringing over this Tamil dude who's wearing an expensive-looking suit and tie, with a trimmed-up stubble beard and short hair.

"How's it going, fellas?" he says, shaking hands with us both.

"Fawad here's got his eyes on becoming a pro basketball player, so I thought he should meet you," says Jerome.

The room is abuzz with conversation and servers going around dishing out more sophisticated things than pizza. Was this guy a scout or something? All of a sudden, I feel my sweat glands working in overdrive.

"Oh yeah, well, I've helped a lot of those guys with setting up their VC firms. They're always banging on my door for investment advice. Just co-invested with Curry in a start-up a couple weeks ago."

Wait! What? What's a VC firm?

. "Like, Steph Curry?" I say, jaw cranked open.

"That's the one."

"Venkatesh has lived a very colorful life. He runs a venture capital firm that funds entrepreneurs to build their businesses, in case you're wondering," says Jerome, putting a hand on his friend's shoulder. "He's got a lot of stories I'm sure he'd be happy to share."

Venkatesh starts smiling. "Absolutely. I've got some time at lunch—come find me."

Jerome starts clapping to get everyone's attention, then lets out a loud whistle. Forgot he can do that. "All right, gentlemen, we're about to start. Let's head into the auditorium and get this show on the road."

"See you later, kid," says Venkatesh. He fixes his suit sleeve and I catch a glimpse of his gold Rolex.

Arif and I are still looking at each other.

"Did that just happen?" I mutter.

"Did you catch his watch?" says Arif.

I nod, then we slowly start moving with the herd into the auditorium, picking up a program booklet with the words "Dream Big" written on the cover.

Arif and I grab good seats in the middle. I don't know what I'm more pumped for: Venkatesh's speech or Yousuf's performance. The stage is set up with lights, a DJ in one corner, and musical instruments on the side. Jerome really did go all-out.

The day starts with Jerome doing a land acknowledgment speech and bringing out a local Chinese hip-hop artist named Li'l Zeng, who's making waves in the city, to get us amped. I've seen some of his YouTube videos. He's going to be big, so I make a mental note to get his autograph during the break.

Jerome comes back on and gives the opening remarks, thanking the sponsors and telling us about how this is the second year he's putting this on, in the hope of inspiring young men from all backgrounds to think bigger than what they've been led to believe about themselves, about their community, and about what they can and cannot accomplish.

He first brings up a Jamaican-Canadian ER doctor who works at Toronto General, who shares some wild stories about what he experiences night-in and night-out: he sees the aftermath of young men trying to murder each other; has to pull out bullets and stitch up open wounds; shuts patients' eyes after the heart monitor stops beeping; tells mothers their sons aren't going to make it. He's got slides up, sharing stats about the rising gun violence problem in the city. I'm sitting on the edge of my seat.

I knew the problem was big—I just didn't know how big. He ends with this closing remark: "Violence begets violence. Most of us are caught in cycles of perpetuating the wrongs done to us, thinking that by inflicting pain onto others, we can feel better. But that feeling never comes. The pain brings only more pain. So I'm asking you young men to be bigger than the pain, to stop it in its tracks and instead, be kind."

He gets a standing ovation, and Jerome comes back up and thanks him once more. Up next is Venkatesh, who gets up and plugs in his laptop before starting his speech. On the opening slide is an old photo of Regent.

"This is the building I grew up in. My family came to Canada as refugees from Sri Lanka, fleeing genocide," he starts, before flipping to another slide of a living room with a mattress. "This is where I slept because there were only two rooms, and between my parents and two sisters, I got the short end of the stick."

He gets a giggle out of us on that one. Then he flips to another slide, one of a janitor sweeping a school hallway. "This is what one teacher said I'd amount to after I got into a fight and he found out I was from Regent."

Then he moves on to a photo of a bay with clear blue skies, sailboats, and a bridge off in the distance. "And this is the view I woke up to from my home in California today."

My brain's gears stop turning for a quick second. I think something exploded inside my mind.

"How'd I get here?" he continues. "I didn't listen to that teacher. Instead, I listened to another teacher, Mr. Davis, God bless his soul, who not only saw my potential in math but also encouraged me to learn programming in this computer lab—before coding was something the cool kids did." He flips the slides to a computer lab with monitors as wide as the desks themselves. "Yes, computers did look like that at one point. I know I'm dating myself. The point is, I had no idea I'd fall in love with programming, but I got into the University of Waterloo and found myself as employee number 245 at a company you might've heard of. It's this small place called Google."

Everyone starts laughing. "And since then, I've taken the hustle mentality I learned from growing up in Regent and applied it to investing, funding a lot of the apps many of you probably have installed on your phones right now." He puts up a slide with logos of apps like Snap, Uber, DoorDash, and Square. "Now, Jerome's a good friend of mine, so when he wanted me to give a talk to you boys, I chartered a flight and put this presentation together on the plane. I kept thinking about what I wanted to leave you with, and I think it's these words . . ."

On the slide, it says, "Belief in Yourself is a Beautiful Armor," with a photo of a knight wearing the full get-up from medieval times. "All my life, there were a whole lot of people telling me I would amount to nothing. Then there were people telling me that I could be whatever I wanted. But one thing that stayed constant was my own belief in myself—that despite fleeing death and eating a steady diet of rice and eggplant because that's all that my parents could afford, I could do whatever I wanted. *That* belief was my armor against all the bullshit, all the negativity, all the garbage I was surrounded by, and that's what I want each and every one of you to think about. Do you believe you're bigger than your circumstances? Because if you don't, good luck. The world's a nasty place."

He then flips to his final slide—a video of him on the court with the Golden State Warriors and shooting around with Steph Curry. "Oh, and I still got a pretty solid jump shot." We watch him nail a three-pointer while wearing a blazer and getting a high-five from Steph, who can't believe his eyes.

Standing ovation. Holy shit, I'm riled up. Everyone's on their feet, clapping. The DJ's spinning Drake in the background. Venkatesh goes back to his seat and Jerome reappears.

"I taught him to shoot like that," he says, and gets a snicker from us. "Up next, we've got a special performance from a talented young man. Give it up for Yousuf."

Oh man, it's time. Yousuf comes out and he's getting help from the DJ to plug his guitar into an amp and get the mic set up in front of a stool. He's rocking a headband, black tee, and gray hoodie.

"Wassup everyone. This is a song I wrote when I was in a dark place . . . still there sometimes, to be honest. It's for my brother, who I lost this past summer. RIP. I'm wearing the headband he used to wear whenever he'd play basketball with me and my friends, and I hope wherever he is, he can hear me and that he's resting. The song's called 'Pieces of Peace.'"

I'm so choked up. My eyes are tearing up. I look over at Arif, who looks like he hasn't blinked in a minute either.

Life's a jigsaw puzzle
that comes with no instructions.
It's up to us to choose to
sow seeds of peace or destruction.

Innocence lost and malice
is found.
How many of us have to go
before we're drowned?

In this sea of blood and
stained Air Force 1s,
looking over our shoulders
and wondering when we'll
be the ones.

We have to believe
in pieces of peace.

It's all we've got when
the future looks bleak.

Pieces of peace,
pieces of peace.

Our loved ones are with us,
they're never too far gone.
I feel my brother's hands
on my shoulder pushing me on.

We can do better, we have
to rise up.
We have to stare at our future
and we have to bless up.

Today's the only day that counts.
Yesterday I saw you,
tomorrow you bounced.

We have to believe
in pieces of peace.

It's all we've got when
the future looks bleak.

Pieces of peace,
pieces of peace . . .

He stops strumming his guitar and there's pin-drop silence.
His voice pierced something inside me. Jerome's got a tissue held
up to his eyes. He's the first to stand, he's the first to clap, but
everyone follows, and with all eyes on Yousuf, I'm just filled with
pride. I hope someone recorded that, because it's going to blow
up the internet.

19

Jerome did have the conference recorded, and he uploaded each talk and performance separately. I'm sharing Yousuf's song *everywhere*.

Ashley finally convinces me to come to her place after school to study. I'm freaking out because I'm going to meet her parents, which is crazy, considering in my culture you only do that when you're ready to get hitched.

My mom asks me where I'm headed looking so "proper" with my schoolbag. I tell her I'm off to Arif's. Oh, and that we'll be going to the mosque after. Two lies equals two more sins.

I think I mentioned the mosque to cheer her up. She's been in the dumps since hearing the news about her brother. If it wasn't for her part-time job at the local thrift store, she might stay in bed all day.

Jamila and I haven't let her step into the kitchen. We've ordered in pizza or made some lame-ass attempts at cooking. Jamila made ground beef tacos one night, which weren't that bad. I also made pasta another night. It turned out really bad. I didn't cook the pasta enough. It was tough and chewy, so we tossed it. That was another night where we ended up ordering pizza.

I've never been inside a Cabbagetown home. I'm anxious, to say the least.

When I arrive at Ashley's house, I admire it. We're deep into fall and the tree out front is glowing in hues of yellow, red, and orange.

When I told Mr. Singh about Ashley and her inviting me to meet her parents, he gave me a scathing look. The kind my dad might've given me. He did tell me to take something and not go empty-handed. I skipped lunch for two days and bought some flowers.

Part of me wants to turn back. It all feels way out of my league, like I should get a reality check. But here goes nothing. I ring the doorbell.

There's a wait, but I can hear someone walking toward the door. Each step is making me feel more nervous. My body feels heavy and I'm rehearsing how to greet her mom. I really want to make a good impression.

Ashley opens the door and her mom stands right behind her; both have big smiles on their faces. Her mom has her straight black hair tied back to reveal some fancy pearl earrings, and is wearing a cozy off-white sweater. I'm still wondering what her parents think of me after Ashley told them I'm from Regent.

"Oh, how lovely. Are those for us?" says Ashley's mom, taking the flowers from me.

"Hi, Mrs. Mitchell. It's nice to meet you."

"That's sweet. You can call me Jena."

I blush because I don't think I *can* call her Jena without it feeling disrespectful. We don't do the whole calling-adults-by-their-first-name thing in my culture. I'm wondering if it's something I'll have to get over. I was expecting her to be a little more strict, like my mom, but I guess not.

"Hiiiiiii," says Ashley, giving me a hug. I'm really awkward, stiff arms at my sides, because I'm not sure if we should be touching or in such close proximity with her mom around.

"Feels like forever since I saw you," she says as I take off my shoes and look around.

"Yeah, one hundred and twenty-four minutes, to be exact," I say, winking and sticking my tongue out.

"All right, Mr. Wiseguy, let's pipe down on the sarcasm," she says, hands on her hips. "Sounds like you clearly didn't miss me?"

I peek inside to make sure Mrs. Mitchell, I mean Jena (agh, feels so weird), isn't around. Then I give Ashley a peck on the cheek. "Did too."

I follow her in and see a staircase going up, and to the left a living room that looks like it belongs in a home decor magazine.

Sometimes I flip through those magazines while waiting for Mom's prescriptions at Shopper's Drug Mart. That's right, I flip through home decor mags. Come at me.

Her mom comes back with two glasses of some light-yellow drinks on a tray and sets it on the coffee table. "Fawad, I think you'll love this turmeric ginger kombucha. You two can get settled in here," says Jena. Okay, I can't: Mrs. Mitchell.

I'm admiring their taste. The coffee table is round, low, and made of solid wood with bronze legs. It sits on this really fluffy black-and-white shag carpet. Then there's this sectional sofa that's the icing on the cake. Okay, I'm going to stop drooling.

We've got the living room to ourselves while Ashley's mom preps dinner. I sit down on the couch and let myself sink in. I don't have anything against the IKEA couches in my home, but this is a whole other level of chill.

"Don't get so comfortable already," says Ashley, pulling me up. "Let me show you around first."

I'm up, and she sneaks in a kiss right on the lips. My head starts turning around for any signs of her mom. Coast clear; I relax. I think she likes seeing me so worked up. She calls it cute, kisses me again, and again sends my nervous system alarm ringing.

We start in the basement, which has a theater room, a ping-pong table, and a sauna. Holy shit! How much money do her parents make?

"We should use the sauna next time you come," she says, all giddy. The thought of us in our swimsuits in a hot, sweaty sauna is too much to bear. "Or we could watch a movie, whatever you want."

I finally realize there's no one around. It's just the two of us in the basement. I get a little daring, tug at her arms, and pull her into mine.

"I think I mostly just want you," I say, before kissing her lips. But then I frantically push her away when I hear her mom yell, "Dinner's almost ready. Don't you kids have homework?"

Ashley laughs at the sight of me freaking out. Real funny.

"We do, I'm just showing him around," Ashley yells toward the kitchen as we go back up to the main floor.

Next up is her room. I don't think I've seen this many books in a library, let alone in someone's bedroom. There's a wall lined with them, and a whole corner occupied by an army of stuffed toys.

"Aren't you afraid they're going to come alive and take over your home?" I say, picking up a stuffed unicorn with a rainbow-colored tail.

"I think my dad could handle them," she says. That smile slays every time.

Okay, I'm getting a little antsy about her mom asking us about homework and wondering what we might be doing in her bedroom.

"Should we study?" I say.

"Fine," she says, pouting. Just as I'm about to turn, she pushes me onto her bed, jumps on me, and starts kissing me. I'm afraid I'm going to lose control. Between wanting to tear her clothes off and the fear of her mom coming up, the fear wins. I wrangle her to the side, get up, and try to compose myself.

I whisper, "What if your mom came up?"

"The door's closed," she says, pointing. I didn't even notice her closing it. I sigh and then confess, "I want to make a good first impression and not get my ass whooped by your dad. Can we just study?"

"You're soooo freaking cute," she says, jumping up and dragging me by the arm down the stairs back to the living room. The two of us settle in, take out our textbooks, and get down to business.

Her notes are written with at least ten different colored pens. Important words are highlighted. Everything is organized in her binder, with dividers, and the binder is propped next to her MacBook Air. Meanwhile, I'm trying to solve some algebra mumbo jumbo with a black Baldwin pen on some loose leaf.

I still have a leg up in math. I'm actually pretty useful as she finishes up an assignment, and there's a lot of "Oh my God, Mrs. Jordan was terrible at explaining that. You're so much better."

A little while later, I hear the door open. Her father comes in and says, "Honey, I'm home." I didn't know that happened outside of TV shows. He's dressed in a three-piece suit, is bald, and has a jawline you could probably use to chop onions.

Mrs. Mitchell (a.k.a. Jena) walks in, and Mr. Mitchell appears. I jump up and stand straight. He gives his wife a kiss on the lips. Did I mention he was tall? He must be at least six foot four.

I smile a half smile because I am straight-up intimidated. I'm afraid to shake his hand. Ash nudges me to go say hi. He doesn't look overly pleased when he sees me. Maybe I'm projecting. Or maybe he used to be a Navy SEAL who will rip me to shreds. Who really knows?

I risk my life and walk up to him. "Hey, Mr. Mitchell," I say, holding out my hand.

He puts his briefcase by the console table and shakes my hand. His handshake is a little too firm, but I don't squirm.

"So, you're Fahd," he says, still not smiling.

"Actually, sir, it's Fawad. Like a-wad with an *F*."

"And you don't have to call me Mr. Mitchell. John will do just fine," he says, walking me over to the couch. "Ashley's been saying your name all wrong, then."

Ashley throws a cushion at him. "Have not, Daddy. Stop it."

He retaliates with a smile and the two of them start laughing.

Meanwhile, I feel like I'm pissing my pants.

"Well, I'll leave you two to it, then," says Mr. Mitchell, giving me a hard pat on the back and my shoulder a squeeze. Ow. "I'll be down for dinner."

Whew. Glad that's over.

He goes upstairs to change out of his suit. We go back to doing homework.

"See, I think he likes you," says Ashley, flicking my cheek.

"Uh-huh. Shall we?" I say, pointing to the math textbook.

"Cutie."

I don't know what's cute about math.

Ten minutes later, Ashley's mom calls us to set the table. Their kitchen has a granite island, stainless steel appliances and pots, and knives that look so sharp that I feel I'll cut myself just by looking at them. I'm trying not to act like it's a big deal. I ask Ashley how I can help, but she waves me off, telling me to take a seat.

We're having steamed vegetables, grilled mahi-mahi, and brown rice for dinner. There's also wine glasses set out for the two adults. Mrs. Mitchell puts a bottle of red Malbec wine on the table. I kinda want to try some but that would be very haram.

We take our seats, and I've got a serious problem. There are two forks, two spoons, and a knife all laid out before me. I have no clue which one to use for what. I'm taking cues from them, watching how they're serving themselves and how they're eating.

I take a bite of the grilled mahi-mahi (also, what a funny name for a fish). It's got some herbs, garlic, and a whole lot of red chili, and I'm trying not to sweat from the spice because the last thing I want them to think is that I can't handle it.

Mr. Mitchell is only eating the fish and vegetables, and to make matters worse, he's putting even more red chili on his plate. What the . . .

"I see you're not a fan of brown rice. It's not my favorite either," I say, hoping to win some brownie points.

"Oh, I like it. I'm just trying this keto diet," he says, putting a forkful of fish into his mouth. "All the guys on my hockey team have been raving about it, so thought I'd give it a shot."

"Cool, I'll have to look that up," I say, struggling to knife through the fish, drinking water after every bite to stave off the burning sensation.

"Oh yeah, you play sports. I forgot all about that," he says, taking a sip of wine. "Ashley was telling us you're on the . . . volleyball team?"

"Basketball, actually."

"Get outta here—we have season tickets to the Raps," he says, slapping his knee. "I tell ya, that Leonard, he's pure gold."

"Yeah, he's good. Not as good as Curry, though," I say, all giddy.

"It'll be one hell of a match-up if we make it to the finals, I'll tell you that much," he says, pointing his fork at me.

"True, true," I say.

I take a few more bites.

Mr. Mitchell clears his throat and says, "So, Ash here was telling us you don't live too far from us."

Here we go. Not this. Not here. Then he winces and bites his tongue. I figure Mrs. Mitchell must've kicked him under the table.

"But Curry, boy, what a jumper," he says.

"Yeah, he makes it look like a work of art," I say, grateful to talk about basketball and not Regent.

After dinner, we have gelato, not ice cream. There's a wafer too. I try not to eat too fast. I think I've discovered my new favorite dessert. It also helps sooth my torched digestive track.

Ashley's parents retreat to the basement to watch Netflix, leaving us to finish up homework in the living room.

"I can hear everything from down there," Mr. Mitchell says in a low voice. "Nice meeting you, Fahd."

I wave and let out another half smile.

"He's such a joker," says Mrs. Mitchell, laughing and following him down the steps with the bottle of wine. "It was nice meeting you, sweetie."

"Sweetie?" I say, looking over at Ash.

"They're adorable, aren't they?"

I nod. "Adorable? I'm afraid your dad could break my spine in two without flinching."

"Oh, c'mon, he likes you," she says. "Trust me, I've had guy friends over. He can smell the bad ones from a mile away. At least, that's what he says."

We're back on the couch for the final stretch of our assignments when Ashley pulls out her phone and snaps a photo of us.

All right, I won't lie, we look pretty great together. She adds it to her Insta Story and sends it to me after making it her phone's background.

I check my phone and realize Mom is probably wondering where the hell I am. The last thing I want is to get a phone call from her.

"I should get going," I say, tidying up. "We should do this again, though."

"Thanks for helping me with this math assignment," she says, fetching a textbook for me from the far end of the coffee table. "You're a good homework buddy."

"Just a good homework buddy, eh?" I say, taking the textbook from her. "I should charge you for my tutoring services, then."

"Okay, but I only pay in kisses," she says, planting another one on my cheek.

"Deal," I say, gushing.

One final kiss and I'm out the door, taking in the fresh air as I start my walk back to Regent. I go past the Mercedes parked in the driveway and catch a glimpse of my reflection in the window. Nothing I can't get if I put in the work. I think back to what Venkatesh said at the conference: belief in yourself really is a beautiful armor.

20

The next day, I drop by Double Take, the thrift store where my mom works. It's a few blocks west on Gerrard Street. I need a suit for the formal, and they just got something in that should fit me perfectly. Jamila pitched in for my outfit too. I went shopping with her and we picked out a fitted white dress shirt and a black bow tie. It wasn't cheap, but I promised her I'd pay her back. Mom is finally going to let me get a job this summer.

I normally wouldn't sweat something like a dance, but Ashley tipped me off that she bought a black vintage flapper dress and expects me to bring my A-game.

At the counter is Mrs. McCowen, or Leslie, as she's told me to call her multiple times. Just like with Ashley's parents, I clearly can't call her by her first name—especially around Mom, unless I want a slap to the back side of the head. She's in her mid-fifties, keeps her graying hair short, and always has a printed blouse underneath her Double Take vest.

There's light country music playing in the background, her favorite. Don't get her started talking about how handsome Tim McGraw is. I had to Google to figure out who he was. She's also always spraying Febreze whenever she goes from one end of the store to the other. When I asked her why, she said it was because not all their customers had access to a shower. I'll second that.

"Hi, Mrs. McCowen," I say as I pass by the checkout counter.

"Oh, you're such a sweet boy. But it's Leslie," she says, ringing items through for a customer.

She doesn't get it.

"Looking for your mom, dear?" she says. "She's in the back, steam-ironing some new arrivals."

I head toward the back of the store. I love browsing and looking at all the stuff people throw away and donate. There are literally racks upon racks of clothes. Women's clothes make up three-quarters of the store, but there's a men's section with stuff that's always three times my size. I spot a beaten-up typewriter, a crazy-looking lamp shaped like a lightning bolt, and a massive disco ball.

I can't wait to sign a multimillion-dollar NBA contract so my mom doesn't have to work here. I'll build her a mansion and hire three or four staff for her so that she never has to lift a finger. If for some odd reason I don't make it, I know I'll at least become a doctor or lawyer or someone who makes good money. Maybe it'll just be one staff member. All I know is that she deserves a break.

I spot her exactly where Mrs. McCowen said she'd be, dressed in a Double Take apron over her traditional shalwar kameez. She doesn't wear a hijab or anything, though. She prefers to keep her hair tied back in a bun.

"Hi, Ammi," I say, dropping my bag off on a chair next to her.

"'Hi, Ammi,' ka bacha," she says, putting aside the dress she was ironing. "You're late."

"Sorry, practice went over."

"That stupid game again."

x

219

I want to point out all the reasons why basketball is not a stupid game, except I still don't think she'd get it.

"Where's the suit you had in mind?" I say, looking through the
rack across from her.

She walks me over to where it's actually hanging. I inspect it
and take a hard look—I think it'll fit me.

I try it on. I'm a bonafide Raja Charming, as my mom puts it.
"Why can't I be Prince Charming?" I say.

"Raja Charming sounds better," she says. "Your baap used to
look just like you whenever he put on a suit."

The thought of Dad wearing a suit puts a smile on my face.
The only problem, though, is the jacket I'm wearing is a tad bit
small. Either that or I've just been getting jacked with all the
training. I figure as long as I don't close the button, it'll look fine.
If anything, it makes my shoulders and chest look buff.

It's the end of Mom's shift. We pay eighty bucks for the suit,
which is a lot for her. I try to be extra nice and good on the walk
home.

. . .

When we get back to the apartment, I try on the whole outfit. I'm
talking dress shirt, bow tie, suit, and even the dress shoes I've got
kicking around that still (surprisingly) fit. Actually, I can feel my
big toe wanting to break through, but whatever.

When I come out of my room, Mom loses her mind. She snaps
photos. My posing game is the greatest, bar none. Obviously.

"Oh, I can't wait to send these to Mohsin," she says, directing
me from one end of the living room to the other. "It'll cheer him
up—and the rest of the family."

"Wait, I don't think that's a good—"

There's an abrupt knock at the door. We're both startled. Jamila won't be home for a while, and I have no idea who else it could be. Another loud knock.

I go to the door and look through the peephole. Standing outside is Imam Aziz with Omar by his side.

I'm a little embarrassed at having to let Omar see me with this suit on—something I know will only give him more ammo for the next time I bump into him.

Except he's not looking too good. I open the door a crack and poke my head out. They're both dressed for prayers at the mosque, wearing thobes and topis.

"Salaam, Imam Saab. What brings you here?" I say.

Imam Aziz gives Omar a slap behind the head and gestures for him to bring something forward. My ball.

"I found this in his room," says Imam Aziz, pointing at the ball. "I saw your name scribbled on it, and he didn't have a convincing excuse as to why he had it. So I made some assumptions."

He turns to Omar and twists part of his ear. "Now hand it over."

Omar winces and pushes the ball into my chest. "Take it, jeez."

"Now tell me, Fawad—did he steal it like I suspect?" Imam says, twisting Omar's arm. "It wouldn't be the first time, you know. I had to go to the police station after he and his friends were caught shoplifting at the dollar store."

I look at Omar. He looks at me. I'm tempted to speak the truth. I'd love to give him his just desserts. But I know it won't solve anything. It would probably just make him come back at me harder. And now, he even knows where I live.

"No, Imam Saab. I must've left it at the rec center."

"See, I told you," says Omar, scowling.

"Liars, both of you," says Imam Saab. He notices my mom in the back. They greet one another from a distance. "I know better than to trust boys your age. Now, if you'll excuse us, I have some more disciplining to do."

He clutches Omar by the arm and starts dragging him off. Before they leave, Omar and I lock eyes. He looks like he'd kill me if he could break free from his father's grip.

I know I shouldn't do what I'm about to do next, but I can't help it. I let out a sly grin, and I can see him seething. I close the door.

I'm dumbfounded, holding my ball while rocking my dope-ass suit. Part of me thinks I'm dreaming. I give it a dribble—it needs a little air, but it'll be okay. *Dad, I got your gift back. No thanks to you, obviously.*

I start passing it from one hand to the other around my hips, and the feel is still the same. I want to grab my gear, head to the gym, and start shooting around to see if it shoots the same. I'm flooded by memories of Dad bringing it out after I cut my birthday cake, and me rushing over to grab it from him. Okay, I gotta go play, like, now.

"Omar's the boy who stole your ball that day?" asks Mom. She chucks her phone to the couch and looks at me accusingly. "Why didn't you say anything to the Imam? Do I need to get involved and talk to him personally about you two?"

"No, Ammi, please don't do that," I say. "It's sorted now. I got my ball back."

"Fawad, do you remember what you looked like when you came home that day?" she says, hands on her hips.

"I know, I know, Ammi."

Lucky for me, her phone starts ringing and she's immediately preoccupied with it. I pick up the ball and dart to my room.

I spin it on my index finger, watching it twirl in the mirror with me looking fly in a suit. I kiss the ball (kinda gross, I know) and do a little slow dance with it. The ball today, Ashley tomorrow. What more could I ask for?

21

I still can't believe cousin marriages are a thing. To be honest, I don't even know why I'm thinking about marriage at all right now. I'm fifteen, for God's sake. Actually, it's probably because I'm afraid Mom might do something drastic with Uncle Mohsin as he's nearing the end of his days.

Seriously, though, I still got undergrad and then law school, if Dad's plan pans out. Even then, what if I get a scholarship to play ball in the States and then get drafted into the NBA? I can't be guilted into marrying my cousin. The press would never let me live that down. Okay, maybe I'm getting ahead of myself, but still.

Whenever I google any pro player, the next search in the drop-down is about their spouse. I mean, it's probably because NBA players marry scorching-hot women and everyone probably just wants to verify. What if I am the next Steph Curry and some kid's googling me? I don't want them to see shit like:

. . . Fawad Chaudhry
. . . Is Fawad Chaudhry married to his cousin?
. . . Who is Fawad Chaudhry's first cousin?
. . . Is Fawad Chaudhry's wife also his first cousin?

That shit could be traumatizing. I don't even want to think about it. It's so stupid. What's worse is I see the two of us dressed up, miserable, and having people dance around us with some random guys playing drums in the back.

On top of that, there are random family members coming around and throwing cash at us like we're strippers, just like the photos of weddings back home that Mom has been showing me nonstop. My mom told me it's supposed to represent blessings, and the money gets donated, but still . . . it's kinda weird. Just saying.

Not to mention there's this Ahmed character I don't even know anything about. What if he comes in on a horse with his gangster boys, uses me as target practice for his shotgun, and then elopes with Nusrat? Both of our lives would be so much easier if I was just out of the picture.

Anyway, thank God it's the night of the winter formal and Jamila is here to make sure I'm looking dapper. The bow tie looks slick once we figure out how to tie it properly. Thanks, YouTube.

Jamila gives me tips for my hair. I use a lot of product, and it's parted and slicked back to one side. DiCaprio ain't got nothing on me.

Mom won't stop taking photos of me. She's too much sometimes. The only reason she's cool with me going is because she thinks I was part of the organizing committee, which I kind of was, and that's a big plus for extracurricular experience I could eventually put on my university application. Jamila also convinced her I'm a terrible dancer and that no girl in her right mind would want to dance with me. Big sisters, I tell ya, can cut and help at the same damn time.

There's a text from Arif.

Still can't believe he got his cousin Nazmul to agree to drive us to the party in his BMW. How he affords that car while living in Regent, I'm not going to get into right now. Word is, he'll shank you if you look at him the wrong way. Meanwhile, my Pakistani crew of one, me, just keeps their head down and plays ball. I'd be a terrible thug anyway. Too nice for all that shit.

I've only met Nazmul once, at Arif's older sister's wedding. I don't even know if he'll remember me.

"All right, you look cute. Now get out of here," says Jamila, pinching my cheek. "Tell Mom you love her before you go."

"Love you, Ammi," I say before closing the door. I wait two seconds for a response. Nothing. Radio silence.

I'm on top of the moon, riding in a BMW. Who would've thought Fawad Chaudhry would be getting chauffeured by Nazmul in a BMW that's got those platinum rims that spin even after the car stops? Damn, I think I've come up in the world.

"I got you some rubber, homie," says Arif, slipping a condom into my hand. He's got a three-piece white suit on, with a red tie and pocket square. Oh, and he's got a fedora with a feather and everything. He's straight-up nuts, but I love it.

"Whoa, I mean, even if we wanted to, where would we do it?" I say, looking at the square packet and reading the label. Durex.

"Bro, there's an after-party at Josh's house," says Arif. "Kate's down to go. I'm sure Ash will be too."

"Man, I miss high school. Now you punks got me thinking about the first girl I ever hooked up with," says Nazmul, turning down the Drake song "In My Feelings" that's playing on the radio. "Now, I'm not bragging, and I've been through a whole lot more since then, but this Caribbean chick I'm seeing right now, she's got me on lockdown, y'all know what I'm sayin'?"

"I feel that," says Arif. "I've seen your girl, though. She's smokin'."

Still in the car, we take a selfie and shoot it over to Yousuf, who responds with some fire emojis.

A couple minutes later, we arrive at the spot where the formal is happening.

"Thanks for dropping us," I say.

"No worries, little man. Just tap some ass. Do your boy proud," says Nazmul in a slow and smooth tone.

Arif and I nod. We bump fists and step out of the car feeling like the shit.

Though I'd be doing a hell of a lot better with Ashley in my arms. I know she's around somewhere—I just have to track her down.

Inside, the decor is next-level. Like, holy shit. I thought Ashley was casually throwing around the whole Great Gatsby thing, but it legit feels like something out of the movie.

There are black, white, and gold balloons behind the registration table, along with a gold sequin backdrop. Tall centerpieces containing gold and black balls are on either end.

I don't want to be eyeing other girls, but I can't help taking a peek here and there. The curves and the cleavage are just too much for me to handle. The dresses are all short and shiny. Many of the girls are rocking headbands with feathers and pearl necklaces. I can't wait to see Ash. She'll blow all these girls out of the water.

Arif and I wait in line to register. The girl at the table butchers my name magnificently.

"Fad Chow-durry," she says.

"Yup, that's me. Thanks, Sa-man-tha."

Still no sign of Ash. Now I'm just antsy. But my jaw drops when I go into the main hall. Each table is decorated with a gold tablecloth, white tableware, and champagne glasses. The centerpieces have crystals and white feathers coming out like they're palm trees or something. The lights are dim and there's some light jazz playing in the background. Fancy.

We walk over to our table, where Nermin and Kate are already hanging out. Kate's decked out in a sequin-embellished minidress and has a green boa around her shoulders. Nermin's rocking a shiny gold hijab that matches her full-sleeve gold lace dress. Classy.

"Well, you're both late, as usual," says Nermin, taking a sip of what looks like Sprite. "But at least you both look good."

"Thanks, yo," says Arif, leaning in to give her a hug. "You're looking pretty good yourself. Wait, is that makeup I see?"

Arif inspects the blush Nermin's applied to her skin. She smiles and for once is at a loss for a witty comeback.

"Come, let's get some drinks," says Kate, putting her arm in Arif's and dragging him away. "We'll see you two shortly. And Nermin, love the posters once again. You're so frickin' talented."

Nermin blushes. It's just me and her left as the hall starts filling up.

"Weren't you going to bring someone from the soccer team?" I say, staring at the empty seat beside her.

"I was, but then he asked me to send him a photo without my hijab on, a couple days ago," says Nermin, rolling her eyes. "I blocked him after that. I think he might even be here."

"What an asshole," I say. "Don't sweat it, there are plenty of other dudes on the soccer team who probably can't keep up with you but would want to try anyway."

"Why aren't you with Ashley?"

"I'm looking . . . I have no idea where she's at."

"You're going to be floored," she says, her eyebrows flashing upwards. "Saw her a little while back. That girl can rock a dress."

And then I see her. Her hair is tied back. She's wearing a black flapper dress with silver sequins, long black gloves, a black boa, and a headband with a silver feather. I'm losing my shit taking in how hot she looks.

She has a clipboard in her hand and a headset on too. As I get closer, I can hear her bossing some dude around to make sure the DJ gets to the venue on time. She's also pointing out where the DJ needs to set up, where the smoke machine goes, and when to dim the lights.

I surprise her from behind, clasping her waist. She doesn't realize it's me at first, and is ready to bitch-slap me as she turns. Once she sees me, she drops her guard.

"Don't do that," she says, smacking me across the arm with the clipboard. "You almost gave me a heart attack."

We're an arm's length apart and it's like there's only the two of us in the hall. I can't stop looking at her.

"You look beautiful," I say.

"Thanks. You did a pretty good job yourself," she says, leaning in to land a kiss on my lips. She tidies up my bow tie. "There."

"Do you want to grab a drink?" I say, pointing at the bar, where they're serving cranberry juice, pop, and mocktails.

"Can't right now. I'm almost done, promise."

Another committee member walks up and whispers something in her ear. Whatever the news is, it makes Ash light up. All I can make out over all the chatter in the background is that something's ahead of schedule. Good news, I suppose.

Ash puts down the clipboard. "Looks like I have a couple of minutes, and I'm thirsty. Let's go get some drinks. I made the drinks menu myself. Mom helped, but still."

"Sure. Let me have you all to myself for all of, like, two minutes," I say, pulling her in close. She cracks a smile.

The earth can part and swallow me whole. I feel pretty darn complete right about now. Well, there's still basketball and the championship. Maybe not entirely done just yet. Sorry, God—I mean, Allah—I take those thoughts back.

We hold hands and walk toward the bar.

"Hey, is that Arif over there?" I say.

Sure enough, it's him, and that douchebag Adam is facing off against him *again*.

"Yeah, wait a sec."

She's already darting through the crowds of kids right toward them. I catch up to her. Kate's looking pissed off, standing next to Arif.

"You got some balls showing up here with her," says Adam, driving his index finger into Arif and shoving him a few inches back.

Arif brushes his hand away. "Why you touching me, bro?"

Before I can say or do anything, Ashley's already in there, getting in between them.

"Is there a problem here?" she says.

"Looks like you let some riffraff make it past security," says Adam, staring down Arif.

I can tell Arif wants to take a swing at him. Adam smirks before walking away with the rest of his boys.

"I'm gonna knock him out," says Arif, fixing up his hair.

"Arif, he's an idiot," says Ashley, putting a hand on his shoulder. "Don't let him get to you."

"Come on, babe. Let's just go back to the table," says Kate, tugging at Arif's arm and pulling him away.

I watch them walk back to our table, and I turn to Ashley with my eyebrows raised.

"Ash, you could've got hurt," I say, hugging her.

"I've sunk way too many hours into tonight for it to get derailed by some bozo," she says, brushing some lint off my suit.

"That's fair," I say.

"Gotta run, Miranda's waving me down," she says, giving me a peck on the cheek before racing off.

I hang out with some of the dudes from the ball team until it's time for dinner. Ashley is running here and there, which is kind of annoying, and I'm trying my best to understand, but seriously, can't other people help out?

I go back to the table and vent to Nermin.

"Just chill out," she says. "Ash put a lot of effort into tonight. It's like if she came to your ball game and wanted you to sit by her in the stands instead of being on the court. How'd you feel?"

To be honest, I didn't think about it that way. Perspective. That's what Nermin is always money for.

Appetizers are brought to the table by servers, and then someone's hands cover my eyes.

"You're not going to guess who," I hear.

I shake my head and grab her hands. "I can sense you a mile away, Ash."

"Fine," she says, taking her seat beside me. "Sorry, Nermin, hope he hasn't been too much of a bother."

Nermin laughs.

"Hey, I'm not a child here, okay?"

Ash strokes my cheek and makes a funny face.

I catch her off guard and go straight for her lips.

Nermin sighs, and Ash and I pull apart. I look at Nermin and feel a bit embarrassed. We eat our mixed greens salad and wait for our main course, which from the menu seems uninspiring. It's even more so when it arrives.

"Ash, who was in charge of the menu? Do they not like flavor or something?" I blurt out, eating some steamed asparagus served with mashed potatoes and grilled salmon.

"You're lucky it wasn't me," says Ashley, cocking her head to the side. "But I'll pass on your feedback. The chicken breast is kinda bland." She picks up some salt and starts shaking it onto her plate.

"I tried some fish Arif brought from home one day," says Kate. "I was stuck in the washroom for the rest of the afternoon."

Everyone laughs.

"Arif's mom's food is too much, even for me," I say.

"That wasn't even that spicy," says Arif, shrugging it off.

There's a choice of cheesecake and chocolate mousse for dessert. Ash and I agree to split the chocolate mousse.

It was the best part of the meal, hands down. Ash wipes some chocolate off the side of my lip with a napkin.

I turn to Arif, who's arguing with Kate over whether or not Drake's the greatest rapper of all time. Tall order.

"Hey, man, you sure it was a good idea for you and Kate to be here?" I whisper into Arif's ear.

We both turn to look a few tables over, to where Adam's chilling with his date and surrounded by dudes twice our size.

"I don't give a fuck, man," he says. "I think he's all talk." He goes back to having his hands all over Kate.

"Okay, whatever you say, bro," I say. I give Nermin a look and I know she's thinking the same thing. What the hell were you thinking, Arif?

. . .

The lights dim and there's an area in the middle of the room cleared for dancing. The DJ starts some tunes and then dials the sound up. The bass is shaking the floor.

Ash grabs me by my bow tie as soon as she hears "Señorita" by Shawn Mendes and Camila Cabello. We're off moving to the beat. There's even a smoke machine and spotlights emitting green and yellow as we make up dance moves.

"I love this song," she's screaming.

It's catchy, I'll give her that much. We're letting loose. All those years of watching Bollywood movies and dancing alone in my room to those songs makes me confident on the dance floor.

Ash is impressed. I smile because I couldn't ask for anything more. Then a slow song plays. We're face-to-face, touching. I can't even think. I'm lost in her. It feels like floating.

It doesn't last long. We both feel a push as kids crowd together, making a circle. Many of them look frightened. My Spidey-sense is tingling. I have a feeling I might know what's going on.

"My turn to be right back," I say, giving Ash's hand a squeeze before she has a chance to say anything.

I push my way through the crowd and find Arif down, holding his gut, while Adam is taking off his jacket and handing it to one of his goons.

Arif stands up, but two of Adam's boys grab him. Adam goes to punch Arif, but before he can sock him, I shove him away. Without thinking twice, I clock him right in the face.

There's blood dripping down his nose onto his crisp white dress shirt. Everyone's staring at him. He is looking at me, bloodthirsty, ready to pounce. His goons let go of Arif and start toward me. I've got my fists up. Paul jumps in after he hands his drink to a girl in the crowd.

"Fellas, what the fuck?" he shouts, holding both of us apart with stiff arms. "Y'all need to calm the hell down."

He's a big dude. I'm not going to get through him to take another crack at Adam. Turns out, I don't need to.

Mrs. Baldwin gets to the scene, along with Mr. Tsang. They break up the fight and escort me, Arif, and Adam out of the venue.

My eyes are searching for Ashley. She's going to kill me—this time, for real. I'm such an idiot. Finally, I spot her just before we're marched out of the main hall.

Her hand's covering her mouth. She looks both frightened and pissed. I see tissues in the other hand. Fuck, I made her cry. Miranda's comforting her.

I messed up big time. We're in the reception area, seated on three chairs, while the two teachers stand a few feet apart talking to each other in hushed voices. I hear the party start back up inside. What I would do to be dancing with Ash right now.

Finally, Mr. Tsang marches up to us, index finger raised as he proceeds to point at each of us, one by one. "You boys are lucky we're not calling the police," he says. "Now call your rides and get yourselves home. You're going to be hearing from the principal's office first thing Monday."

"Sir, I just want to say Fawad shouldn't be here," says Arif, standing up to plead his case. "This is between me and that punk."

"Watch your mouth—" Adam sneers.

"That's enough out of you, Adam, and sit back down, Arif," says Mr. Tsang, before turning to face me. "Adam is nursing what could be a broken nose. I don't think that happened out of thin air."

Adam's got an icepack for his face. There's some bruising and swelling, but nothing he doesn't deserve. If anything, I wish I could've done more damage.

"And if there's any more trouble out those doors, in the parking lot or wherever," says Mrs. Baldwin, "there will be severe consequences."

Fuck. Arif calls Nazmul, who sounds pissed on the other end of the line. He's probably never playing babysitter with us again. Adam's on the phone with his dad.

I'm imagining Ash spending the rest of the dance on the sidelines or back in the middle of the dance floor, this time with someone else. Both scenarios send shivers down my spine. At the same time, I couldn't just let Adam and those fools get away with hurting Arif like that. He'd never let that happen to me. I don't know anymore. I pick up my phone to see if she's texted. Nothing. I'm wondering what I could write to her. I type out words like "I'm sorry" . . . then hit backspace a handful of times.

Inside Nazmul's car, Arif's going on about how I sucker-punched Adam.

"You should've seen Fawad tonight," he says, simulating the whole thing. "He nearly broke Adam's nose. I owe him for real."

Arif then has to talk Nazmul out of any further retaliation, saying cops could get involved, he could expelled . . . it wouldn't be worth it.

I'm sitting in the back seat, silent. No pride. Just staring at my phone and still thinking about what I could text Ashley.

I give up. I can't think of anything. I stare out the window and watch the streetlights, storefronts, and traffic pass by.

I wish I could invent a time machine and go back to dancing with Ashley. I'd put that moment on pause forever.

22

Ashley hasn't responded to my texts, calls, or DMs on Insta all weekend. Forty-eight hours of radio silence is hitting me hard. It's Monday morning. I'm hoping that everything will magically go back to normal.

First thing's first, though. Arif and I are sitting outside the principal's office, and it's nerve-racking. The door opens and out comes Adam with a smug expression on his face. The bridge of his nose is a blackish-blue with a bandage on top of it. He acts like we're invisible and walks past us without so much as a look.

"Mr. Chaudhry, Mr. Mohammed, please come inside," we hear from the office.

The principal is a woman named Mrs. Stone. She's a hefty lady with short brown hair, today wearing a teal blouse and black cardigan. I've only seen her at assemblies and in the hall. Now, we're squaring off. I'm worried about being suspended, expelled, kicked off the basketball team, and worse yet, my mom finding out about any of this.

"Please sit," she says, gesturing to the chairs across from her big, executive-style mahogany desk. "Do you boys have anything to say for yourselves?"

We're silent for a few seconds. I look over at Arif, who finally says, "Miss, we're both really sorry."

"Now, as I understand, boys," she says, picking up a piece of paper with notes scribbled on it, "Mr. Tsang and Mrs. Baldwin found you both fighting with Adam. Is that correct?"

I lean forward and interlace my fingers. "Kind of. Adam had started it," I say, watching her look at me with a straight face. "He punched Arif and I jumped in."

"I see," she says again, looking down at the note. "And you, Mr. Mohammed, you did nothing to provoke Mr. Williams into punching you?"

"Oh, you mean Adam," says Arif. "Nothing, ma'am. Everyone there is basically an eyewitness to that. He attacked me first."

"I see," says Mrs. Stone, making some more notes. "And you boys just had to go along with it. Did you not have a choice to stop the altercation at any given moment?"

"We tried," I say.

The principal leans back and looks at us, bemused. "Did you, now? From what I can tell, you almost broke Mr. Williams's nose. His dad was livid in our phone conversation. You boys are lucky I was able to dissuade him from pressing charges."

"Pressing charges?" I say, slamming my fist on her desk. "If anything, we should be the ones—"

"You sound like we started it," Arif cuts me off. "I just want to be clear it was very much Adam."

Mrs. Stone picks up two other file folders sitting on her desk and begins to page through them.

"Boys, boys, I am well aware from looking at your files of the circumstances you come from," she says, closing the folders. "But there are other ways to handle conflicts."

What the fuck does she mean by *circumstances*? That just because we're from Regent, we're thugs or some shit? That this poor white boy was a victim? This shit is fucked. I grit my teeth and don't say anything more—I just slouch back and cross my arms. Venkatesh's speech is playing in my head. This is what people expect. I'm not going to listen; I'm bigger than that. It's more fuel for the fire.

The two of us nod, clench our fists where she can't see them, and stare at the floor.

"Well, you two will still need to be disciplined," she says, crossing her arms. "Charges or no charges, you're looking at a month of detention. That'll be all."

I can deal with that. Not the end of the world. Ashley not responding is the end of my world.

"Okay, ma'am," I say, picking up my bag and standing up.

"I haven't dismissed you boys just yet," she says. I sit back down. "But yes, we're done. You can head on to class."

We leave the office. I'm glad we weren't suspended—my mom would've whooped my ass if she'd found out. I wonder if the office called her. Shit, I should've asked.

"Well, guess that wasn't that bad," says Arif. He's dragging his feet and sulking.

"What a bitch, telling us she knows our 'circumstances,' eh?"

"Forget it, dude. You know how they are," says Arif, which makes me even angrier. "Kate said she wanted to break up over the weekend."

That'll get him in the dumps for sure. "Damn, that's rough, bro. Ashley's been ghosting me all weekend. I have no idea what's going on in that girl's head right now."

"Join the club," he says. "You should go find Ash."

"Yeah, you're right. I'm going to see if she's at her locker before class starts. I'll catch you later. Wish me luck."

We bump fists and I start jogging in the opposite direction. I get lucky and spot Ashley taking a textbook out of her locker.

I speed-walk toward her, scared she's going to run off. I know she sees me, but she doesn't look at me and turns away as if I wasn't there. She's already walking the other way.

"Ash, wait up," I say. She turns and throws up her middle finger. Savage.

"Whoa, what's up?" I say, grabbing her hand. "Ash, at least talk to me."

"Fawad, let go," she says, brushing off my hand. "You need to learn to keep your hands to yourself."

She's clearly mad about me punching Adam.

"He punched my best friend," I say, keeping up with her. "I don't think you'd just stand around if something happened to Miranda, would you?"

"That's not the point, Fawad," she says, stopping mid-stride. "Listen, I told my parents what happened. They think it's best if we stop seeing each other."

"But why? You're acting like I started the whole thing."

"They don't want me dating a boy from Regent Park," she says. Those words pierce me like icicles. They left her mouth so nonchalantly.

"So that's it? I'm just another boy from Regent?" I shout, still in disbelief that she of all people would say that to me. "Fine then, we're done."

"Wait . . ." she says. But I'm already gone. I storm off and run down the steps to get away from her.

I've been called a lot of things in the past. For some reason, "boy from Regent" hits me hardest. I hate her.

After reaching the main floor, I go to the washroom. I take a hard look at myself.

My clothes are not all brand-name. My skin is not colorless. My features don't look like anything I see on TV, in movies, or on magazine covers. I may even come from a single-parent family living in a grimy neighborhood.

But all that aside: I'm not going to let myself be boxed into anyone else's idea of who or what I can be. I will do me, Ash and the rest of the world be damned.

Hear that, Dad? I will do me. That means law school may or may not be on the table. I'm going to pretend like you'd love me anyway, even though I have serious doubts about that. But since you're not around, I can think whatever I want.

. . .

It's the last game of the season, against St. Mary Catholic Academy in the west end of the city. I still have that damn conversation with Ashley playing like a broken record in my head. I text Yousuf about it and he tells me not to get hung up. Nermin thinks Arif and I are idiots for what we did at the dance, but also that Adam deserved it. She tells me to give Ash some space, that she's just reacting and it might be different in a few days. I want to believe Nermin, but it's hard. I can't bring myself to talk it over with Jamila, and Mom . . . well, she's still trying to hitch me to Nusrat, so yeah.

I try tuning it all out while warming up. I'm jacking up shots, practicing my handles, and guarding Spence, who can jump twice as high as me, trying to block his shot. Anything to get my mind off Ashley.

I don't want to think about her again. It's over. She's over. I'm going to play basketball all of the time. It'll be like she never existed.

My heart rate's off the charts. I'm sweating way more than anyone else warming up on the court right now. Out of the corner of my eye, I catch Mr. Singh and Andrew having a little heart-to-heart away from everyone. Guess they're discussing game-time strategies or something.

There's a point guard on the other team who's supposed to be *really* good. He's from the east end of the city. I've seen him play before and the dude has some serious game.

I'm launching and hitting those threes like Curry; plus, I know I can steal the ball like Kawhi now too. Call me a double threat or the best of both worlds.

Okay, maybe I'm exaggerating by comparing my game to two of the best players in the world, but who says I can't dream?

The whole team's taking notice. Spence is throwing me the ball and the swish at the very end of each shot is as satisfying as eating Mom's special rice pudding on Eid.

"Woooohooo, someone's on fire," yells Luke. That's after five made threes.

"Yo, let's just change Chaudhry's name to Curry, man," says Isiah. "I like the ring of that. Fawad Curry."

He throws me the ball. Net.

"All right, he's gon' miss this one," says Scott, lobbing me the ball again. Net.

"One more," yells Spence, throwing me the ball. Net.

I think breaking up with Ashley might be doing me some good. I'm so in the zone. It's me and the net. The net and I. Sounds fucking poetic.

At least the net won't ever tell me not to shoot in it because of where I'm from. It'll give me a chance. Not put me in a box. Not label me. Not judge me.

Just me, the ball, and the net. Now the other team is taking notice. That's nine. Ten. Eleven. Twelve. Fuck, what's happening?

Finally, the ref blows his whistle and the game's about to start in ten. My teammates are all over me, high-fiving me and shit. It's just pregame warm-up stuff. I really don't know what the big deal is. Seriously.

In the huddle, I notice the starters taking off their jumpers and doing a little more stretching. Except for Andrew. That's really weird.

"Bring it in, boys," yells Mr. Singh. "Last game of the season. We've got the best record in our division. It's a testament to everyone's hard work."

We all look around and take it in. It's been a journey, even though it's only been a couple of months. I feel like I've known these guys for years. We're basically family.

"We got a little bit of a change for today's game," says Mr. Singh. "Andrew and I both think that Fawad should start."

I'm going to start a game? My jaw goes slack and I'm frozen with my eyes wide. I want to jump up and down, but I don't want everyone to think I've gone crazy and get benched.

"'Go Northern' on three."

"One, two . . ."

"Go Northern!" everyone yells.

Andrew comes up to me as the huddle breaks. "You deserve it," he says as we do a little shake and man-hug. "Now go get 'em."

"Thanks, man," I say. "You know I will."

Boy, do I let 'em have it. The stat sheet at the end clocks me in at twenty-two points, eight assists, and five boards. We win by ten. Everyone's ecstatic after the game and going wild.

They all want to go out for dinner. Mr. Singh agrees. I tell them my mom's expecting me at home and skip out.

The truth is, even though starting, winning, and celebrating feels sweet, I can't stop thinking about Ashley. I feel like maybe I stormed off too early. That maybe somewhere there's a chance that we can still work things out. Nermin's right—she's probably just reacting. I think it could still work.

. . .

On the streetcar ride from the subway station, I whip out a loose sheet of paper and a pen. Dad used to say if you can't say it, write it, and if you can't write it, it's probably not worth saying anyway.

So here I am writing Ashley's parents a note. I think I'm just going to slip it under their door to make them feel bad. They're going to have to feel guilty after they read what I write. That's going to make Ashley feel bad about not talking sense into them. All three of them will realize that Ashley and I are perfect together.

It sounds highly impractical. I feel like I've seen some variation of this in several dozen Bollywood films. In the end, the girl and guy get together . . . most of the time, anyway. The few times they don't, at the very least they die together. Bollywood is obsessed with *Romeo and Juliet* dramas. Every movie is basically a variation on that plotline.

I'm tired from the game. The blood doesn't seem to be rushing to my head fast enough for me to come up with something to write. I write a sentence, cross it out. Write another sentence, cross it out. Fifth time's the charm. Here goes:

Dear Mr. & Mrs. Mitchell,

I apologized to your daughter about my conduct the other night. I think it's only right that I do the same for both of you. It wasn't my intention to ruin the night for Ashley. We all know how hard she'd been working to organize the event and make sure everything went according to plan.

Before you judge me for starting a fight, punching a boy, and possibly breaking his nose, I just want to be clear that the boy assaulted my best friend. I think any best friend would do what I did in that situation, regardless of which neighborhood they come from.

I may live in Regent Park today, but I can guarantee you that I will not live here forever. I have an 89% average (don't tell my mom that since it's 90% or bust for her) and a 96% in math.

Besides being smart, I'm also on the school basketball team, and if you ask any of my teammates, they'll tell you that I'm a great point guard. Sorry to go off listing all the things I'm good at. I don't like bragging, but I hope it helps me make my case.

If you'd like to see my test scores or attend one of our upcoming playoff games to verify any of what I've written above, please feel welcome.

Sincerely,
Fawad A. Chaudhry

Beauty. That hit the spot. I have a smile that's a mile wide right now.

It's a long streetcar ride, and I'm just staring off into the traffic when someone taps me on the shoulder. I turn my head quickly and it's Yousuf with his guitar slung across his shoulder. That punk.

"You nearly gave me a heart attack, man," I say.

He sits down next to me. "C'mon, bro, it wasn't that bad," he says, setting the guitar in between his legs.

"Where you coming from, slinging that guitar around?"

"Remember that rapper at the conference, Li'l Zeng?"

"Yeah, what about him?"

"Well, he hit me up after the show and asked me to record with him."

"What?" I say, ready to jump to my feet and scream. Instead, I stay seated and give him props. Gotta keep it cool. "Bro, that's amazing. I'm so pumped for this. You got a name? Or you gon' keep it as Yousuf?"

"I'm thinking Nafs. It's gotta a nice ring to it."

We reach the intersection of Sumach and Gerrard Streets, and I'm pitching him ideas for his music video for "Pieces of Peace."

We're still chatting at the intersection. I can see my building and the lights peering out from our first-floor apartment windows.

Instead of heading home, I get this itch to go to Ashley's house right there and then. Even though it's pitch-black out and Mom's probably worrying her brains out. I wonder if Yousuf will come with. Knowing him, probably.

Just as I'm about to ask, I notice a group of guys in black hoodies and puffy black jackets coming our way from the east, where both our homes are. It's not just any group of guys.

It's goddamn Omar, Steven, and Johnny. Not to mention a few other dudes. Damn it. Yousuf gestures to me to cross the street, but it's too late. We start walking and see they're tailing behind.

This is not good. My duffel bag is too heavy. I won't be able to run full speed with my basketball gear. They've started speed-walking. Okay, now or never.

"We need to jet."

I throw my gear into a bush, hoping I can get it tomorrow morning, and Yousuf does the same with his guitar. I start sprinting as fast as I can. They're on our tail, all six of them.

I'm not paying attention, thinking Yousuf's keeping up until I realize after putting a few blocks between us that they've caught up with him. Would they do anything to him? Even if Abshir wasn't around, I don't think Omar would fuck with him. Me, on the other hand? I'm fair game any season.

"Get that bitch too," I hear Omar yell behind me. I'm faster than all of them. I turn to run but then I hear it.

"Hey, Fuckwad, you forgetting someone?"

I turn and stare. Johnny and another dude have Yousuf by the arms on both sides. Omar punches Yousuf right in the gut, sending him to his knees.

"That's your boy, ain't it?" he shouts.

Fuck. Me. There's a voice in my head that's telling me it's a really bad idea to do what I'm thinking of doing. But goddamn it, agh.

"Leave him alone," I yell.

"Oh yeah, what you gon' do about it?" says Omar, kicking Yousuf in the head. That sends him flying back into the concrete. I hear a loud thud, then see Omar gesture to the rest of them to start beating on Yousuf.

They crowd around him, taking turns getting their kicks in.

"Yo, Fawad, just run, man," garbles Yousuf, under their stomps. "I'm good. These snakes can't do nothin' to me."

I can't leave him there like that. I want to run in the other direction but I'm frozen. There's only one direction that my body is willing to travel in and that's toward Omar. I'm already anticipating a lot of pain. I'm sizing up the guys. The odds are definitely not in my favor.

"Fucking leave him alone," I yell as I run up to Omar and sock him in the jaw. His boys back off Yousuf and start rushing toward me. I brace myself and flinch.

"Easy, easy boys," says Omar, holding them back. He's got that ugly grin on his face now. "I've been waiting for this day for too long. I need to enjoy this."

"What the ... hell's ... your problem?" I stutter. "I didn't snitch to your dad, if that's what you're mad about."

"Oh yeah? But I bet you liked seeing him hit me," says Omar, scrunching his knuckles. "Well, tell me how it feels now."

He gets me square in the jaw. I'm flung back a few feet. I wobble, but I'm okay. I should run. I really should. The other way. Not toward Omar, which is what I'm doing as I tackle him to the ground.

He's been fucking with me for so many years. It's all just coming out. I knock him to the floor, get a few solid punches in, and draw some blood. Steven whips me off him and Johnny pushes me to the ground. The other dudes are having a tougher time pinning Yousuf down.

I hear Yousuf scream, "Help, someone help!"

The next thing I know I'm on the ground in a fetal position. I'm covering my head and face with my arms. Broken bones will heal but broken noses require plastic surgery.

"How's that feel, you piece of shit?" yells Omar, kicking me.

His Timbs make me feel like he's taken out a rib. Agh. Someone else is kicking snow into my face. My hands feel brittle from the cold. Motherfuckers.

I start screaming and crying. They don't listen and the blows don't stop. Then another guy jabs me right in the back of the head. That's when things start to feel fuzzy. The little I can see starts to blur. I see red on the snow next to my face.

There are sirens in the background. Someone must've called the cops.

A few moments later, everything starts fading to black. I feel broken in every way. The last thing I remember is feeling the cold of the concrete and hearing Yousuf's voice. By then, I'd lost the strength to keep my head up. I let go as I see bodies in uniforms rushing toward me.

23

My eyes open slowly when I come to. The light blinds me. I see a few dark, blurry figures start to come into focus.

I follow the drip that's going from my arm to an IV. I'm in a hospital bed wearing a gown, with a blue sheet covering me. It's tight quarters. A curtain is drawn as a separator. The figures I notice are Jamila and my mom, both stirring from their chairs and coming to stand over me.

"Fawad, thank goodness you're all right," Jamila says, taking my hand. "How are you feeling, kiddo?"

Her voice sounds raspy, and the sentences take a bit to process. I stare at the tips of my toes poking up from under the sheets. Little by little, I feel all the parts of my body that are bruised or broken.

"Ammi, he's up, he's up," says Jamila.

"Oof, Allah, my little boy," says Mom, throwing her arms around me. "Look what they've done to you." She starts sobbing.

"Easy, Ammi," says Jamila, slowly pulling her off me. Thank God, because I'm in so much pain I can't speak. Even breathing feels like a chore. The right side of my torso still feels like it has one of Omar's Timberland boots lodged in it.

"I'm okay, Ammi Jaan, honest," I say as I try to shift into more of an upright position, but Jamila places a hand on my chest.

"Yeah, let's not push our luck here," she says, helping me settle back down.

"How'd I get here?" I'm trying hard to recall the last few moments of the beatdown. "Where's Yousuf?"

"An ambulance," says Jamila. "Yousuf's family just took him home a few minutes ago. He had a broken arm. They put it in a cast and let him go."

"He was okay otherwise?"

"He didn't want to leave till you woke up," says Jamila, stroking my hair. "But the doctors needed to free up a bed."

Mom's still in tears watching me from her seat. She has her tasbih, prayer beads, strung on a teal string with a golden tassel. I see her whispering the ninety-nine names of Allah.

Before I can dig deeper on the Yousuf situation, a doctor arrives.

"Okay, let's see what we've got here," he says as he gestures to Jamila and my mom to give him some space. They push their seats back. He checks my vitals, looks at a few pages on my chart, and starts explaining to me what the damage is.

"You had a deep gouge behind your ear," he says. "We've stitched that up. The stitches should dissolve on their own."

"That's it?"

"Not quite. You also suffered a few broken ribs and a dislocated shoulder," he says, continuing to look at his clipboard and not at me. "The shoulder, we've fixed up. You'll need to see a physiotherapist for a few weeks. The ribs, on the other hand, require bed rest for a minimum of two weeks and downtime of six to eight weeks. With no physically straining activity, that is."

"But I have playoffs after the holidays. That's, like, three weeks away," I say. "There's no way I'm going to miss those."

"I'm afraid you're going to have to," he says. "I'll give your sister a prescription for the pain medication. We can discharge you after the nurse comes back, removes your IV, and replaces your bandages. Any questions?"

I shake my head.

I'm having Mr. Singh, my team, Jerome, Kingsley, and the entire season flashing through my head. All down the drain. Fuck Omar and those bastards.

By the time we're all done at the hospital, I've got a little sling on and bandages wrapped across my torso. Not to mention the stitches behind my ear, which pinch and tug at my skin.

"Ray said he'll pick us up," says Jamila, checking her phone. "He's not too far."

"Why don't we just take a taxi?" says Mom. "Why do we need *him* to come now?"

"Ammi, he volunteered," she says. "It's not like I told him to. He won't take no for an answer. So you'll just have to put up with him for ten minutes. Is that too much to ask?"

This is the first time either my mom or I will be meeting Ray. It feels like Jamila cracking open a window to her personal world that is otherwise a vault.

Jamila's phone buzzes and she says, "He's here."

We exit the waiting area for the Emergency Room, past a man vomiting into a trash can.

There's a Honda Civic parked outside the entrance. Ray gets out. He's muscular, Filipino, and has perfect hair. Always figured Jamila would only date studs. I wonder if it'd be weird if I asked him what hair product he uses. I decide against it.

"Hey, little guy, I'm sorry for what happened," he says, looking me up and down. "Those guys really did a number on you."

He puts my good arm over his shoulder and walks me to the car. He then helps me get seated in the back.

"Hi, Aunty, nice to finally meet you," he says, holding out his hand.

She doesn't bring out her hand. She does say hi, coupled with a very noticeably forced smile. It's good enough for Jamila. Ray smiles nervously before saying, "Shall we?"

The drive home is quiet. Ray puts on the radio and we listen to some soothing jazz. I hear him and Jamila whispering to each other. They're actually really cute together.

She directs him, and when we arrive outside our building, I wonder if Ray has ever seen where we live before. Maybe Jamila also pretends she lives in Cabbagetown and asks to be dropped off a block north. I know that's what I would do.

He helps me again all the way to my room. I like him already. The three of them stand there looking at me awkwardly as I struggle to get comfortable in my bed. I clear my throat. Mom puts my comforter over me. I don't want to be rude, but I want to be alone.

Luckily, Ray breaks the silence. "I've gotta go," he says. "Get better, Fawad. I'll see you later, Jams."

I notice he catches himself going for a kiss and hesitates as he takes a step back. Jamila blushes and quickly glances back to see if Mom caught that. Luckily, I don't think she did.

"Bye, Aunty," he says, sticking out and then quickly withdrawing his hand. "Really nice to meet you." He waves.

My mom again gives a fake smile and nods half-heartedly to acknowledge him, her lips pursed.

Jamila sees him out. When she returns, my mom says, "He's good-looking."

"Yeah, Jams, good choice," I blurt out, trying not to crack up at her nickname, mostly because it hurts when I laugh. I can tell she wants to throw something at me.

"Don't call me that again," she says, rubbing her eyes and yawning. "I'm going to get some shut-eye. It's been a long night."

My mom doesn't leave. She pulls a chair next to my bedside, recites prayers, and thumbs through her tasbih.

"You should go to bed too," I say. She waves me off. There's no arguing with this woman.

Finally, I doze off. When I wake up, I see a little makeshift bundle of blankets on the floor next to my bed where Mom is curled up, sleeping.

I attempt to fix my position and balk at the pain that moving causes. This is going to be hell for a while.

I imagine Dad walking in right about now and holding my hand. He used to say that nothing was unbearable. That difficulty was how Allah tested us. Those words comfort me as I drift off again. I wonder if he can see or hear me right now. Though if he could, maybe he should've pulled some strings up there so that I wouldn't have got my ass whooped a few hours ago.

Sometimes I wish I could tell him I need him and that it really sucks he never came back from Pakistan. Sometimes I wish I could've warned him never to go in the first place.

. . .

I wake up groggy and my head feels like it's filled with bricks. My muscles feel stiff, and with each breath going in, I wince as the pain in my ribs spikes. I remove my blanket and inspect the bruises that have turned purple on my arms.

It's late into the afternoon when I check the time on my phone. There's, like, a hundred messages from Yousuf, Arif, and Nermin. I text them the same thing back—that I'm okay and will call in a bit.

Mom is no longer sleeping on the makeshift bed on the floor. Now it's just a tidied-up pile of blankets layered on top of one another with a pillow. I really hope she doesn't pull this again tonight.

I fidget a teeny bit. I need to go to the washroom—my bladder is going to explode. I slowly inch my way over to the edge of the bed, panting with shallow breaths to minimize the chest pain. I get myself up so that I'm standing. My first steps are shaky, but I firm up. There's shooting pain down my shoulder now.

One step. Little breath. Another step. Little breath. Eventually, I make it to the washroom, struggle to pull my pants down, and manage to relieve myself. Everything is a whole lot more awkward with a sling.

On my way back to my room, I see Mom passed out on her own bed. She probably missed work today because of me.

As I attempt to lie back down, it hits me . . . where the fuck is that letter I wrote? My brain is going haywire trying to remember.

Was it in my bag? My jacket pocket? Or was it in the back pocket of my jeans? There are too many places to check. I can barely move, and I can't rest until I make sure I still have it.

I check my clothes, which are torn and tattered from the attack. There are bloodstains. I can almost feel the boots, elbows, and punches again as I go through them. No letter. Check my jacket. Nothing. Check my school bag. Again, I come up empty. Fuck.

I could write another one. I take out a piece of paper and a pen, which I grip with my left hand. My dominant hand is stuck in that dumb sling. I attempt to write, but instead of letters, all I get are scribbles.

I give it another shot, this time focusing on getting the precision just right. Still illegible doodles. One last time . . . Fuck. This.

I throw the pen and it hits the wall. I scrunch up the piece of paper, and when I open my hand, it rolls onto the floor. I feel broken.

Winded, I lie back down. On the exhale, there are tears. Lots of them. And it hurts.

The tears are boulders rolling down, crushing everything in their path. When I'm done, I'm left with a mountain of tissues, and for a good half hour afterwards, I stare blankly at the wall.

When I get up to discard the tissues, I notice a photo album buried beneath a pile of papers and old binders at the bottom of my bookshelf. It looks ancient. I pry it out and use my sling to wipe the dust off. The cover's got illustrations of flowers over a background of pink and white stripes. Super corny.

I open it and I'm transported to a whole other age. I see photos of my father from when he was an engineer working for the Pakistani Navy. There's one of him with his squadron, another of him posing with his aviators next to a ship, and another with him posing with mom and Jamila when she was probably about two years old. Damn, why have I never seen these before?

As I flip through the pages, I'm flooded with faint memories of Pakistan, our village, our house in the city, and the few years of school I did there. Then I see a photo of me wearing Dad's aviators . . . I'm on his lap as he snuggles me. He's got that scruffy mustache of his. Always did wish he'd shave that thing off.

But I think my favorite is of him holding my little body up in the air and me pretending like I'm flying. Looking at him then and comparing it with the last image I remember of him is crazy.

Scenes from my father's funeral start coming to mind. I was eleven when it happened. A courtyard full of neighbors and relatives from our village packed into the home my father grew up in.

I wore a white shalwar kameez. Jamila and I watched as our father's body, with a white cloth spread over it, was brought out on what looked like a stretcher and laid down in the middle of the room. They uncovered his face. His nostrils and ears had been stuffed with white cotton balls after he'd been showered.

Everyone had just finished the meal that my mother, her sisters, and a few other women had cooked. The pots they used were so big they could have fit me and a few of my cousins, who were my age, inside. There were also huge tankards filled with Rooh Afza lemonade.

Then we watched as a group of men composed of uncles and older cousins came toward his lifeless body. Four of them took the stretcher bearing the body of my father and heaved it above their shoulders.

Only the men went to the ancestral graveyard. A grave had already been dug—I don't know by whom. He was placed in it and the men started shoving dirt onto him.

I had snot dripping down my face. My eyes were blood-red from all the crying.

It started raining. The dirt turned to mud and so too do my memories of everything that followed. Mom arguing with Dad's mom and his brother, all of it having to do with what was to be done with some farmland. I never understood any of it, and no one bothered to fill me in.

I turn the page and there's a photo of all four of us at Lahore Tikka House from the first week we moved to Canada. A tear falls onto the page and I wipe it off.

Mom walks in, dark bags under her eyes, looking exhausted. "Fawad, what do you want for dinner, beta?"

She walks over to see what I'm crouched over. "Where'd you find that? I'd been looking for it." Eventually my legs give and I sit with my back to a wall, legs spread out and photo album on my lap now.

"On my bookshelf," I say, flipping to another page. "It was under all these loose sheets of paper."

"Oh, look at that one," she says, sitting next to me. "That's the first time we went to Niagara Falls."

We're smiling and posing in front of the falls, with Dad holding a Tim Hortons coffee cup. It's a rite of passage for every immigrant family to have said photo.

"I miss him," I say. Another tear falls onto the photo album.

"Aww, beta, come here," Mom says, hugging me to her chest. "He loved you both so much. Before he left, you know what he said to me?"

I shake my head. "What?"

"He said he was the luckiest father in the world to have kids like you," she says.

I'm full-on sobbing now, trying to spot the box of tissues from the corner of my eye.

"Why'd he leave, then?" I whisper. "He shouldn't have gone to Pakistan. We should've stopped him."

"Beta, these things are out of our hands," she says, stroking my head. "Allah has his own plans for each of us. We all come here only for a specific time. It's up to us to decide what to do with what we're given."

"It's not fair," I say, breaking down.

"You know what he used to say about you?"

I shake my head again.

"He once told me you reminded him of himself when he was a boy," she says. "Both of you, stubborn as bulls. That you have no quit in you."

"I love you, Ammi Jaan," I say. Feels like forever since I've told her that.

"I love you too, beta," she says, kissing my forehead. "Lie down now and I'll make your favorite aloo keema parathas."

I nod and dry off my tears. I hobble back to bed, and Mom puts my blanket over me. My mind conjures up an image of me high above the clouds, my dad holding me up with his strong arms, both of us flying toward the moon.

24

A few days after, Arif, Nermin, and Yousuf are on their way over. It was impossible to say no. It's a week before Christmas break, so I'm going to need to ask Nermin and Arif to get me notes and assignments and whatnot anyway.

I'm a little more mobile but not a whole lot. I still can't get up when the three of them walk into my room and pull up chairs beside my bed. The last time the four of us hung out was on my birthday, when we went to Paramount together—their chicken shawarma is tops. Damn it, now I'm hungry.

"Oh my God, Fawad, I didn't think it'd be this bad," says Nermin, gasping. "What did the doctors say? When will they take off the splint and bandages?"

"I think in about a week," I say, wincing as I try to turn toward them. "But I'm doing way better, honest. It's good to see you guys." I pause. "How's your arm?" I ask Yousuf.

"It's all right, man, it'll heal. Them dudes really did a number on you," he says, getting up to inspect my cuts and bruises. "Guess this is one of those times when being a bigger guy comes in handy."

I laugh. "Yeah, guess you could say that."

"You both should've seen the way Fawad came at Omar when his crew was holding me down."

"He's just kicking butt left, right, and center. You should've seen what he did to that kid Adam," says Arif, giving me a slight slap on the right arm. It makes me jerk back with pain.

"Arif," yells Nermin. "Careful."

"Sorry, sorry, sorry."

"It's okay," I say, rubbing the sling over my right arm. "I just think you both would do the same for me, that's all."

Arif starts laughing. "Dude, do you remember that ridiculously stupid line from that Bollywood movie? That's so Fawad right now."

"Agh, don't remind me. How'd I let you suckers convince me to sit through that?" says Yousuf, massaging his forehead and looking down.

"What stupid line?" says Nermin.

"Don't say it, Arif," I'm quick to say. It's the most annoying piece of dialogue ever. It's literally something stupid like, "Others don't have it (*hero-ness*), and it never leaves me." I know: ridiculous.

Arif perks up and in his best Tiger Shroff impersonation says, "Dosron ko aati nahi, meri jaati nahin."

"From *Heropanti*?" says Nermin. "That movie made me want to throw up."

"It wasn't that bad," says Arif, frowning. His taste really is suspect.

Nermin rolls her eyes. Then she looks back at me and when our gazes meet, she suddenly starts to sob. "I was really scared when I heard. I'm glad you're both okay."

"Agh, Nermin, you're going to make me cry now," says Arif, handing her a tissue. "Get your shit together, girl."

She wipes her tears. There's some mascara smudged under her eyes.

"Also, when did you start wearing mascara?" says Arif, getting close and wiping away some new tears.

She gives him a death stare, which zips him right up. He sits back in his chair and almost tips over backward.

Mom walks in with a tray of cumin seed biscuits, and Rooh Afza mixed into lemonade. My favorite drink. Arif stands up and takes the tray from her.

"This pink stuff is straight-up crack," says Yousuf, picking up a glass with his good hand.

"Thank you, Aunty," says Nermin. My mom just smiles at her. She's not super comfortable with the idea of a friend who is a girl being in my room.

Arif takes one sip. "Oh man, I love this stuff. We only make it at home during Ramadan."

"Same," blurts Nermin after taking a drink. "It's so good."

Arif clears his throat. "So, I finally saw Ashley," he says.

Did he just say what I think he said? I push back against my pillow to pull myself upright.

"Whoa, calm down, guy," he says. "She gave me this letter to give to you. I asked her why both y'all be wasting paper when you have phones. Anyways, she stopped listening and walked away."

"Yeah, I don't blame her," says Nermin, giggling.

"Why'd she write me a letter?" I hold out my hand for it.

"Probably as, like, a response to the letter you wrote her. I mean, I did give it to her. That's the least she could do. Right?"

His words hit me like a tsunami. How in the blue hell did he get that letter and give it to her without telling me? If I could, I'd strangle him right now.

"You what? When did that happen?" I say, my face tightening from the frustration.

"Whoa, calm down, guy. Drink some more of this," he says, handing me my glass of Rooh Afza. "Didn't Jamila tell you? She found it the night you got beat up, and she gave it to me to give to Ashley. Though she did say not to tell you until I got a response."

I take a sip, but it's not helping. I'm still glaring at him. "And you're telling me now?"

That's also totally something Jamila would do. I'm having a hard time processing any of this. I've been trying so hard to push Ashley out of my mind, and now this. Arif holds out the paper, and I snatch it out of his hand.

"Jeez," says Arif. "It's not like I was going to read it. Otherwise, I would've already."

I look at it for a moment, trying to guess what's inside. Part of me wants to know what she wrote. Part of me doesn't. I open the letter.

Dear Fawad,

I showed my parents your letter. First off, they were surprised kids still wrote on paper. ☺

I'm sorry for reacting the way I did. My parents also didn't mean to judge you so harshly. I was furious and upset that night over what happened, and I know it wasn't ALL your fault.

Anyways, forget all that. Arif told me what happened to you. You have to message me right after you get this so I can make sure you're not dead. Okay?

I can't wait to hug you and kiss you in the New Year. I'd come over, but I don't think your mom would be too happy about that.

XOXO,
Ashley M.

Agh, what does she mean that it wasn't *all* my fault? That still means *some* of it was my fault. My eyes skip over to the next line again, telling me to forget it. Now she's concerned about me? It's been, like, two weeks.

My eyes track the last sentence, about her wanting to hug and kiss me. Do I want her to? I do and I don't. I go back to the top and realize she said sorry. I don't know about the "messaging her" part. Her face flashes before me. I miss her.

"Well, what did she write?" says Nermin, leaning forward to catch a glimpse.

"You are going to tell us, right?" says Yousuf.

I shield it from their eyes, tucking it away under the pillow next to me.

"Yeah, bro, spill it already," says Arif, shaking my leg. "Or at least wipe that smile off your face. It's kinda gross."

I stick my tongue out at him. "I think she wants to get back together."

"Awww, I think I'm going to start crying again," says Nermin, reaching for another tissue.

"Jeez, you're killing us here," says Arif. Nermin punches him in the arm.

"Where is the washroom?" says Nermin. I give her directions, and she leaves the room.

It's just the three of us now.

"I still can't believe those dudes would hit you," I say to Yousuf.

Yousuf shakes his head. "Omar's an idiot. Got his ass handed to him when my brother's boys found out. They told him if he ever comes around me or you again, he won't be able to show his face in Regent."

I see the scene unfolding and I can't lie, I wish I could've been there to see Omar whimpering and being given a taste of his own medicine. But this is how shit spins out of control here. I'm worrying about what he might do next.

"And you think Omar's going to listen?"

Arif leans back in his chair with a grin. "If he knows what's good for him."

I throw my left arm up and say, "How am I ever supposed to leave home now? I'll be paranoid crossing the street."

"I'm telling you, man, you're good now," Yousuf says. "You ain't gotta worry about shit."

"That's what you think."

"That's what I know, bro."

"Just listen to what he's saying, man," says Arif.

"Arif's telling someone to listen," says Nermin as she strolls back in and sits down. "That's a new one."

Arif makes a funny face at her.

"What were you guys talking about?" she says, picking up a biscuit and munching down.

"The Jays," I blurt out.

"Okay, I'm not an idiot."

Right. I probably should've said the Raptors.

"You know, that math quiz Fawad missed," says Arif, picking up his bag and going through it like he's looking for the quiz. He picks out a piece of paper and holds it up. "Maybe we should walk through the answer key with him."

She snatches the paper out of his hand and gives it a hard look. "This is your science quiz, and you guys are the worst liars ever. Now spill the beans."

Before Nermin can grill us some more, Mom walks in and gestures for Arif to follow her to the kitchen. The two of them return with plates of homemade naan and Yousuf's favorite: seekh kababs with lots of raita and some raw onions. If Abshir was still around, Mom would pack him some. Yousuf knows that too. I see his face, and I know he's thinking the same thing.

I try to change the subject. "When'd the doctor say you could get back to playing guitar?" I say, straightening up as Arif and Mom place the trays on the bed, and we coordinate plates and cutlery.

"Couple of weeks," says Yousuf.

"Aunty, these look amazing," says Nermin.

"Best in the city," says Arif.

"I'll second that," says Yousuf. "Thanks, Aunty." He takes a bite and says, "Hey, Fawad, remember the first time I came over after school because my mom had a doctor's appointment, and you were, like, mad new to Regent and still tucked in your shirt and had that poofy comb-over hairstyle?"

"Let's not go there," I say, flustered.

"Oh, we definitely should," says Nermin, taking a bite. "Who's got photos?"

266

"Actually, I think I might have a few," says Yousuf, setting his plate down and pulling out his phone, then doing some scrolling. "Here, check this."

Oh no. Here we go. "Nermin, I'll get you back for this," I say.

We all start cracking up as Yousuf starts his little slideshow presentation.

Those days were not my best, but seeing us then and now, it's hard not to feel grateful for these three clowns. They can each be annoying as fuck, but I wouldn't want it any other way.

And yeah, I was a legitimate nerd. I give Nermin a little sideways glance when she finds a pic of us in the library, my hair half a head tall and going in directions that probably kept other girls a mile away. Not my finest moment, to say the least.

. . .

I'm starting to feel a little better. I can now almost go to the washroom and relieve myself without excruciating pain. Both Yousuf and Arif have been coming around more often too, pigging out on Mom's food and conspiring to let me crush them in *NBA 2K19.* I keep telling them to not take it easy on me, and they act all nonchalant, like it's going to make me feel better. Okay, so it kinda does. Still.

One evening after they leave, I get a call from Nusrat.

"Salaam, bhai," she says in a quiet tone.

"Nusrat?" I say. "How are you? I'm sorry about your dad. I've been meaning to call but . . ."

"It's okay, bhai. Aunty told me," she says. "Thank God there weren't any serious injuries."

"Thanks. What's up? You sound like you're hiding in a corner somewhere."

"I am," she says. I hear her sobbing. "I heard Abbu and Khala talking. They want us to do a little ceremony. You know, before he . . ."

"Oh man," I say. "Listen, Ammi's been a little off. I'm sorry, I should've spoken to her earlier. You shouldn't have been having to deal with that on top of everything going on with mamu."

I hear her sniffle and sob some more. "Ahmed wants to talk to Abbu, but I'm scared it's going to make things worse."

"Listen, I'm going to take care of it right now. No more lies."

"Thanks, bhai."

I hear someone call her name in the back. "I have to go. Salaam."

Oh man, Mom's nuts. *Dad, help me out—how would you talk sense into her?* Actually, the two of them argued about almost everything. Wrong person to be asking.

My body's shaking. I'm afraid the words that need to come out of my mouth won't. That I'll be swallowed whole by guilt or whatever else Mom can throw my way. Then I think of Jamila. I try to channel her. Okay, game time.

I go out into the living room, where she's seated and scrolling through her phone. Her glasses are sitting low on the bridge of her nose as she squints to make out whatever is on her screen. Probably a message someone from Pakistan forwarded to her.

"Fawad, beta, why are you up?" she says, looking up at me. "If you needed water, you should've asked."

"No, Ammi, I'm not thirsty," I say. "I needed to tal—"

"C'mon, there's something I needed to tell you."

I bite my tongue, hoping to keep my cool, and sit down beside her.

"Beta, you know I was thinking . . ." she says. "Your mamu doesn't have long to live, and it would be such a—"

"Ammi, stop," I say.

She looks shocked.

"I know what you're going to say," I continue.

"Let me finish, Fawad," she says. "You know I've had my eyes on Nusrat since—"

"She was born," I say, finishing her sentence. "I know, Ammi. You've told me about a million times."

"I wanted the two of you to get—"

Okay, here goes. "I'm not going to do it."

"What do you mean?" she says, tossing up her hands. "Her father's going to die. Don't you think he deserves a little happiness before he—"

"You're doing it again," I say, this time my tone a little louder. "Ammi, don't you think I deserve to choose who I end up with?"

"Fawad, you think I had any choice in marrying your father?"

"It's different now, Ammi. Why can't you see that?" I say, pacing in front of her. "We don't live in Pakistan anymore. I love you, but I can't go through with this."

"Think about Nusrat, beta. What'll happen to her? It's so difficult to survive there as a girl. Without a father, it's impossible."

"Ammi," I say, with a deep sigh. I stand up. "You don't get it. You think about mamu, you think about Nusrat. When was the last time you thought about me?"

Her face gets tense. "What do you think I've been doing here all these years in this stupid, cold country? Cooking, cleaning, working. You think it's for me?"

I groan. "Ammi, jeez, for one second can you not see how ridiculous this whole thing is? It's not just me—Nusrat doesn't want to end up with me either. And I have a . . . girlfriend."

That catches her off guard. "What? Nonsense."

"Ammi, Nusrat has someone, and I've been dating someone too."

"It doesn't matter, Fawad. I've already talked with Mohsin and it's settled."

"No, Ammi, it's not. You can't make that decision for us."

"Fawad. Do not talk to your mother like that," she yells, standing up and slapping me across the face.

It forces me to take a step back, but I don't lower my head. I don't cower. I don't cry.

"Fine, hit me again," I yell. "You think that'll solve anything? You think it's fair that Jamila can date whoever she wants, and I have to settle for my cousin back in our village?"

"I won't be living with her," she yells. "She's going to move out the first chance she gets. It's you and your wife I have to end up with."

"So that's it," I yell back. "It's all about you and your convenience."

"You stupid boy," she screams. "You think it's easy to be in my shoes?"

"Ammi, stop it," I yell, something inside me breaking. I start tearing up. "Just stop it. What happened to you is not my fault. Abbu dying is not my fault. Us moving here is not my fault. You can't blame me for everything. And I hate you for making me feel like this. You hear that, Ammi? I hate you."

Jamila opens the apartment door.

"What the hell is going on?" she says, stepping between us. "Why do you both look like you're about to kill each other?"

I point at Mom. "She thinks it's a great idea to get me engaged to Nusrat because mamu is dying."

"Ammi," says Jamila, smacking her forehead. "We talked about this."

Mom looks like she's about to blow a fuse. Jamila goes over and puts an arm around her to get her seated. She's already got blood pressure issues. I'm worried she's going to snap.

"I know you think no one's going to take care of you when you get old," says Jamila, stroking her arm. Her words cut straight to the heart of the matter, and Mom starts crying. "But it's not like that. You don't need Nusrat for that. What do you think we're going to do? Just abandon you on a street or something?"

"You don't know what it's like," starts Mom, with the rest of her words coming out in slurs from the sobbing. "Toiling your entire life, and for what?"

"Hey, hey, come here," says Jamila, placing her hand on Mom's head and pulling her into a hug. "We're here for you. Doesn't matter who we end up with. We love you."

"Yeah, Ammi Jaan, don't be silly," I say, sitting on the opposite side of her. "No one can come between us. We're in it together."

Jamila and I are hugging her from both sides and now everyone's in tears. Great, just what we needed. But actually, it *is* just what we needed. I don't know if Dad can see us now, but I get the feeling he's smiling somewhere, wherever he is.

25

There are only a few more days left before school is back in session. I can't wait. If I lie on this bed for a day more, I think I might lose it. I never want to lie down again.

Hell, I'd be okay sleeping vertically like a vampire at this point. There's only so many Steph Curry highlights and Twitch streams of people playing *Fortnite* or *NBA 2K19* my brain can handle.

On top of that, I can't wait to see Ashley. We did do a video call this one day. She was as red as a tomato from sunbathing in Florida, where her grandparents live. They go every winter break.

She was scuba diving, snorkeling, and doing yoga with her mom on the beach. She had trouble believing me when I confessed that I wasn't a very good swimmer. And that I had never stepped into the ocean.

I don't think we slept that whole night. We just stayed up talking and laughing.

Jamila took me to the doctor's again. I got the splint off my arm—no more sling!—and the bandages removed from my shoulders and ribs.

The only thing is, I have to be super careful about not getting too winded or having my ribcage take any impact on account of it still healing. I still want to think the doctor was exaggerating the whole "no basketball" thing and just trying to be on the safe side.

Like, I really thought I was going to get right back into it with the playoffs on deck and help Northern win a championship.

Then I realized I could barely walk for twenty minutes before feeling broken inside. Damn. Couldn't I wear a brace or something? NBA players do that type of shit all the time, don't they? I know I could play through it if I just got the chance.

When we get home, Jamila goes to her room to rest. I sit next to Mom as she scrolls through WhatsApp. No surprise there. Mohsin Mamu is on his final legs. Mom has been doing everything she can to make arrangements and be there for the family back home.

"Another engagement?" I say, putting an arm around her. "Don't people have anything better to do there?"

I look a little closer at the bride and groom. "Wait, is that . . ."

My mom nods.

"But . . ." I say, taking the phone from her hand and looking at the photos up close. "That's . . ."

"Nusrat and Ahmed. Besides, it's just an engagement," Mom says, roughing up my hair. "They'll get married after she finishes school. Nusrat's going to be a doctor, you know."

I catch a photo of Mohsin Mamu beside the two of them. He's in really bad shape. I see how my mom cringes and starts tearing up every time she sees his picture. I try to comfort her, but I know there's not much that can be done.

"At least he'll rest in peace knowing everything's taken care of after he leaves," says Mom, letting out a heavy sigh.

"You know I'll always take care of you, don't you, Ammi?" I rub her back.

She wipes a few tears, nods, and lets out a half smile.

I go into my room and message Nusrat.

ME: Congrats!!! So happy for you guys.

NUSRAT: :) Thanks. Come visit us soon. Ahmed wants to meet you.

ME: For sure. I will.

I put my phone away and think about how funny life is sometimes. Even with all the shit we go through, there's always something to smile about.

. . .

It's 2:00 a.m. and I can't fall asleep. I doze off but then wake up because I have to go take a piss. One of the reasons I avoid drinking water right before bed. It's so annoying. I roll off the bed and drag my feet toward the washroom. I've never seen a Pakistani zombie. The stuff I think about when I'm tired.

I stop outside my mother's room when I see the light under the door. It's odd, considering she went to bed way before me. I put my ear to the door and hear sobbing.

I push it open and see Mom rocking back and forth.

Jamila's already at the scene. She's by her side, comforting her and trying to get her to take deep breaths. I feel like a deer caught in the headlights. I don't know what to do or say.

"Mohsin Mamu passed away," says Jamila when she sees me. "Ammi got the call a few minutes ago."

Gulp. That's it, then. He's gone. Off to meet his maker. I can't imagine what Mom's going through right now. Her whole body is shaking. The last time I saw her like that was when we got the call about Dad.

"Ammi Jaan," I say. "Are you okay?"

"Can you bring her a glass of water?" says Jamila. "Also, she's got a massive headache. Bring the Advil too."

I run to the washroom, then do as I'm told and run back. Mom's got to the point where she can formulate sentences and make sounds I understand. Her eyes are puffy, her nose red, her entire body wrapped tightly by the grip of grief.

"Oof, Allah, why him? Why so soon?" she says repeatedly, massaging her temples. I can feel her migraine pulsating through as I try to stroke her hair to help soothe her.

Jamila finally manages to get her to drink the water and take the Advil.

Mom's phone rings again. It's more family from back home. The rest of the night she's weeping with them over speaker-phone. I imagine them thousands of miles across the Atlantic in this remote village where my family has its roots. There's a lot of relatives wanting to pay their respects, console each other, and weep together.

Jamila is pressing Mom's arms and rubbing her back like she's the child and not the other way around. I do the same. This goes on till sunrise and then, after the seventh or eighth call, the three of us collapse. We're all huddled on Mom's bed.

Jamila and Mom pass out. My eyes can't stay open for a second longer either. Before I let them close, I take out my phone, bring up Nusrat in my WhatsApp, and send her a message:

ME: We're all praying for him and are here for you.
May he attain Jannat and always watch over you.

I don't expect her to respond.

The last time we all passed out on the same bed was the night Dad was just as excited as we were to rewatch *Kabhi Khushi Kabhie Gham* for the ninety-ninth time after we'd come home from eating at an Indian restaurant way out in Mississauga.

Somehow, it feels like he's here with us now. I swear I can feel him taking up space on the bed. I put my phone away, and I'm out cold.

26

Mom, Jamila, and I spend a lot of quality time together after Mohsin Mamu passes away. We watch really old Bollywood movies, eat tons of popcorn, and even spend a few nights out in Little India on Gerrard Street to eat dinner. Lahore Tikka House all the way.

We try to insist Mom go back to Pakistan and visit. She doesn't want to, telling us things are too political back home. Plus, she'd rather keep her nose out of it while grieving.

Jamila makes a joke about how our noses are so big they're hard to keep out of anything. That at least makes Mom smile. Also, what does Jamila know about having a big nose? Hers isn't even that big.

Then it's the first day back to school. I'm bundled up in my parka with a fake Canada Goose–looking brand on the side of the arm. I spot Ashley waiting for me. But the memory of our last in-person conversation creeps in, and those words "boy from Regent Park" hit me. My mood goes sour.

"Hi," she says as I stand a few feet away. There's awkwardness, for sure. I don't know if I should make the first move or let her.

She puts her bag down, takes a few steps forward, and reaches in for a hug. My body is stiff and cold. The warmth radiating from her makes me want to melt.

I didn't realize how much I missed her. I actually want to cry but obviously, I don't. I hug her back. She squeezes harder. I squeeze back even harder. Then she squeezes harder. I forgot that my ribs were still healing and I let out an "Ow. Easy there."

"Oops, I'm so sorry," she says, checking to see if I'm okay and giggling simultaneously. I drop my guard. She gets a quick peck in.

"Careful there," I say, holding out a stiff arm. "You just kissed a boy from Regent."

She grabs my hands. "I didn't mean it. It all just came out wrong . . ."

"I'm kidding, we're good." I want us to be good.

We hug again, this time a little more gently, and kiss. Her lips taste sweeter than gulab jamuns on my birthday, which is saying a lot, since gulab jamuns are balls of dough deep-fried in sugar syrup.

"Oh, this is for you. It's your Christmas present," she says, picking her bag up and holding it in front of her. "Open it. I've been freezing here waiting for you."

"For one, let's get inside. Second, why'd you . . ." I say, flustered. "Also, I can't. I didn't get you a gift. Let me do that first."

"Don't be silly," she says, pressuring me to take the bag from her hands. "I want to know if you like them or not. You can get me a gift anytime. These are timely. You'll see in a second."

We go indoors. Here goes. Even if I don't like what's in there, I can sure as hell pretend.

I open the bag. Past all the paper stuffing, I can feel the corners of a box. I pull it out. The gift wrapping has cartoon reindeers on it. There's even a bow with a little tag.

I'm trying to suppress my excitement as I gently tear open the wrapping. It's a shoebox. Not just any shoebox, though. I look up at her and she seems just as excited for me to see what's inside as I am. I lean forward and give her another kiss.

Inside, there are a pair of Stephen Curry's new Under Armour sneakers customized to match the school's colors of red, blue, and gold. Wow. I'm floored and not able to speak. I'm looking at her like she's nuts. She didn't have to do this. Damn. All I want to do is put on those shoes and shoot around.

"They're for you to wear during the playoffs," she says, gently touching one side of my face. "You're going to win it, I just know you are."

"Ash, I wish," I say, suddenly deflated at the thought of not being able to play. "The thing is, the doctor told me I gotta sit out the rest of the season."

"Oh," she says, squeezing my arm. "That's okay. You know there's, like, two more years, right? You'll get your chance."

"Yeah, I guess so."

"All right, no sulking. The important thing is you're back on your feet," she says, picking up my chin with her hand. "Even more important, though, is that we have each other."

We kiss. She's right. The world's not as bleak as I think it is.

I take another look at my new sneakers. I can't wait to torch whoever I play against when I get back on the court.

I put them back in the box, hatching plans in my head to not let this season slip out from under me.

. . .

Even though I thought I'd come to terms with my injuries, I'm itching to get back on the court. Something about having those sneakers sitting in my locker is getting to me. There's practice after school. I can't help but think that maybe, just maybe, I could play during the playoffs.

I mean, I'd have to be super careful obviously but, like, pro players do it all the time. Now all I need to do is convince Mr. Singh. I can pull it off. The man must have a heart.

When the last bell rings for the day, I walk over to the gym and poke my head in. Hearing the sounds of my teammates dribbling and warming up is the sweetest thing ever. It's perfect. There's no other word to describe it.

My heart starts beating faster because I'm afraid my plan isn't going to work. Spence notices me, drops the ball, and rushes over, yelling, "Yo, Fawad's back."

I'm surrounded by the guys I went to war with on the court, fielding questions left, right, and center about my health. They're all over me. They all want to know whether I'll be better in time for the first playoff game next week. Mr. Singh emerges from his office and blows his whistle.

"Let the boy breathe," he says, shooing them away. "Get back to warming up. Practice starts in five. Fawad, come with me."

I high-five, fist-bump, and man-hug as many of the guys as I can. I missed them so damn much. Now, the hard part.

I follow Mr. Singh back into his office. He takes a seat, still thumbing through some papers, looking occupied while I sit across from him. After he finishes signing some documents, he looks up.

"Before I let you say what I know you're going to say," he says, interlacing his hands and looking at me like he's about to do some cross-examination, "what did the doctors say?"

Agh, I knew he'd bring that into the mix. I hesitate. I want to lie. I casually lean back in my chair. "They said I just needed some rest," I say.

He homes in on me, leaning forward. Fuck, I feel like I'm being interrogated. "How much rest?"

My chair feels like it's going to tip back. I quickly clutch the desk and bring it back on all fours. I should've prepared a little more for this. Flustered, I start mumbling, "Well . . . I've been resting for like . . . the past month." I pause to look at him, then shrug. "That's probably the right amount."

"Uh-huh." He leans back and crosses his arms. He's not buying any of it.

"Okay, my shoulder's back to normal. I've been to physio and everything. Plus, my ribs are like eighty-five percent there. So I can basically play."

"Uh-huh. You know you remind me a lot of this boy I used to know," he says, getting up and walking over to pick up a framed photo. "One day, he twisted his ankle playing pickup in the streets and instead of letting it heal, you know what he did?"

Gulp. I shake my head.

"He went to practice the next day and played a game," he says, looking intently at the photo. "You want to know what happened?"

I don't. I really don't. He doesn't take my lack of an answer as an answer.

"He hurt it again grabbing a rebound. Even after two surgeries and years of physio, he could never play ball at that level again. You want to know who that kid was?" he says.

Still silent. I seriously want this storytime to end. Instead, he hands me the frame with a photo of him posing with the rest of his university team and points at where he's sitting. "Me. So if you think I'm going to risk putting you out there, you're wasting your time."

I put the photo on his desk. "But Coach . . ."

"But nothing," he says, sitting back down and taking out a little sheet of paper to hold up. "The only way to get on the court is to show me a doctor's note. Till I see one, you're benched. You're welcome to come to cheer the squad on, obviously."

I want to curl up into a ball. I'm pulling my hair out. "But . . ."

This time he gives me a stern look. I know the conversation is over.

Mr. Singh: 1. Fawad: 0.

As I leave his office, my head's spinning; I'm wondering if my old family doctor, who's this really old lady and good friends with my mom, would write me a doctor's note.

I head out and sit on the bleachers to watch the guys practice. Spence's crossovers are so deadly he nearly causes Andrew to drop. Scott and Luke are oohing and aahing over the two of them going at each other. Meanwhile, Isiah goes in for a dunk and almost makes it. Every bit of me would do anything to be out there.

. . .

Two and a half weeks pass. I swear I have never been on such an emotional roller coaster as I have been lately, watching my team play without me. They crush our first-round match-up. Then they nearly lose and come back to win the second-round game. Lastly, they hold on to win by a single point in the third round to make it to the championship game. That'll be against Central Tech, Omar's school.

That's right—the school where Omar is top dog and has been ripping opponents to shreds. I've been keeping tabs.

At the end of next week, we'll be tipping off against him. I'm still not cleared to play. Nothing about that makes any sense.

My attempt to get my family doctor to write me a note was unsuccessful. Even after I took her some ladoos drizzled with ghee that I'd bought from Little India and that I knew she had a weak spot for, she still said no. I mean, she did put a stethoscope to my chest, pressed it to my rib cage area, and then waited to see whether it caused any pain or not.

I did my best poker face. If she was pressing gently, I didn't flinch. Then she increased the pressure just a teensy bit. I couldn't help it. My body gave in. I winced in pain, which sealed the deal . . . and my fate. Bullshit.

Coach let me start shooting around with the team, at least. He had to show some pity. My shot was still wet. I don't think there's a sweeter sound in the universe than *swish*.

I just can't run for long without feeling winded. My conditioning is way out of whack after having been in bed for three weeks and getting, like, zero physical activity.

Feeling like I'm down for the count, I stroll over to the only place that comes to mind: the South Regent community center. I know Jerome will be training Kingsley.

I think he's about the only person who'd know how badly I want to play right now. No one else gets it. Not Mom, not Jamila, not Arif, Nermin, or Yousuf. Not even Ashley.

I open the door to the gym and watch Kingsley, with his weighted vest hooked up to what looks like a parachute, run sprints back and forth.

I can't wait to see how far he's going to go in his ball career. Like, how cool would it be to turn on the TV and be watching him play for the NBA?

Jerome notices me and blows his whistle, telling Kingsley to continue as he gets up from the bench and walks over.

"Hey, Fawad. How are you? I heard what happened. I swear, I don't know what it's going to take to change this neighborhood, but it's gotta be done."

He sizes me up and puts one of his heavy hands on my shoulder.

"I'm okay, Coach. I meant to let you know sooner . . ." I start, gazing down, thinking back to that night.

"So, what's the damage?"

"Well, I had a dislocated shoulder and fractured some ribs," I point out. "But most of that's dealt with. Minus the ribs. They're still a li'l bit sore when I run."

He nods. "I see. So, big game next week. Are you thinking of playing? CT, and Omar. I know you probably don't want to be sitting it out, that's for sure. Not after what happened. But it's just tenth grade, and there's two more solid years to go."

"That's what everyone else is saying. Jerome, I thought you might see things differently."

"I lost my entire pro career to an injury. I'd be the last person to tell you to risk it."

I'm sulking. "So that's it? I should call it quits?"

He puts both hands on my shoulders and looks me square in the eyes. "Fawad, let me tell you something. There's a quote I love from Malcolm X. I even have it on a T-shirt," he says. "'The future belongs to those who prepare for it today.'"

I'm looking at him with my head tilted because I have no idea what that has to do with my present situation. "Huh?"

"Start doing some rehab," he says. "You'll probably be back in shape to play in the summer league, and in the meantime, there's no shortage of dribbling and shooting drills you can do without running much."

"I guess but . . ."

"It'll be fine. I know the game means the world to you—it means the world to me—but to win at it takes more than just throwing yourself at it. You have to be strategic too. Let me show you a couple of drills you can do at home to keep those handles tight."

He grabs a ball and starts demonstrating some exercises like shuffling the ball around my body, shows me how I can practice my shooting form and a few other things.

"I totally forgot to tell you. You remember Venkatesh?"

"Yeah," I say, nodding.

"He'll be in Toronto when the Warriors play the Raptors. He's got box seats for a handful of kids for the game. You in?"

"Is that even a question? Of course."

"All right, I'll let him know. Tell Arif and Yousuf too."

Kingsley finishes his drill and walks up to me. "You're a warrior, homie," he says, pumping his fist, sweat dripping down every bit of his body as he takes a breather. "You got this."

Amen to that. Also, me and Kingsley, homies? Box seats to the Warriors? Sign me up. Best. Day. Ever.

27

I know I'm not supposed to, but I train every day at the North Regent recreation center—after school, on the weekend, and in every spare moment I can find leading up to the big game. It's not pretty. I wince when I'm out of wind, but that's not enough to keep me sidelined. I have a different immediate future in mind, and I'm just preparing for it. Coach may not put me in. But even if there's, like, a 0.01 percent chance that I'll get to play, I want to make sure I'm up for it.

The day of the big game, I leave last period early to get to the gym before anyone else. There's something about being the only one dribbling on the hardwood that sends shivers down my spine.

I have my gear ready to go in my duffel bag, with the sneakers Ashley gifted me. I come out of the changeroom and start shooting around. I'm warming up with my own ball, since Mr. Singh hasn't put out any just yet.

Feeling the ball in my palms, something tells me that no matter how today unfolds, my dad, wherever he is, would be proud. I mean, I'm not playing cricket like he always wanted me to, but I think this is close enough.

As I start warming up, I get into a rhythm. It feels like no matter where I shoot from, the ball finds its way to the bottom of the net. The rest of the guys start piling in and are ecstatic to see me ready to go in the Northern colors.

"Hey, Fawad, you gon' play today or what?" Spence says as I drill another three.

"Game-time decision," I say, smirking and knowing it's a long shot. I'm here in case I get a chance, and that's all that matters.

"Oh word, fingers crossed, homie," he says before going into the locker room and emerging a few minutes later in his uniform.

Everyone else follows suit, and soon I'm running a few drills with Luke and Scott, practicing plays we haven't practiced since before my injury.

For a hot minute, we get into the twins throwing me the ball around the three-point line. I'm putting on a show, drilling each and every shot. As I release the last shot, I hear a whistle and Coach yells, "All right, team, gather around."

I turn to face Mr. Singh, who finally notices that I'm changed and ready to go. He gives me a disconcerting look, shaking his head.

"Come here, kid," he says, gesturing with his index finger for me to come closer. I do. He puts an arm around me and walks me away from the rest of the team. "What are you doing dressed for the game?"

"Coach, I've been meaning to tell you," I mumble. "I've been training for the last week and a half. I think I'm ready to go."

"Sorry, kid, I can't risk it," he says. "Wouldn't be able to live it down if something happened."

"But Coach . . ."

"'But Coach' nothing," he says firmly. "Now, you're going to cheer on your team from the bench, and God willing, we're going to win. We wouldn't have got this far without you. Just know no matter what, you had a hand to play in getting us here."

I nod, pretending to understand, when really I don't. Shouldn't I be the one clearing me to play? I'm the one inside my body. Don't know why adults think they can call all the shots without all the information.

Central Tech's team starts marching in. A busload of students, teachers, and parents in the stands cheer them on.

There are already kids from Northern who've claimed all the best spots. As the stands fill up, my heart sinks even more. I wish I could play to the rhythm of their cheers.

Locking eyes with Omar shocks my system. A mix of panic, fear, and anger swells up inside me. I want to charge and tackle him to the ground, then get a few good punches in and beat his face to a pulp.

The best thing would've been beating him on the court. That's what I really want. To show him that he can't break my spirit.

"What up, Fuckwad?" he says, stopping a few feet away from me as he and his crew make their way to their changeroom. He's got that damn grin on his face that I wish I could wipe off for good.

"Eh man, watch your lip," says Isiah, stepping next to me.

Omar takes a few steps back but then homes in on me again. "You gon' play with that sorry-ass team of yours today or what?"

"Don't worry about it," I say, crossing my arms. "Either way, you're not leaving here with the trophy."

"Psh, like you suckers have a chance," he says, laughing before turning his back and entering the changeroom.

I want to scream, run after him, and take him on in a one-on-one fight. I don't care if he'd beat the shit out of me again. I just want to land another punch.

Isiah taps me on the back. "C'mon on, Fawad, it's not worth it." He puts a ball in my hands and walks off. I dribble and launch from at least two feet outside the three-point line. *Swish.*

T-minus two minutes to tip-off. We're huddled around Coach by our bench. He's got a school tracksuit on, with a red turban.

"Fellas, you will be pushed to the edge today," he says. "Don't be afraid when you get there. Lean over. Feel the fear and keep pushing."

I exchange glances with the rest of my team members. We're ready to push, all right.

"Now, this game won't be easy, but nothing worthwhile is," Coach continues. "Savor the challenge and give it everything you've got. What do you say?"

We scream, "Yeah!"

"All right, bring it in," he shouts. "'Northern' on three."

"One, two . . . Northern!"

We break and the starters get on the court, continuing to stretch and get ready for tip-off as I watch from the sidelines.

I look toward the gym entrance and see Ashley walk in with her dad. That totally throws me off. She points me out, and he waves at me. I don't know why she would bring him to a game I told her I wouldn't be playing in. I wave back but feel super embarrassed.

Behind them, Nermin and Arif stroll in. They're holding hands. What the fuck? When did that happen?

I'm making gestures and crazy faces at them when I catch their attention, thinking it's some kind of a joke. They realize I'm losing my shit, shrug, and laugh it off.

Yousuf's right behind them, except instead of sitting with the CT fans, he's sitting next to Nermin and Arif. Solidarity. We catch each others' eyes and raise our fists.

I watch both teams now warming up. On Central's side, besides Omar, there's a shooting guard that's been on a tear. His lean, athletic build paired with quick off-the-dribble jump shots don't give me a good feeling about our chances. Especially considering how well that complements Omar's mid-range and post-up game.

"Look, he's over there!" I hear.

I look around and see it's Jamila, Ray, and my mom taking their seats in the bleachers. Mom's got one of her cute shalwar kameez on, along with a black shawl wrapped around her head. What in the world is going on? I run up to speak to them.

"What are you guys doing here?" I say, excited and even more disheartened knowing they came all the way and I won't even be playing. "You know I'm not playing, right?"

"We're here to cheer on your team, kiddo," says Jamila.

"Fawad, why didn't you get a haircut for today?" says Mom. Here she goes. "Especially with this many people watching. Also, why isn't your jersey tucked in like the rest of the boys'?"

"Ammi!"

"Anyways, I made dua this morning that your team will win. Allah always answers my prayers."

I smile. Of course, there's nothing like my mom's prayer to give me more confidence in our chances.

"Thanks for coming, Ray," I say, the two of us exchanging fist bumps.

His hair game is next-level. I make a note to get some styling tips one of these days. Or at least figure out what product he uses.

"Is that her?" says Jamila, pointing a few seats away. I turn to see Ashley quickly look away. "She's prettier in person. Introduce us after."

I turn to see Mom's reaction. At first, her face is stern, but then she allows herself a smile. "Mashallah, now don't get distracted. Focus on the game."

Sage words. Also, the thought of Ash meeting my fam sends me over the moon. I look over toward her and smile to let her know that all's good. She and her dad send a wave our way and everyone waves back. What a day.

I hear the ref blow a whistle and I realize the game is going to start. I give my mom a hug because I never thought she'd want to come see me play, then I think of Dad for a moment and look up at the ceiling. I've got a feeling he's watching real close.

. . .

Back on the bench, I watch the opening tip-off, which Isiah loses. I cringe as the shooting guard on the other team shakes off Andrew so quickly that he's in a daze, before pulling up and knocking in a jump shot to put Central up by two.

It doesn't get better from there. Spence keeps us in it, but Omar and that guard are torching us. They're up by ten at the end of the first quarter. My stomach is churning, telling me it's too late, that they're the better team, and that there's no way we're going to pull it off.

"Andrew, that kid has your number," says Coach in our huddle. "You gotta stay on him."

"Force him left," I say. "He doesn't look all that comfortable with his nondominant hand."

Mr. Singh looks at me, impressed. Andrew nods.

"Luke, double-team that Omar kid when he gets the ball. Even if their center gets a shot off, we should make him shoot."

The second quarter starts. We're not faring any better a few minutes in. Luke gets a few buckets, but that's about it from our side. Omar and his team are still lighting it up. Halfway through, Andrew's got the ball up top and there's a switch. He's got Omar on him. He loses him momentarily with a crossover, sees an opening, and drives in hard to get a layup.

The other team's center jumps in. As Andrew lobs up a floater, he lands on their big man's foot. We all see his ankle twist as he stumbles hard to the floor.

The ref blows the whistle and Andrew's clutching his ankle, writhing in pain. A few of us rush over. After several minutes of everyone hovering around him, Scott and Luke help bring him back to the bench. There's a standing ovation from Northern's side.

Damn. I glance over at Tim, a skinny white kid who's the only other candidate to play point guard for us. He looks even paler than usual. I can tell instantly by the way he's sweating that the last thing he wants is to be out there right now.

I glance at Coach. I know he knows what I'm thinking. I hop over and quickly unzip my track jacket, revealing my Northern jersey.

"Coach, I got this."

"Kid, for God's sake, if something happens—"

"I'll take full responsibility. I swear. You gotta put me in."

He looks around, searching the bench for another option. A few painstaking seconds later, he nods and says no more.

The other guys are as excited as I am. I walk over to Andrew before going onto the court, look him in the eye, and tell him, "This one's for you."

He smiles despite the obvious pain he's in and nods. Oh boy, as soon as my new sneakers touch the hardwood, there's electricity going through my body.

I glance over at the stands and see that Ash looks worried. I give her a thumbs-up and hope it calms her down. Then I zone in on the game. It's our ball.

Spence lobs it to Luke, who swings it over to me. Omar switches to me too. Staring at him face-to-face with the ball in my hand is all I've wished for this year.

I pump fake, getting him off his feet, step back behind the three, and launch a shot that makes the loudest swish of any of the shots I've ever taken. We're down by eight. The game's on.

Omar yells for his teammate to pass him the ball, and he drives in looking to bulldoze anyone who gets in the way. Luke steps in with a clean stance and draws the offensive foul. Omar's on the floor, yelling at the ref.

I bring up the ball with that guard on me, his hands poking and prodding, looking for that steal. He reaches one way. I leave him behind, finding an open Spence in the corner, who throws it up for Isiah in the paint. He gets an easy two.

On the other end, I can tell the dude I'm guarding is pissed. He's dribbling this way and that, unable to shake me. I poke the ball away and run after the loose ball; it's just me on the other side. Rather than drive in all the way and get the easy layup, I stop a foot behind the three-point line and jack up a shot. Net.

The crowd's going crazy, and I look up to see Ashley's dad whistling. I let him know that was for him. Central's team is pissed, now only up by three.

The rest of the second quarter is a seesaw battle in which we exchange blows. Their coach calls a time-out and reins them in. They recalibrate, and so do we.

They still lead all the way up to the middle of the fourth quarter. We're down by five with a few minutes remaining. This possession, I catch the ball in the corner behind the arc and have two guys running at me as they see me squaring up to shoot.

I pump fake one of them and step to the side. As I release the jump shot, a defender fouls me. We both watch the arc of the ball as it goes in. *And one*, baby. I shoot the free throw. It's a one-point game. "Let's go, Northern," the crowd chants.

"Fuck," I hear Omar yell. He exchanges some words with his teammates. Doesn't seem like they're all too happy with each other right about now.

A player inbounds to Omar and yells for him to pass the ball back. Omar waves him off. It's five-on-one, as far as I can tell. He's double-teamed but refuses to give up the ball.

He gets around and throws up what looks like a prayer. *Clank.* Hits the side of the rim, and Luke grabs the board. He shoots me a pass. I look up to see how much time is left on the clock.

A minute remaining and Central's still up by one. We can do this. I hear Jerome's voice in my head. *I gotta leave it all on the court.*

Scott sets me a pick; I roll off it and have Omar on me now. Just what I was hoping for. I fake a shot, he jumps, and as soon as I see his feet leave the ground, I dash past him. I see a clearing to drive all the way to the rim.

But as soon as I attempt to get a shot up, I feel his arm swipe across my chest. Fuck.

Just like that, I'm winded and on the floor, desperately trying to catch my breath. I can't breathe.

The ref blows the whistle. Isiah gives Omar a shove, ready to go to blows. The coaches jump in. Both sides break it off.

Coach runs over to where I'm kneeling and yells, "Hey, kid! Fawad, you okay?"

I need a minute. I squint, look over at him, and nod. He's grumbling something to the ref now. I look over at the crowd.

It's blurry, but somewhere there are Ashley, my mom, Jamila, and my best friends. I wipe the sweat from my eyes and take a deep breath in.

Spence helps me to my feet. Two free throws and a chance to put us ahead. I got this.

At the line, I dribble the ball and look at the rim. Feels like it's just me and the net right now. I look at the ball, feel it in my hands, and I have Abshir's voice in the back of my head, reminding me how to hold it with my fingertips, how I need to leave a space between my palm and the ball. This first one's for him.

I shoot and knock it down. Tie game. This next one will put us ahead. All we'll have to do is keep Central from scoring in the final seconds, and the championship is ours.

Omar comes through crisp and clear in the corner of my eye, but I block him out. Instead, I think of riding on Dad's shoulders and the time he got me the basketball. This second free throw's for him.

I shoot and again get the bucket. Now we're up by one. My team scrambles to get into a defensive position. Central inbounds and Omar's yelling for the ball across the half-court mark. I stay with the guard as he brings it up in a mad rush.

Finally, he finds Omar with Scott on him. Luke rushes over to double-team. He dribbles right through them; he's got two open teammates, though I doubt he sees them.

Once again, he puts up a shot. I watch as the ball hits the back of the rim, rolls around once, bounces, and then just when it looks like it's going in, it rolls out. The buzzer sounds. Holy shit, we won!

My team's huddled around me, jumping and cheering like crazy. Coach pushes his way through.

"Easy now, boys, we need him for next season too."

I look up at him, beaming. "Told you I got this, Coach," I say.

"You do, kid. You one hundred percent do."

The team's huddled around me and we're jumping frantically up and down.

"Eh yo, Fawad," I hear from a few feet away. The correct pronunciation of my name and that voice don't go together.

I break away from the team and turn to see Omar. The win somehow sucks the hatred out of me.

"Respect, guy," he says, holding out his fist. We bump, but before he heads off, he adds, "Coming for you next year."

"You know where to find me," I say, smiling a mile wide. "Right here on the court. All day, every day."

28

Box seats at the Scotiabank Arena for the Warriors game were almost as good as winning the championship. Venkatesh told me to stay in touch—he lost his dad last year from heart failure, and tells me I can reach out anytime. I owe Jerome big. Mr. Singh too, though winning the championship and ending Northern's drought is pretty solid.

We're almost winding down the school year, and it's the month of Ramadan. That means a couple of things. For one, getting up before dawn and stuffing my face with as many of my mother's parathas as possible.

For another, not eating or drinking anything until sunset. Though when we do eat, it's a feast, and the best part is how Yousuf, Arif, and I take turns eating iftar (the meal after sunset) at each other's houses. It's a good break for Yousuf too—he's been recording his debut EP after school and is planning on dropping it this summer. I think it's going to be straight fire. The icing on top, though, is that he's switching schools to Northern next year. Boom!

Lastly, it means no swearing, kissing, touching, hugging, music, shows, lying, violence, and a whole list of other things that good *practicing* Muslims should follow. My mom makes it a point to repeat all of the above, especially now that she knows about Ash.

I'm not perfect. Not like Nermin, anyway. I do what I can—mostly the getting up before sunrise. Oh, and the not putting anything in my body till I come home, nap, and wake up to the smell of my mother's amazing iftar.

The other thing is that in my home, I'm the only one who fasts. Jamila's given up on the whole religion thing, and Mom's too old. Plus, she has way too many medical conditions for it to be plausible.

She'll try to sneak in a day or two. Even then, she's pushing it, so I gotta take one for the team and carry the family on my shoulders.

On the real, though, the best part about that is my mom goes nuts preparing iftar just for me. Jamila reaps the fruits of my labor, but that's okay.

I'm not talking about everyday food items. I'm talking fancy haleem, chicken biryani, home-cooked naan, kabobs, nihari, paya, pakoras, samosas, and more.

Not all on the same night, but still. Of course, it's not *all* for me. I gotta distribute it to the neighbors, who send food in return.

A couple weeks into it, I head into school and as usual, catch up with Ashley by her locker. She gets all giddy when she sees me and attempts to pounce on me. I dodge just in time. She blushes and remembers.

"Oops, you'd think I'd have figured it out by now," she says, giggling. We air-kiss.

"All good. Trust me, sometimes I forget too."

I brought in a big container of my mom's biryani because that evening, we have a special iftar at the school put on by the Muslim Student Association, headed up by Nermin, no less.

Ashley grabs her bag and we head off to meet up with Arif and Nermin.

We find them at our usual spot by our lockers.

Arif is splattered flat on the floor. He's fasting today, no doubt, and looking for attention. The more, the better in his books. Drama queen to the max.

Nermin, on the other hand, has her textbooks open and is doing some math homework. De facto nerd.

"C'mon, it's only, like, eight forty-five," I say, kicking Arif.

"Agh, leave me alone."

"I brought some of my mom's biryani for the iftar tonight."

He immediately sits up and inspects the contents of the bag I'm holding.

"All right, I can do this. Only eight hours, twenty-seven minutes, and forty seconds," he says.

It's a bad sign when he's talking to himself. I'm wagering he'll give up around 2:00 p.m., but hey, I could be wrong.

Nermin closes her textbook and rolls her eyes. She crumples up a piece of paper and throws it at Arif. "Jeez, you're such an attention hog."

"Am not," says Arif, picking up the piece of paper and retaliating. His aim's way off, though.

"Ashley, is Arif an attention hog or not?"

"I'm not getting into this again," says Ashley. "Also, you guys are adorable. Nermin, did you match your hijab to his shirt again?"

"Nope, total coincidence. Unless he's spying on me."

"Damn it, Ashley," says Arif. "It's supposed to be a secret operation."

We sit across from them. I continue making fun of Arif.

"You guys are—"

"We know," they both yell. "Crazy."

The four of us crack up. Ashley snorts. I swear it's the cutest thing I've ever heard in my whole entire life. I can't take my eyes off her.

"Look, he's doing it again," says Nermin, elbowing Arif to pay attention. "What a creep."

Arif rolls up another piece of paper and whips it at me.

"Dude, you guys have been dating for a minute already," he says.

I shrug, blushing.

"It's okay, I'm used to it," says Ashley, looking at me with her wide eyes and beautiful smile, stroking my cheek.

I clear my throat. She pulls her hand back with a sly smirk.

Nermin and Arif continue berating me for living too much in my head, but to be honest, I've already tuned them out.

All I can see is Ashley. The only thing running through my mind is what a crazy year it's been. I never in my wildest dreams thought I'd make the school team, let alone win a championship, or be able to talk to a girl, and here I am sitting next to Ash. It's not easy for my mom to swallow—I'm sure she would've preferred I'd agreed to get engaged to Nusrat—but that's okay. I think she's been pretty happy ever since I showed her I was on track to finish the year with a 92 percent average.

Also, Jamila and I remind her as often as possible how much we love her. That helps too. Though Jamila got into a fancy art university, and seeing as how she's probably not going to be Picasso right away, I'm thinking about Venkatesh's story.

We seem like we're pretty alike; maybe I could study computer science and work for the next Google—if I don't get drafted into the NBA, that is. What was it he said again? "Belief in yourself is a beautiful armor"—mine's already been hit with a lot of shit, and yet here I am.

The bell for first period rings.

I help Arif to his feet, Nermin puts her books away, and Ash is waiting for me to walk her to class. I'd walk her to the moon if I could, but hey, one step at a time. I remember my dad lifting me up in the air, and I feel like I'm high above the clouds, and all I want to do is climb down and thank him.

ACKNOWLEDGMENTS

Thank you to my agent and eternal cheerleader, Stacey Kondla. Being in the trenches with you made the entire journey enjoyable, and your enthusiasm for the project kept me going when it felt like we were doing the impossible. A huge thank-you as well to the entire Rights Factory team, including Sam Hiyate, for believing in me and the project, and to Liza Demaison for handling foreign rights.

Thank you to Lynne Missen and Peter Phillips, my incredibly talented editors at Penguin Teen who helped take the project to heights unforeseeable by me. Your patience and trust during this process was incredibly heartwarming.

Thank you to my grade-twelve writing craft teacher, David Reed, who helped kindle my love for storytelling and who I once frantically ran into in the hall and explained my anxiety about the final-year project, to which he said the words, "one percent inspiration, ninety-nine percent perspiration," and told me to keep at it. You are something out of a Robin Williams movie and you responded when I reached out to you after all these years telling you about this story. We met at a café and you were bluntly honest with me and guided me in taking the necessary steps to making this project a reality.

This project would still be a pipe dream were it not for David's push for me to sign up for Humber's Creative Writing Graduate Certificate program where the stars aligned and I got matched with a mentor who helped shaped the book into what it is today. Tim Wynne-Jones, your feedback made all the difference and your guidance helped me take this project from a rough draft into something that got people excited.

Thank you to my family, there's a lot of them, but firstly my younger brother Mohsin Khan for sharing your stories with me and for not hating me despite my big-brother antics growing up.

My sister, Erum, you're one of the most incredible women I know, and if it were not for your love of literature and leaving books around the house that you didn't mind me reading, I never would've discovered my love for stories. You've forever opened my horizons.

My mom: Wow, you are a rock and I don't know how you raised seven kids in a foreign country in a social housing project on welfare, but your steadfast dedication to your children allowed us all to blossom into the human beings we are today.

My dad, for setting his sights high and never letting us meander, for pushing us to believe we could accomplish great things despite our circumstances, and for the bravado to get us out of a rural village in Pakistan to Canada.

Meenu for reading early drafts and letting your older brother know what was and wasn't in vogue with the youth.

Kousar, Babar, Annie, Manisha, Ghazala, and my entire army of nephews and nieces for your tireless encouragement and support throughout the process.

Matt McQuillen, who taught me about grit and perseverance and took the time to read a "very" early rough draft and for being supportive all the while I worked as a product manager at Xello.

My friends Adam McNamara, Lauren Kluge, and Safia Lakhani for being early readers and never tiring of reading draft after draft with utmost enthusiasm.

Lastly, a huge shout-out to Regent Park and all the people I met while growing up there. You helped shape me into who I am today. The friends, mentors, and memories helped me pour the necessary love into sharing this story with the world.

31901067833279